Dark Mission

by

Susan Vaughan

The DARK Files, Book 1

Dark Mission

Contact Information: info@thewildrosepress.com

Cover Art by *Kim Mendoza*
The Wild Rose Press, Inc.
PO Box 708
Adams Basin, NY 14410-0708
Visit us at www.thewildrosepress.com

Publishing History
First Edition, 2023
Trade Paperback ISBN 978-1-5092-5216-9
Digital ISBN 978-1-5092-5217-6

The DARK Files, Book 1
Published in the United States of America
Previously Published 2004, Silhouette Books (Intimate Moments), Harlequin

The bike roared up beside her. When it threatened to bump her, she pulled into the parking lot.

As her dad said, the best defense was an offense. She rolled down the window. "Cowboy, you're in my way."

"If you're out for a Sunday drive, it's only Wednesday." He looked too good in the worn jeans, snug on his muscular thighs, and a black t-shirt. "We never finished our talk. Imagine my shock when you pulled out in that excuse for a car."

"I couldn't sleep," she said.

"Me, neither. The ground behind your cabin is harder than this pavement." He rolled his shoulders.

She recoiled. "You slept behind my cabin?"

He sighed. "Keeping watch. That's what I'm here for, 24/7."

She felt unbalanced, as though her protective layers were peeling away. "I gave you my answer yesterday. What part of no don't you understand?"

"Oldie lyrics don't cut it. Neither does no. Markos may have already found you. If you won't go to a safe house, come back and we'll talk. DARK wants Markos. You want to be safe from him. We can work out… something."

Safe, yes, dear God, she wanted to be safe, but with Cole? How could that be safer? His nearness was devastating to her pulse. His low voice sent heat eddying through her veins.

Dedication

For my friends Virginia Kantra, Virginia Kelly, Sharon Mignerey, Ann Voss Peterson, Sheila Seabrook, Linda Style, Sue Swift, and the members of Maine Romance Writers for all your support and encouragement.

Chapter One

"SO, LAURA, I see you're still holding court."

The racquet slipped from Laura's shaking fingers to clatter on the tennis court. Ten years vanished in a heartbeat. Only one man's smoky rumble could hum like that through her nerve endings.

"Thank you, Kay," she said to the girl who retrieved the racquet. "Um, you girls switch opponents and keep practicing."

Simmering with awareness and trepidation, she scarcely noticed whether they complied or not. She turned to face him.

Cole Stratton lounged against the gate. Self-assured and arrogant, yet elements of his rebellious youth remained.

The last time she'd seen him he wore leather. His present garb of charcoal T-shirt and khaki cargo pants appeared almost respectable, except for the scuffed boots. Military, not the chain-draped motorcycle boots she expected.

Why was he in Maine? She had to get rid of him fast, before he revealed her identity. If he lingered, she'd have to run again, to find a new sanctuary and a new identity. Her life was in danger. She'd take no chances with a wild card like Cole.

And what consummate gall he had to approach her after dumping her like a worn-out tire on his Harley-

Davidson. Her pride wouldn't allow her to reveal how much he'd hurt her, how much damage his betrayal had caused. She couldn't trust him.

Her stomach knotted, and her heart raced. It took a minute for controlled breathing, learned in therapy, to ease the tension.

She clutched her racquet in front of her—useless as protection —as she walked to the fence. "What are you doing here? Hart's Inn is a family resort, not a biker bash. Did your motorcycle dump you, or are you lost?"

His ice-blue eyes drilled her without a hint of the humor she'd discerned in his mocking greeting. His expression was as chilly and unrelenting as the North Atlantic tide.

He hooked his fingers in the fence above the opening. "Can't a guy take a vacation?"

"Here? That makes a lot of sense." She propped one hand on a hip. "The Cole Stratton I knew traveled only to motorcycle races, certainly not to a staid old Maine resort. Your idea of vacation was a six-pack and a Saturday afternoon."

She blinked under his scrutiny. What did he think about the changes time had wrought in her? Cole might be tracing her shape with his gaze, but at least she could keep her scars—physical and emotional—hidden from him. She closed the shirt collar around her throat.

Heat leaped in his eyes, and tension flattened the skin across his angular features as though he were struggling with his thoughts or emotions. His scent, a mingling of aftershave and soap, and another musky essence purely Cole, wafted to her, a lure to buried emotions and memories.

Oh God. She couldn't let her awareness of him

erode her vigilance. She had much more at stake than pride and resurfacing anger.

He plunged a hand into his dark hair, spiking it into disarray. "Hell, I'm not here to hassle you. General Nolan sent me to protect you."

Laura grasped the fence for support. Trent Nolan? Her breath came in shallow gulps, and she willed her lungs to drag in air. "Why on earth would the director of a Homeland Security agency approach you about me?"

"You don't want these happy vacationers to know how you got those scars you're trying to hide. Or how Alexei Markos is hunting the only murder witness against him." He jerked a nod toward the goggle-eyed kids on the court. "Lose the audience. We need to talk. In private."

A tornado twisted through Laura, leaving in its path the wrecked illusion of anonymity and safety at this quiet lake. "But how do you know all this? Why are you here?"

"Hey, Laura, how's the tennis going?" Burt Elwell waved to her from a golf cart laden with garden tools and painting supplies. His curious gaze earned no response from Cole, who gave him a stony stare.

"Terrific." She waved off the young handyman. The fewer people who noticed her with Cole the better.

"Laura, are you coming?" one of the girls called.

"Can he come and play too?" Kay cooed.

Although consumed with curiosity, Laura knew she couldn't cut short the lesson. Some parent would complain to her boss, and she didn't want to have to explain Cole. Even if she could.

"I have to finish the lesson," she said to him. "Then you'd better have a good explanation." Hoping that was the final word, she retreated to her class.

Like birds to a feeder, her flock of students gathered around her, clamoring for her to observe their progress. Kay, the oldest girl at thirteen, said, "Who's the hottie? Your boyfriend?"

"Just someone I used to know." A friend. A lifetime ago. It had been friendship, at least at first. Maybe she should have remained a timid rabbit like the other girls and not have approached the leather-jacketed rebel in senior history class.

Then she wouldn't have fallen for him two years later.

For the next half hour, Laura could scarcely focus on what she did. A robot, she shot balls to each girl in turn. As they swatted at them, she mumbled inane phrases of praise and critique.

Her brain swirled with questions. How did Cole know General Nolan? How did he know about Alexei Markos? And how could she get rid of this dangerous man?

For a while Cole stood beside the closed gate. When the parents of one girl arrived to watch the practice, he strolled away and leaned against a tree.

Keeping him in sight as she tried to pay attention to her charges, Laura observed wryly that Cole Stratton never actually strolled. He prowled.

He wasn't overly tall, about six feet, but God knew what kind of labor must have augmented his lean muscle to render him more imposing than ever. His hair was still as black as night but clipped ruthlessly short, no longer in a thong-tied ponytail. What had been taut lines at eighteen and twenty stretched into deep creases down the lean planes of his tanned cheeks. Thin white scars slashed his chin and right temple. He'd matured into a man who would invariably draw female eyes. He looked hard, dangerous and—uch as she hated to admit —sexier than ever.

She used to call him cowboy. The soubriquet still fit.

Unbidden, the memory of his rescuing her at their all-night, unsanctioned graduation party leaped to her mind. When some of Cole's drunken biker pals had rolled in, he stopped one from harassing her. He wore a black Western hat instead of a helmet, and she called him cowboy. Seeing through his tough-guy biker persona, she was attracted to his protective nature and sense of honor.

But that was before he'd broken her heart.

When the tennis lesson ended and the girls dashed away to their cabins, she turned to confront him.

He was gone.

Not knowing whether to be relieved or frightened, she froze. Swimmers' carefree squeals and the tang of pine scent floated on the light breeze, cooling the perspiration on her forehead.

Thank God, she thought, giddy with conflicting emotions. Maybe she'd dreamed him up, this ghost from her past. Or from one of her nightmares. She emitted a bitter laugh that stopped just short of a sob. Like a ghost, he'd dematerialized. In a puff of exhaust from his bike, he vanished from her life.

He must have.

After zippering her racquet in its case, she hurried toward her cabin.

Chapter Two

HELL, STRATTON, YOU handled that like a professional. A professional grade-A ass.

Cole kicked at the dirt beneath the big tamarack tree beside Laura's cabin. From there, he had a view of the tennis court, but she probably couldn't see him.

The sight of her knocked him back with a sucker punch to the gut. As if the chasm of years didn't exist, he wanted her with the sharp hunger of his youth. And he loathed her with the same intensity. He suppressed a groan.

Why did protecting her have to be his latest assignment?

He clenched his fist so tightly around the multi-tool in his pocket that his knuckles popped.

Concentrating on his mission, he scanned the area. Hell. The DARK advance team was right. This damn resort was an assassin's dream. Trees all around the cabins and lake. Rambling outbuildings. Plenty of cover and lots of sunbathing civilians to hide among.

Laura's cabin was smaller than the tourist accommodations and set back from the lake, like the other employee cabins, all simple frame structures. Front door, side door. Both locked up tight. Both adjacent cabins were empty.

Not secure, but not bad.

Flowers overflowed her small window box. Red and

white round-petaled flowers — the colors of blood and purity. Purity — that was a laugh.

An older model two-door hatchback was parked at the side. So she still liked old heaps. They had character, she used to insist. An odd quirk of such an otherwise sharp woman. It had made her more intriguing. But he bet she wasn't any better at remembering to change the oil or fill the gas tank.

He started to smile, recalling how he'd teased her about expecting mechanical things to take care of themselves. But that was in the past. Better left there. His mouth tightened.

Memories were a distraction from the mission.

He had to get her away from Maine. Fast. If Markos's man found Laura here, Cole and the rest of his team would have a hell of a time protecting her.

Protect her. Right.

But who would protect Cole from her?

He peered around the tree. Demonstrating an overhead swing, she arched with long-limbed grace to whack the ball precisely where she wanted it. Pressed white shorts and a blue polo. Hair sleeked back with a clip that wouldn't dare let a strand slip out of place.

Everything perfect and classy.

Too good for the likes of a Harley hoodlum.

With the glow of her skin, the golden blond of her hair and eyes the color of maple syrup, she was King Midas's daughter in living flesh. Beside her regal beauty, the preteens posed as gawky pretenders.

Damn. What was it about this woman that turned his thoughts poetic? Or to fantasy. Because that's what their ancient affair had been. A fantasy.

Their dreams together—a fantasy all right. Laura

7

had killed all the dreams. Betrayed the future they planned.

He slapped the mosquito drilling his arm, flicked it away. A Maine one big as the ones in the Colombian jungle. Bigger.

He never should have agreed to this assignment. He should've tried harder to persuade Nolan to send him back to Colombia. Combating narco-terrorists, a man knew his enemies and the dangers involved. Cole spoke Spanish well enough to catch the nuances of deception, of treachery.

Did he and Laura speak the same language anymore?

Besides, the narco-terrorists were making deals with the government, so Nolan probably wouldn't go for it.

A trip in the countryside had sounded like a chance to unwind after a tough assignment and the end to his latest romantic entanglement. That woman had pushed for more than dinner and sex.

He never let a woman any closer. Only once had he been that vulnerable.

But he was over her, past his feelings for her. He'd put all that behind him long ago.

From the studious, classy girl he remembered, she'd grown into a serious, classy woman. Educated. A museum curator.

That didn't surprise him.

Eight months ago, this curvy, elegant female had walked away from a vicious attack that would have sent some Marines he knew cowering under their beds.

That shocked the hell out of him.

When the cop guarding her room was found dead in the hospital stairwell, she fled in the middle of the night.

No one had seen or heard from her. Until a traced phone call led his agency to her here.

He'd known it was her as soon as he saw the name Laura Murphy. Murphy was the cat at the stables where ten years ago she rode and he worked. He used to wish she'd cuddle him the way she did that furball.

How did a pampered princess survive underground?

When gravel crunched on the path, he levered away from the tree. Drawing on years of discipline, he produced a professional facade. He would think of her as only an assignment.

Her mouth was tight and her shoulders rigid. Amber flames burned in her eyes. He'd never known her at a loss for words. What she must be thinking, he couldn't guess.

At that thought, he allowed one corner of his mouth to quirk up. "Cabin doesn't have much of a lock. Or much of a door, for that matter." He indicated the single wood panel with a window.

She glared at him. "Explain yourself. I want answers. Right now. Then leave me alone."

He yanked his ID from a pocket and held it up. "General Nolan's my boss." Let her absorb that fact first. Then he'd hit her with the rest.

Her eyes widened at the sight of the leather case. After she'd stared at it long enough to memorize the damn thing, she gaped at him as if at a stranger. Which he guessed he was, after so many years.

"You're a federal agent?"

"Officer, not agent."

"A federal officer," she repeated, as if trying to absorb it. "Isn't that hiring the wolf to guard the sheep?"

He swallowed the caustic response that burned his

tongue. He needed her cooperation. "Who better to know what the other wolves are up to?"

Wariness again sharpened her gaze as he pocketed the ID case. "How did you find me? I was extremely careful not to leave a trail. I told no one where I am."

"But you telephoned your parents twice from the pay phone at the inn. Second one was last week to their villa on the Amalfi Coast."

"I had to let them know I was all right. Oh. You traced the call." She lifted an exasperated gaze to the tree branches arching overhead. "I thought Markos would find me if I had a cell phone. And anyway, I can't afford one."

"After the first call, we tapped the phone at your father's request. They want you protected."

"I should have guessed." She inhaled sharply. "But Markos could get to them."

"Don't worry. They're under federal protection."

Chattering rent the peace of the wooded clearing. Two red squirrels scurried past them and scrambled up a spruce tree.

A frown etched Laura's forehead. "Attempted murder isn't a national security issue. Why is your agency—DARK or something —involved? My father plays golf with General Nolan, but I can't believe he would send in the Feds at the request of a retired state department official."

He was tempted to make a smart-ass rich-girl comment, but restrained himself. The idea of family favors appalled her as much as him. "You may not be a national security issue, but your boyfriend Alexei Markos is."

A shudder twitched her shoulders. "Don't call him

my boyfriend. We were social acquaintances, a relationship he severed with murder. He's merely Markos, no first name for me."

"Markos has some unpleasant playmates. You heard of the New Dawn Warriors?"

"Vaguely. It's an extremist group, an obscure sect. From the Middle Eastern country of Yamar, I believe."

He arched a brow. "Most people wouldn't know that much. New Dawn are militant extremists, itching to eradicate anyone East or West who doesn't adhere to their strict code. They're suspected in an attempted airplane hijacking and the embassy bombing in Monrovia. Fortunately, they don't yet have the financial clout of other groups like ISIS."

"Ah, that's where Markos comes in. The charming and greedy import-export tycoon." An angry crimson stained her fine cheekbones. "Let me guess. The art and antiquities he had me authenticate were part of building their bankroll. And he knew all along. A deal with the devil."

"I always did admire your quick mind." He planted one foot on the top step of her cabin and propped a forearm on his knee. "A deal with the devil is right. Markos's client was Husam Al-Din. He's a fanatic bent on building his group into a world power. To locate him and stop New Dawn, we need leverage with Markos."

"And I am that leverage."

"Exactly. We think he knows where Al-Din is. A credible witness against him for murder and attempted murder might encourage him to sing like the arrogant peacock he is."

"Peacocks don't sing. They screech."

"I didn't say it would be pretty."

Fear and doubt clouded her eyes before she turned to the window box. Doubt about nailing Markos. Doubt about Cole's ability to protect her. She pinched two dead blossoms and dropped them on the ground. Her hand trembled and she shoved it into the pocket of her shorts.

"Why you, Cole? Why did Nolan send you?"

"He said because we went to school together, you'd know me. Trust me." Hell, there was a laugh and a half.

He'd refused, but Nolan insisted he needed Cole's expert undercover skills and sixth sense for danger. So here he was.

Rationalizing that he wanted only to comfort her, he eased over behind her, let his hands hover above her slender shoulders. He shouldn't touch her. He should keep his hands and all other body parts strictly away. He needed discipline to do his job. Yet he could no more keep his hands from her than he could've refused the general's orders. The temptation of her skin and her fragrance wove the old spell.

He cupped her shoulders and turned her to face him. "An informant spotted Markos in Boston. We believe he's traced you. Pack up, and we can leave in an hour. I'm to take you to a safe house out West."

She was in danger here, and soon, if reports were accurate. His gut clenched with fear that she wouldn't trust him. Hell, from the looks of things, she wouldn't trust him as far as the door, much less Utah.

Emotions chased across her features—fear, fury, determination. She twisted from his grasp. "I'm going nowhere with you. After the way you treated me, I have no reason to trust you."

"What the hell? You have things backward." She was the one who dumped him, left him strung out for the vultures. And *she* was ticked off? But this wasn't the time. He held up his hands. "This doesn't have to be personal."

"No, and it's not going to be. Trent Nolan can send someone else to protect me. I'll even give him a call, so you're off the hook. You've had your say. Now leave."

She ducked past him and unlocked the door with a key slipped from her shorts pocket.

This mission couldn't fold before he even began. "No can do. Arrangements have been made. A DARK team is in place, not just me. Markos could already know you're at this resort." He racked his brain for anything that would keep her talking to him. He gestured at the keys in her hand. "Good your survival instincts have you buttoning up."

"Old habits die hard. I'm used to keeping my doors locked." Clearly ready to shut him out, she glared at him from the doorway. "I'm perfectly safe here in Maine. At least I was. Now please go. I have no more to say to you."

****

Once inside the cabin, the impact of the encounter slammed into Laura, and she sank onto a chair. She stared into space and hugged herself.

He was gone, but where he'd touched her, sensation still lifted the hairs. The attraction remained, undimmed by years. It was only chemical, sexual. Once she'd thought Cole was Mr. Right, but he was Mr. Wrong after all. She'd thought so then and she *knew* so now.

His very presence here threatened her safety. If the Feds could find her, so could Markos. Cole was right about that.

She'd fled Washington, D.C., last October with few belongings and little cash. She hated forfeiting her career and leaving her family and friends. After months alone on the run and in hiding, her previous life seemed a distant dream.

But fear crouched in her mind and in her belly, like a hibernating beast, ready to roar to life.

Twice she'd defied death. Twice something in her clung to life. Double jeopardy. She didn't relish a triple. She didn't have nine lives to risk like the feline name she adopted. But she could do nothing except remain in hiding until she could return and testify.

A month ago, she'd found this secluded Maine resort, a haven to a woman on the run. Teaching tennis and sailing here provided a focus… and kept the beast at bay. But oh, God, she was so tired of dodging, dissembling, hiding.

She wanted Alexei Markos behind bars.

She wanted to be Laura Rossiter again. To be safe.

But she couldn't tolerate even one day of bodyguarding by Cole Stratton.

Tears welled, and she blinked them away. Tears would accomplish nothing. Resolve and determination would keep her strong. She squared her shoulders and stood.

The last thing she wanted was for Cole to probe their past, to learn the secret she'd kept for ten years.

That left her only one choice.

Chapter Three

AS DAWN'S LIGHT peeked over the ridge, Laura coaxed her rusty hatchback up Deer Mountain on the road from Hart's Inn Resort as far as the scenic turnout. In her rearview mirror, she spied a black-and-silver motorcycle zooming out of nowhere, on her tail. Cole. She slumped. She should've known.

The bike roared up beside her. When it threatened to bump her, she pulled into the overlook parking lot.

As her dad said, the best defense was an offense. She rolled down the window. "Cowboy, you're in my way."

"If you're out for a Sunday drive, it's only Wednesday." He looked too good in the worn jeans, snug on his muscular thighs, and a black T-shirt with the Harley eagle logo. "We never finished our talk. Imagine my shock when you pulled out in that excuse for a car."

"I couldn't sleep," she said.

"Me, neither. The ground behind your cabin is harder than this pavement." He rolled his shoulders.

She recoiled, not liking the implications. "You slept behind my cabin?"

He sighed. "Keeping watch. That's what I'm here for, 24/7."

Did he know the turmoil that idea generated inside her? Her head swam, and she felt unbalanced, as though her protective layers were peeling away. "I gave you my answer yesterday. What part of no don't you understand?"

"Oldie lyrics don't cut it. Neither does no. Markos may have already found you. If you won't go to a safe house, come back and we'll talk. DARK wants Markos. You want to be safe from him. We can work out... something."

Safe, yes, dear God, she wanted to be safe, but working out something with Cole? How could that be safer than the situation she was in? His nearness was devastating to her pulse. His low voice sent heat eddying through her veins.

Just like old times.

She gripped the steering wheel and fought for the logic and control that had been her bulwark over the years. He had her under surveillance, so she couldn't get away, down the other side of the mountain to Alderport or anywhere else. She had no escape. "What choice do I have?"

"I'll follow you back to the resort." He waited as she turned the hatchback and pulled onto the two-lane country road.

****

Cole pounded a fist into the other palm. Damn! Yesterday when she'd railed at him, life had sparkled in her eyes and pushed away the fear. Now he saw only fear.

Grimacing, he rolled his shoulders. He didn't need much sleep, but too much rough duty had taken its toll. His bones and muscles objected big time to the outdoor stakeout. Otherwise, duty in DARK challenged him, satisfied him and made him who he was now. Made him who he needed to be, not a biker bum, like his old man had always said.

You'll never do more'n scrape up enough to buy the next pint, his father had raved at him. *You'll be lucky to keep working at that cycle shop. You're just like me.*

No, he wasn't. He wouldn't be. He'd escaped that fate in spite of his old man's booze and abuse. This op was another brick in building his life.

Except for the general's devious U-turn.

Cole had gotten his contact officer to check with Nolan on Laura's refusal to budge. This morning the contact said Nolan was happy as a Maine clam at high tide that she stay put. The safe house was no longer part of the plan. They could work out something.

The *something* was a trap, with Laura as bait.

Cole might have a bone to pick with her, but he couldn't condone staking her out like the poor damn goat fed to T-Rex in *Jurassic Park.*

Restful stay in the country, hell.

One DARK officer had already moved into a rental cabin as a guest. The second ensconced at the inn was code-named the Confessor, for an ability to make friends and encourage people to talk. Not that a pro hit man would fall for that, but having an operative on the inside could eliminate suspects. The rest of his team would be deployed at the resort today.

Meanwhile, guarding Laura was his responsibility. He had to stick as close to the sacrificial lamb as a conjoined twin, but how the hell could he convince her to let him protect her? She considered him the wolf, not the shepherd.

As he clamped on his helmet, he noticed the sheen of a viscous fluid on the pavement beside him. Small puddles and drips glistened where the old hatchback had stood. A trail of sparkling drops led out of the parking area.

Brake fluid.

Sputtering oaths, he spun onto the pavement. Had someone done this? Or was she still not maintaining her vehicles? The thought of Laura tearing down that mountain road with no brakes raked his spine.

He prayed he reached her before it was too late.

He leaned into the turns and followed the trail of fluid weaving down the slope. He cast a wary eye at what took the place of a guard rail—boulders nearly as big as her car.

What would she do when she reached the bottom? What was there? He couldn't remember. Damn. He gunned the bike.

A screech of tires followed by the shriek and crunch of metal had his heart racing as fast as his engine.

Around the next turn were the rocks she'd hit. One fender, sheared off as if by a can opener, lay beside a scarred boulder. Miraculously, she was still descending.

Halfway down the hill, he caught up to her as she steered wide on a gentle turn.

The trail of fluid showed she was handling the curving down-grade damned well. She downshifted so the engine slowed her. But the car was still gaining speed.

At the foot of the hill, her car shot across the path of an unwitting truck driver. The wild-eyed man slammed on the brakes.

His worked.

Veering wildly, Laura careened past a shed and through a wooden fence. Slowed by the impact with the fence, the hatchback plowed on into a farm field. The car ground to a halt axle deep in grass and mud.

Cole jumped off his motorcycle and wrenched open the car door. He allowed himself a deep breath when he saw no blood, no twisted limbs.

Laura clutched her belly and groaned.

"Are you hurt?"

She groaned again, but shook her head.

He had to get her out of there. What if the car blew? Rare, but it could happen. Gently, his throat constricted, he checked for injuries. When he found none, he unbuckled her seat belt and cradled her to him. "Here we go. Let me carry you." With her trembling in his arms, he trudged away from the car.

She curled into his chest, murmuring in a wrenching tone that tore at his heart. "My…" A sob obscured the rest of her words.

"What is it, Laura? What did you say?"

She shook her head, then raised it a little. "N-nothing. I'm… okay." Eyes closed, she inhaled slowly, then exhaled in what he figured was a calming tactic.

He set her down on a log near the bike. He squatted in front of her and checked her pupils, her face. Reassured she was whole, he pressed his shaking hands to her knees.

She gulped down tears. "If you hadn't stopped me and made me turn around to go back to the resort, I'd have driven down the other side—"

"And over the cliff." His words left no room for doubting the outcome.

She'd been through hell already. He wished he could shield her, wrap her up and cart her off to safety. But she wouldn't have it. Nor would the general, damn him.

"You saved my life. I —" A sob cut off her words.

So many emotions whirled and tumbled through Laura that she could scarcely get her bearings. Fear and fury at Markos's latest attempt on her life were only part. Harder to accept was her treacherous relief that Cole was the one to pull her from the car and hold her in his arms.

"Don't thank me yet," he growled. "That may be only his first attempt. I bet my saddlebags that those brake lines have man-made holes. If we had doubt about Markos trying to kill you, this is proof."

He sprang to his feet and stalked to the hatchback, buckled into the muddy field like a permanent growth. He stared as though X-ray vision would reveal the reason for the brake failure.

Deep breaths gradually calmed her. She smoothed back her hair and tried to stand.

"Whoa, babe." Arm around her shoulders, he eased her back down. "Take it easy. Maybe we should get you to a hospital."

"No hospital." She just wanted to get away from him.

He peered at her, clearly still worried. "I know better than to argue with that tone, but you shouldn't ride back to the resort on a motorcycle." He flicked on his cell phone. "Stan can send somebody."

She eyed the Harley as if it were a fire-breathing monster. Ride back with him, on that, her knees pressed to his hips? She was relieved she didn't have to create an excuse. "I can't leave my suitcase and other box in the car. It's everything I own."

"Everything you own? A downsized princess." He stood, shaking his head in disbelief. "I'll load them myself when your carriage arrives."

As he waited for a response, she caught him

watching her, puzzlement on his face. "Laura, what was that you said when I pulled you out of the car? 'My' something?"

Her heart stopped at the fear he'd puzzle out her garbled cry. Then she'd have no choice but to reveal the secret locked in her mangled heart. Only six months after they'd broken up had come her first brush with death.

She dropped her gaze to the ground. "I … I don't know."

****

It wasn't Stan who arrived in a resort pickup truck, but the hot-eyed kid Burt. An amazingly perked-up Laura installed herself in the truck's passenger seat before Cole could object.

He followed them on his bike. He didn't trust anybody where Laura was concerned. The shifty-eyed Burt especially.

He ached to grill her about what she said as he pulled her out of the wreckage. My … something, but what? She knew all right, but she didn't want him to know.

Opening that can of tarantulas would get them nowhere fast. Yesterday he'd blown it, and she'd run. Not from a killer, but from him. So he had to tiptoe a tightrope with her. And after today's so-called accident, the present—not the pas —demanded one hundred percent of his attention.

Desiring her and remembering how she'd *gotten* him better than anyone before or since were logical consequences of being near her. But she'd dumped him long ago. He had to put personal concerns aside until the threat to her life ended.

Sure.

Later a visit to Libby's Garage where the hatchback

was towed confirmed his suspicions about the car being sabotaged. The mechanic pointed at tiny holes along the brake lines. He said in his laconic Down-East drawl that corrosion could cause the fluid to drain out slowly and, "Ayuh, might be a accident. Might not."

But it was no accident. So Cole was sticking to Laura the rest of the day like ugly on a warthog.

He stood to the side of the tennis court as she stowed the ball machine in the adjacent shed. "You should see a doctor. At least rest for a while."

"I'm perfectly fine. Coaching tennis beats sitting around like a caged bird." She juggled her sunglasses and racquet and stepped forward to face him. A white visor with the Hart's Inn logo shaded her expression. She'd had to miss the sailing class, but chafed at any other rescheduling. "Besides, the accident wasn't that bad."

"If you say so, but you have a shadow. After this morning, I'm not letting you out of my sight." At that thought, his blood simmered. The clear challenge of her golden-brown eyes and her familiar scent reminded him of the power she once had over him. Damn.

Resisting her was essential to her safety. Essential to his sanity.

With a resigned huff, she strode down the path. She wore longer dark-blue shorts that didn't show nearly enough of her legs. Like her pink-striped shirt, the shorts looked preppy perfect. And like yesterday, she had the collar turned up to conceal the scars where Markos's hit man had cut her.

The thought of the asshole importer or his goons manhandling her churned within him. DARK had better snatch up Markos before he could try anything more. If Cole ever got his hands on the bastard, there wouldn't be even a smudge left.

He shoved away his urges and fell into step with her. "The brake failure was no accident. At the garage, I insisted it was corrosion to keep the local cops out of it except as an accident. But a tool like an ice pick or awl was used to puncture the lines. Sabotage, not pure, but simple. Markos has found you. Or his paid killer has."

"Then why make it look like an accident? Why not a... bullet?" Her chin trembled, but her voice remained calm.

"An accident would let Markos avoid two murder charges—the murder you witnessed and yours. Without you, there's little evidence against him. The only accidental part was timing. The sabotage could've happened anytime in the last few days." Not knowing how the killer might strike next cranked up the risk factor. And he couldn't rule out a direct attack.

When they reached her cabin, he said, "I'm not leaving you at the door again, Laura. We have more to talk about."

"You have to talk, I suppose. General's orders. And I suppose I have to listen." She unlocked the door and leaned her racquet against the wall inside. "But we don't have to do it here. Let's take a walk. If you think it's safe."

"Safe enough." His DARK team would back him up. But she didn't need to know about that yet.

Through the open door, he noted one great room with a kitchenette. Bathroom and bedroom in the back. Her refined touches to the tag sale furnishings— flowered pillows on the faded sofa and wildflowers on the painted table.

"Not the Ritz Hotel." He and Laura may have been

in the same high school class in Potomac, Maryland, but a chasm bigger than the Gulf of Maine yawned between them in every other way.

"It's adequate." She relocked the door and pocketed her key. Chin raised, she cloaked herself in cool dignity as she led the way to the lake.

A smiling man in a warm-up suit came toward them on the path. With his erect bearing and brush haircut, he should've been jogging to a military cadence. Instead he hobbled with a cane.

Not bad duty for a DARK officer. A stroll around the resort two times a day, once at night, report in, relax around the lake.

Glorious morning, isn't it?" Snow's gaze slid neutrally over Cole.

"Beautiful," Laura sang out.

Cole gave him a casual salute as he passed them.

A dragonfly dipped a wing before darting across the glittering blue surface of the lake. Bees hummed in the flower beds, and a jogger passed them, humming along with the tune playing in his ear. Cole was about to suggest this location wasn't private enough for their conversation when Laura veered off on a diverging path into the woods.

"This leads around behind the cabins and west along an old farm road," she explained.

On their left, birch and other trees leaned over a small stream that babbled beside the path. On the other side stretched a partially overgrown field, dotted with saplings. At its edge, massive branches from a dead elm tree had fallen over a stone wall. The bare hulk stood like a ghostly sentinel, lending the clearing an ominous air.

Crossing her arms, Laura sat on a boulder. She

glared at him down her nose. "You said we have to talk. So talk."

Her princess manner peeled away his professional resolve. Was he angry at things he couldn't change, or at her?

"Seeing you on that tennis court takes me back. Sports for rich kids who don't have to work." Like that summer after she started college. He'd mucked out stalls for horses he never rode while she and her preppy friends learned jumps.

Rolling her eyes, she shook her head. "Are you still hung up on that rich-girl image of me that your biker buddies put in your head?"

He gave a derisive snort. "Hell, if I forgot, my old man reminded me." She was rich in lots of ways he couldn't even begin to express. *Outta your league, boy.* He shoved his dad's slurred put-down back into the vault where it belonged. "They just voiced what I already knew."

He'd lived with his drunken father in a two-room garage apartment smaller and way grubbier than her cabin here. No family. No real home. Had never had. Never would have. He scooped up pebbles and leaned against a birch to toss them into the stream.

"I know you had a rough time. But you excelled in your AP courses and later at the community college no matter how long or hard you worked outside school." Her earlier reserve had eased a notch.

"Yeah, at the stables and the cycle shop. Biker bums don't get white-collar jobs. Right, Laura?" Hell. That was his old man talking. Seeing her exhumed the defeatist attitude he thought he'd buried.

Her eyes shot sparks. "I know all that. You

practically raised yourself. But, as the kids say, get over yourself. You seem to be doing all right these days. And I meant what I said yesterday. General Nolan can send someone else. After the way you treated me ten years ago, why would I want anything to do with you?"

The unfair remarks heated his simmering enmity to a boil. He dumped his remaining pebbles at his feet. "The way *I* treated *you*? I didn't notice you complaining when we made love in front of the fireplace. Or twice in the bed. Afterward you wouldn't even accept my calls. When I really needed you."

Before he could draw another breath, she leaped to her feet. She waved a fist and yelled back at him. "Needed me? For what? To post bail? Of course I didn't take your calls. I knew that bike gang was trouble. Did you think I'd help you get out of jail after what you did to me?"

"All I did was make love to you. And it *was* love, dammit." He was rolling now, roaring with all the invective he could muster. "I thought we had plans. But I was just stud service, wasn't I, babe? So you could return to campus with experience and enjoy the high life."

Tears welled in her eyes, and she held her arms close to her middle as if trying to hold herself together. "Stud service? If that's the way you looked at it, no wonder you decided to pass me around to your friends."

The stream burbled over rocks and fallen branches. A light breeze stirred the pale green birch leaves.

The only other sound was his heart thudding in his ears. "What the hell do you mean, pass you around to my friends?"

Chapter Four

FOR THE FIRST time, a sliver of doubt crept into Laura's mind. "You know, Ray Valesko. He…um." Oh, how could she say the words? "He came to see me that Monday morning. Sent by you."

The set of his jaw and the fierce scowl that drew his ebony brows together were her answer. He stepped closer and grasped her shoulders. "I sent nobody. What did that weasel-faced bastard do? Tell me."

She shot him a wary glance and tried to pull away. She'd never told a living soul, not even her cousin Angela, in whom she always confided. For ten years, she'd believed the worst of Cole.

Doubt wedged a splinter into her heart. Was it possible Valesko had acted on his own? "We were supposed to meet at that commuter parking lot beside the Metro stop. Remember?"

"It's seared in my brain. Go on."

"A guy on a Harley roared up and parked beside me. He had a helmet like yours, the custom one that was stolen."

"My helmet. Oh, yeah. And Valesko knew your sportscar." Cole held her firmly, but with gentle hands. His blue gaze drilled into her as though he could see the scene on her pupils.

She'd waited outside the car in the fresh air. The old car lacked air conditioning. Valesko sneered at her as he leaned against the door and lit a cigarette. He grabbed her and anchored her to his side. Alarm tightening her throat, she focused on a home-done tattoo below the rolled-up sleeve of his dirty t-shirt. A scorpion.

She shivered at the vivid memory. "He … he said you'd sent him. That you were a real pal." Tears burned her eyes, and she fought them down.

"This is tough, Laura, but I need to know." Cole's voice was even, but sharp-edged as a sword. "I didn't send him."

She forced herself to look him in the eyes, so she'd see the truth. "He said I should be nice to him. You said I was a great lay and you had me all primed and ready for him. He was… graphic about how I should be nice to him."

"That lying son of a bitch. I should've killed him." His eyes adamantine, he touched her cheek. "Did he hurt you? Did the bastard—"

"No. I didn't give him the chance." The expression, seeing red, had taken on new meaning as Valesko pawed her. Rage had spread in a hot scarlet smear, whirling her into action. "I think adrenaline kicked in. I pushed him so hard he toppled backward over his bike. Somehow I managed to start the car and drive away." With her heart fissuring in an emotional earthquake.

She drew a deep breath for courage to finish. "Hearing you were in jail delivered the final blow. I was ashamed to tell anyone about Valesko, about us. About any of it."

Cole flung away from her and stalked to the edge of the stream. His hands flexed. "It didn't take much for you to decide I was finally showing my true colors."

When he faced her, in his ice-blue eyes, she

glimpsed a mirror of her own pain.

Valesko had fabricated everything. Cole hadn't known.

And she saw a new truth. For years, he'd thought her a snob, but he was the snob, in reverse. His misgiving was that he couldn't be good enough for her, that a hardscrabble background with an alcoholic father and his biker reputation would slap him down every time. No matter how often he proved himself, how high he climbed, it wouldn't be enough.

His mother had died when he was five, and his father, drowning in his own problems, taught him not to count on people. She doubted he trusted anyone enough to let them past his barriers. Except for anger. Considering how she'd protected her own emotions for the past ten years, she understood.

She wanted to tell him that she'd loved him and shouldn't have doubted him. But he probably wouldn't believe her.

After all, why should he? She was keeping secrets from him. She owed him the truth, at least most of it. This little talk shone light in the dark voids in both their hearts. And if Cole knew the rest of the truth…

She couldn't deal with more now. These revelations were painful enough. She dragged in a ragged breath. "Valesko was so convincing. After being with you, I was so high, and he brought me so low. I thought it was your way of getting rid of me, that you'd gotten all you wanted from me. How else would he know about us, and that we spent the weekend together?"

"Hell, they all knew I was with you. Valesko especially. Who do you think framed me?"

"You mean jail? He was responsible for that?"

He paced to and from the stone wall. "For ten years, I've been certain you deliberately let me sweat it out alone. I hated you for it."

His words tore at her. Cole was right. She'd accepted everything bad she heard. Her mistaken beliefs fell away, leaving only raw wounds. "I did refuse your calls. But how could I have helped?"

"You were my alibi. That Monday morning the cops came to Daddy Bo's Cycle Shop to arrest me for dealing cocaine. A police informant bought drugs Saturday night at the bike rally from a guy wearing my helmet with the reflective visor down."

The news hit her with the force of a punch. She collapsed onto the rock. "The helmet. Oh my God, he didn't have one like yours. It *was* yours."

He nodded. "The custom-made, one-of-a-kind helmet."

"And you were with me."

"But because Valesko lied to you, you wouldn't help me. The cops called your house, but you were gone."

She nodded miserably. If only she had known. "After... after that, I was desperate to get away. I was so distraught that Mom sent me to Europe with my cousin. We left right away. I didn't return home for two months."

"I left for Marine boot camp before you came back." Cole stopped pacing and stood expectantly before her.

She longed to go into his arms, but she couldn't allow herself to act on the impulse. "Why did he do it?"

"Jealousy. Envy. Greed. His drug habit. I kept trying to steer the gang away from that stuff, but he went his own way. Like with alcohol, he never knew when to quit. Valesko took my helmet and did the drug deal. Later he ditched it in the garbage bin behind my apartment.

"I don't know if he really thought he could have you or if he was just making sure you wouldn't help me. I sat in that stinking jail for three days before one of the other guys ratted on him."

"If only—"

"Shh, Laura. No if-onlys. We can't go back. We can only go forward." Tugging her from the boulder, he cradled her in his arms. With one finger, he wiped a tear from her cheek.

For her the if-onlys wouldn't go away. They ripped at her heart and squeezed her throat. If only she hadn't listened to Valesko. If only she'd taken Cole's phone calls. The tragedy that crippled her life and haunted her every moment, waking and sleeping, wouldn't have happened.

Absorbing his scent and his strength, she let him hold her. Only for a minute, for comfort, for old times' sake. Nothing more was possible.

No longer arctic, his eyes burned with desire. No mask over his emotions, no barrier between them. Except the barrier she must keep between them. The barrier protecting her. And her secrets. And Cole.

She allowed herself to exult in the realization that he didn't reject her, didn't betray her. Perhaps he'd loved her a little. He assured her more than once he'd never hurt her. He spoke the truth. The shock of those terrible events blinded her to it.

In Cole, in addition to the other qualities she'd loved, honor and integrity ran true. She was the one with nothing to offer. No good would result from renewing their failed affair.

She saw in his eyes that he was about to kiss her. Her pulse skipped. In spite of herself, she swayed closer

31

to him.

Before his mouth could touch hers, she averted her face and drew away. "You, the self-styled biker hoodlum, were trustworthy after all. Ironic, isn't it, that I didn't trust you. And you didn't trust me. We didn't know each other as well as we thought."

Cole's heart raced. The truth spun his wheels. "I came to protect you, not attack you. But I feel like I just survived a firefight."

"I know what you mean." She smiled, apparently accepting the olive branch. He noted the sheen of tears, the tight mouth. "And I seem to be thirsty. Would you like a cup of tea? Or is that a snobby drink?"

"I used to think so. That was before I spent months in places like Mazar-I-Sharif where meetings with everybody from shop owners to village elders begin by sitting on rug-covered dirt to sip tea. I drank enough tea for three lifetimes."

Her eyes widened, but she didn't ask. "Then is diet cola okay?"

"No problem."

They headed back on the path through the sunny woods. He watched the sexy sway of her hips as she strolled ahead of him. Heaviness tightened his groin.

God, she was beautiful, head tilted to one side, her hair loose around her shoulders. He wanted to run his hands through it, touching it... touching her... She looked delicious in the striped shirt, like a peach sundae. Damn, he still wanted her.

From the first time he'd seen her, she attracted him. Her classic beauty and unconscious sensuality. Her long, lean legs. And surprisingly, her lively intellect. They found common ground senior year with their interest in history. That was the start. In spite of her snobby friends' disapproval, they cobbled together a sort of friendship.

Then during the summers of her first two college years, friendship evolved into more. In stolen moments, they shared hopes and fears and dreams.

And finally, their bodies and souls.

He saw in her now the same qualities that had called to him then. Not much deterred her. The warm glow of her eyes sprang from the vibrant life within her, from her agile mind, from her self-possession and security in who she was.

But she was right to push him away now.

He stared past her as they neared her cabin. Only green shadows stared back. Valesko's story about him had seemed credible, so she felt betrayed. She left without giving him a chance.

Back then, his brain had slipped below his belt. He couldn't afford to fall for her again. Their lives, their backgrounds differed too much. Her actions then only reminded him of what he should have tattooed on his chest—that he could trust only himself.

"Marines and DARK. How? You were such a rebel." Laura turned on the gas burner under the teakettle. Fine lines furrowed between her brows, a sign she was thinking hard.

"I decided after that drug arrest. The cops didn't railroad me, treated me okay. When I was cleared, I joined the Marines to serve the country where a no-account guy got a fair shake. I did a four-year tour, finished a college diploma."

"I'm glad. Do you remember what you told me when I said you were smart, that you should do more than the occasional poli-sci or engineering course at the community college?"

That had been at the all-night graduation party. He remembered their conversation word for word. "When Hogs have wings to jockey up to the moon."

She chuckled at his slang term for Harleys. "Maybe I should check out the moon for new two-wheeled satellites."

He grinned. Her words touched off a spark in his chest. She'd known then, saw the best in him when no one else had. Including his father. "My old man never understood why I wasted my time with those college courses."

She narrowed her eyes as she extracted a tea bag from a canister. "His problem with your bettering yourself was just that—his problem. He kept trying to cut you down to his size. He was afraid."

That made him blink. "He was afraid of nothing. Bitter as hell and a sloppy drunk, but afraid? Afraid of what?"

"For one, that you'd leave him."

The truth of that hit him between the eyes. Why hadn't he seen it? "Like my mom dying. That's when the real drinking started. Hell, in the long run, I did leave him." Guilt gnawed at the edge of his consciousness, but he shook it away. *Don't even go there.*

"You're meant to leave. Parent birds teach their chicks to fly so they can leave the nest. We humans are the same. Or we should be. You had to find your wings the hard way."

"I guess we both did." He managed another grin.

"As for your current status, let's see if I recall exactly what DARK is." A sly gleam lit her eyes. He suspected where she was headed, but couldn't stop her.

"An agency in the Homeland Security Department. It's an elite corps made up of talented people from other agencies, like the FBI, CIA, ATF and DEA."

"Also military intelligence and Border Patrol," he added.

"General Nolan has never told me what the acronym stands for. Division of something? Or is it secret and if you told me, you'd have to—never mind." She flushed as she realized what she'd almost said.

"No secret, but the director prefers we not broadcast it. Domestic Antiterrorism Risk Corps."

"*D-A-R-C?*" she spelled.

"Yup." He ran fingers through his hair. "The general thought DARC didn't seem um…" He searched for a term that matched Nolan's but wasn't obscene.

She smiled sweetly. "Clandestine or dark ops enough?"

"That'll do." He'd remember that next time.

"So you must have been in some other alphabet-heavy agency before DARK." Her eyes shone with curiosity and something like respect. This was the way he remembered her best, her passionate intellect focused. Breathtaking and beautiful, she tied him in knots. But passionate was an unfortunate word. Passionate conjured up other images, memories of naked limbs and love-scented sheets.

Damn. He said nothing.

Her smile hit him like a laser beam. "I'm impressed. You never had any breaks as a kid. You had dreams, but not goals. The striking success you enjoy you've earned on your own. That's quite an accomplishment."

He'd achieved more than he ever thought possible. His heart swelled at her praise. "Hard work paid off." But then he got it, and he deflated. She was placating him for her desertion, for being the unattainable princess. Whatever the biker bum did made no damn difference.

"I believe the CIA sends officers as advisors to Afghanistan, and both the CIA and DARK are in Colombia. Or were until recently."

"Is that right?" He groaned inwardly. She'd already inferred more than he should divulge.

"And let's see. You excelled in Spanish in school. I remember hearing you chatter away with the Guatemalan boy in our class. Esteban, I think, was his name. And is it Pashtun they speak in Afghanistan?"

"Pashtun is an ethnic group. Their language is Pashto."

She smiled, a slow, knowing curve of lips that streaked blood to his lower body and had him squirming. "I see. Remember, I'm the daughter of a diplomat. I know when to stop asking questions." She slid the soda can from the refrigerator and reached for a glass.

"Can's fine. I don't need a glass." He ambled over to lean against the sink.

"You never would let me tame you. You haven't changed too much." A smile crinkling her eyes, she wiped off the can with a damp cloth, then handed it to him.

As he accepted the drink, his fingers brushed her graceful ones. Fiery tingles leaped from her touch and darted up his arm. She spun away nearly as fast as he did. Had she felt the electric awareness too?

"You're wrong there. We've both changed." He raised the can to her. "What you did to escape Markos's thug after losing so much blood took more grit than I've seen in many leathernecks."

Her chin lifted. "I did what I had to do. I couldn't let someone else be killed because of me." She looked away, sorrow darkening her eyes. "That poor policeman. He didn't deserve…"

She'd once told him that when she was a child, at the embassy where the family was stationed, a Marine had been killed preventing her from being kidnapped. And she'd witnessed the violence. No wonder she fled from Markos. And no point in telling her now that the Feds could've protected her.

He shook his head. "Your bloodstained clothing was police evidence. What did you hit the road in after you ran away from the hospital? Not a bare-butt johnny."

"I gave an aide money to buy some things. A pair of jeans, a shirt and sneakers."

In the middle of the night, she'd slipped away and disappeared. Bandaged. Weak. The image of this elegant, vulnerable woman on those dark streets running for her life chewed at his gut. "How did you manage? Did you see a doctor about your wounds?"

She licked her lips, and his traitorous gaze followed the sweep of her pink tongue. "I suppose I should have. I'd have been in trouble if infection had set in. But it didn't. I removed the stitches myself." She reached up to close the collar over her scarred neck.

Why couldn't he just do his job and not care about her? Why was she making this so damn hard? The pain in her eyes made him ache. Enough. She shouldn't have to endure more. Maybe he could convince the general that a safe house was the better plan.

"Setting a trap for Markos could backfire. Maybe I can wangle something else. Let me help you. We can go to a safe house. You won't have to look over your shoulder anymore."

Chapter Five

LAURA TURNED TO the sink, her shoulders tight as if clamped by steel bands. She ran water and scrubbed at a stain on the worn porcelain.

Her battered heart thudded at the prospect of running again. She'd have to leave in the fall anyway, when the resort closed. That prospect loomed over her too. How long could she keep up the pretense, the lies? Always being someone else, finding anonymous work? And how much longer could she hide on her own before Markos found her?

Emotions tangled in her soul. Finally she pivoted back to Cole. "Enough running, enough hiding. If you must protect me, you'll have to do it here. I'm going nowhere with you or anyone else."

Cole froze, his features turned to stone. Before she could develop a Medusa complex, he shook his head and swore.

"Dammit, that amounts to setting a trap—with you as bait. When you wouldn't go with me yesterday, my contact informed me DARK would prefer exactly that. But a trap is damned dangerous. Let me get you to safety. Even without you as bait, we should snatch up Markos soon."

"You lost him before. They let him out of jail."

His mouth flattened. "Hell. A high-priced lawyer sprang him soon after the cops arrested him."

"He called me in the hospital. He threatened me and my family. That's why I ran." Bruised, with broken ribs and stitches in her stab wounds, she'd ached more from terror than her wounds. If she was wise, fear would guide her now.

"I figured as much. Before the agency picked up on his New Dawn ties, he vanished. Kovar too, the pit bull he sicced on you. So when a Yamari illegal washed up at Great Falls, dead of strangulation not drowning, the cops could find no suspect and no witness."

Discussing this with him seemed so strange. But tough as he'd been—still was—he'd always had little patience for injustice or bullies. She remembered— *No, I don't want to remember.*

"In or out of jail," she said, "his contacts and money give him an advantage."

He stared at her hard, as if the power of his gaze could change her mind. "We think he's hired someone to silence you. A professional."

A professional. The monster she'd mostly banished crept out of the closet in the back of her mind and clawed at her soul. But she would not allow Alexei Markos to win. Or to chase her around the country anymore. If he found her once, he could find her again. She had to convince Cole of that.

Shutting herself up in a safe house with him would be beyond torture. He filled a room with his sensuality, his male power. Larger than life, he was a warrior and the honorable man she once knew he could be. The attraction that had spiraled into lust still tugged at her. The touch of his big, capable hand jolted her with awareness. Attraction meant too great a risk to her heart, too great a risk to her secret.

Telling him the rest of what happened would mean reliving the agony and grief, ripping open her scars and bleeding on the floor. Could she trust him?

She trusted him in one way. He would protect her with his life in spite of their past. But their past would be another trap too great to chance. Remaining here in Maine gave her some measure of freedom, some power over what happened.

And some distance from Cole.

She clenched her hands into fists and glared back. "A professional. But the thug would then lead you to his boss, wouldn't he? I want this ended. I saw Alexei Markos strangle a man because the artifact he offered was a fake. I see that poor little man's bulging eyes, hear the horrible gurgling sounds in my nightmares. Markos must be punished."

"We'll roll him up. Soon. We have a lead."

"Because of me. You'll need bait. Me."

"A trap is too risky, too unreliable. I'll convince Nolan to hide you, not set you up. Come away with me. We have places he'd never think of."

She shuddered. "And do what? Pace the floor like a mouse in a maze? No, thank you."

"And how is what you suggest different?"

Heart clattering, she tamped down the panic threatening to paralyze her. To have survived so far, she'd learned to be smart and alert. She needed to think clearly. Cole's nearness fogged her brain.

"I want to *do* something. For nearly seven months, I walked, hitched, and drove all over the East Coast. I chopped vegetables, packed fish, and delivered pizza."

His mouth dropped open. If it hadn't been attached, his jaw might have fallen on the floor. "You, street savvy? Working menial jobs? I can't picture it. How'd you get the jobs?"

"I had one reference, the director at the community center in D.C., where I'd volunteered. Stan Hart, the resort owner here, was the only employer who bothered to make the call."

Cole shook his head. "That director kept your secret well."

Pleased she'd covered her tracks, she said, "In that part of D.C., people keep what they know close to the vest."

He flicked a finger at the designer logo on her shirt pocket. "I didn't know pizza delivery or tennis lessons paid well enough for designer wear."

She'd always taken pride in her appearance, and she wouldn't allow his sarcasm to diminish that. She learned a lot in her time on the road—about going without and about herself. And she didn't mind admitting how she managed. "You'd be surprised what bargains one can find at Salvation Army and Goodwill thrift shops."

"You beat all. I already knew your determination and self-confidence. You've had a damned tough time."

She looked away from the unnervingly tender look in his eyes to the jar of flowers on the table and the living room of the small cabin. "Teaching tennis and sailing here is the best job I've had. But Hart's Inn Resort isn't home. I achieved a meaningful career. Markos stole it from me. Turning the tables on him will help me get my life back. I've played his game of cat and mouse for eight months. I want to be the cat for a change. You have to build the trap."

"When you've made up your mind, you're rooted like a Maine birch tree. Setting a trap is easy. Catching the rat when he goes for the cheese means the cat doesn't sleep. Make no mistake, Laura. You're the cheese, not the cat. And you're not going to shake this cat—" he jabbed a finger at his sternum "—loose until I know you're safe."

His acquiescence came too quickly to allay all her suspicions. She didn't used to be cynical or skeptical of people's motives, but that seemed a long time ago.

In the filtered light through the scratched window, he reminded her of a predator. He stood with his legs wide, his arms hanging loosely at his sides, ready for action. When she'd first known him, he kept a distance, some barrier between them. It was like befriending a wild animal. One did not cross his line of acceptance. Not a cat, though. In a wildlife magazine photo she'd seen, a huge timber wolf's eyes stared into the camera with frightening effect.

Cole had the same piercing gaze, mesmerizing, patient, and acutely perceptive.

Although he might never be domesticated, he was civilized enough to be a federal officer. But she couldn't take a chance that intimate proximity and his perception might cut through her protective shell to the secrets and pain inside. Space, she needed space.

"If you're arranging a trap, you can do your job at a distance. We've cleared up the misunderstandings of the past, but your skills are all I want from you. Keep away from me until this is over, and everything will be just fine."

He didn't reply, merely fixed her with his wolf's stare.

She whisked to the door and held it open. "Don't you have to go report in or something?"

Sighing in an exasperated manner, he closed his eyes briefly. When he opened them, his face was a neutral mask. He'd changed from the bad biker, more than she wanted to admit. The control and protectiveness didn't surprise her, but who was the man with the official face and aura of cool worldliness?

"You can complain all you want about my presence," he said, "but distant doesn't cut it. I can't protect you if I don't know what's going on, who's who around here and what you're up to. Markos's man is already in place. And I don't have to answer to you. I have to answer to—"

She put up her hand. "I know, General Trent Nolan. Tell it to him."

He started toward the door, but something halted him in his tracks. His nose twitched. "What's that I smell? Gas?"

"Oh, probably." She waved a hand dismissively and crossed to the gas heater against the wall. "This thing seems to have a loose valve." A little like her.

"You should get that fixed."

She gave him a saccharine smile. "Wouldn't want me to do Markos's job for him, would we?"

"He came close today. You were lucky that old junker got you down the mountain in one piece. You never were big on maintenance."

He had his nerve. Her chin shot up. "And you're still as arrogant as ever."

"I'll check the outside tank before I go." He grinned as he ambled to the door. "See you later."

"Don't bother. I'll be perfectly safe. I have an early sailing class. I doubt my eleven-year-olds will attack me."

"No problem. I've always wanted to learn to sail."

A sudden thought skittered panic down her spine. "Cole, what about the children? Will my staying here endanger them?"

His brows drew together in a fierce scowl. "If I said yes, would that change your mind about a safe house?"

She cocked a hip at him. "You'd have to convince Nolan as well, wouldn't you? The truth, please."

He heaved a sigh. "I doubt this hit man would try something in a crowd. The kids are safe. Just don't take a couple of them for a hike without escort. That means me and my team's surveillance for backup." He tossed the key onto the table. "Lock up behind me."

The teakettle whistled to end round two, and she wanted to throw it at him. But, acknowledging reluctantly the wisdom of his advice, she did as he'd instructed.

Not instructed. Ordered.

Her heart still pounded from their confrontation, and she sank onto a chair. She stared into space and hugged herself. She'd long ago cut him from her heart, from what was left of it after she believed he tossed her away. She believed Valesko's lies and ran away. Cole saw her actions as abandonment, and he ran away too. Neither one trusted the other enough to weather their first storm. Without trust, love could not survive.

She'd barely survived. Hiding the truth from Cole and protecting her heart from his sensuality and strength might use up another of those imaginary feline lives. After today's crash, how many did she have left?

She wouldn't—couldn't—allow Cole to touch her again. Her eyes and chest ached as tears flowed. She would keep her distance. He might crash her sailing lesson tomorrow morning, but he wouldn't know about tonight's stage-crew work session at the theater.

****

"What possible reason could *I* have for murder?" the quavering soprano said.

"Exactly the right amount of indignation, Doris," boomed the director. "Now Martin. Comforting but anxious."

Actors and stage crew scurried around backstage at the Hart's Inn Barn Theater. Three children played tag among the heavy curtains and backdrops. Paint smells and the cacophony of hammers and voices caromed through the stage wings and up the stairwell at the rear. The stage manager swept through, sprinkling "good job" and "not that color" as she went.

Laura shoved up the sleeves of her Hart's Inn sweatshirt for the fiftieth time. Slapping golden-oak stain on the wooden back of the diner booth, she tried not to clench her teeth with every hammer bang behind her.

Cole.

The blasted man had somehow found her. Not only did the bad penny turn up again tonight, he joined the stage crew. Only in her cabin could she escape him.

Not a bad penny, a loose cannon. Why did he have to be her protector? She couldn't bear it. His very presence unearthed painful memories she habitually kept buried.

And since he'd raised the specter of a hit man, at every step she looked behind her, around her, expecting an attack. Maine was safe. She'd never given a thought to walking alone from her cabin along the wooded path to the rambling inn and the theater beyond. But tonight at the first scrabble in the murky twilight shadows, she sprinted for the theater's stage door.

Good sense told her she needed Cole's protection, but why did it have to be at close range?

"If that man's eyes had laser beams, you'd have a hole in your back. You and our new hunk have a problem?" an amused feminine voice whispered.

Laura recognized the redhead about her own age. An inn guest, she too had recently joined the stage crew. "Vanessa, oh, hi. No, no problem. We… knew each other in high school."

The friendly woman smothered a laugh into the blue-checked curtains she carried. "Why do I have the feeling that's as complete as saying Romeo and Juliet met at a party?"

Vanessa's laughing green eyes and warm candor invited sharing. Laura could use a friendly shoulder, but she had hit the wall with what she could divulge about Cole. "Romeo and Juliet about says it." A tragedy. She'd rather not think about the ending. "Let's leave it at that."

Acting as bait meant she needed protection. She could handle his presence. She couldn't block her awareness of him, but she didn't have to talk to him.

Chapter Six

BY THE TIME the stage crew took a break, Laura
had had enough of Cole's laser stare and overbearing
attitude. When his back was turned, she slipped down the
backstage stairway. A few minutes to herself would
restore her equilibrium.

The lower floor used to be the stable of the old barn.
Storage and dressing rooms lined a hall through the
former horse stalls. She inhaled the fragrance of long-
removed hay, its essence embedded in the wood. No one
seemed to be working in any of the rooms. All was dark
except for a bare bulb in the long hall.

She sank into the comfort of the old rocking chair
used in *Arsenic and Old Lace*. More than one of the
gentlemen callers had drunk the ladies' elderberry wine
and died in its embrace. Morbid thought. Not what she
needed as a mood changer.

The wooden stairway creaked. A second tread
creaked.

Someone was coming.

Alarm bells rang in her head. How stupid! She'd
done exactly what Cole warned her not to do. She'd gone
off by herself. Heart pounding, she eased to her feet.

Perhaps it was only one of the stage crew. Or Cole.
But perhaps it wasn't.

Where could she hide?

As the unknown person continued down the stairs,

she ducked among the hanging costumes in the nearest storage room. She held her breath and waited. Sweat trickled down her back.

Rubber soles squeaked on the cement floor. Someone was walking along the hall, just as she had. As the footsteps approached, she peered between a silk cloak and a velvet doublet.

Vanessa walked by the door, a bucket of paint in one hand.

Laura exhaled slowly, her hand on her chest. Safe enough, but she might not have been. She wouldn't be so foolish again. Extricating herself from the soft fabrics, she strolled out into the hall.

"Oh, hi, Vanessa. What're you doing down here?" She tried to sound casual, but could hear a wobble in her voice.

The redhead turned from the doorway where she stood, alarm on her freckled face. She slid a hand from her jeans pocket and pointed. "Extra paint. I left it in here since I don't know where it goes. What're you up to?"

Laura shrugged. "Checking to see if we could use any of these costumes. Nothing more modern than Shakespeare's time, I'm afraid."

Vanessa gestured toward the stairs. "After you."

When the two women emerged backstage, Cole's disapproving countenance zeroed in on Laura.

Making a show of ignoring him, she grabbed her brush and slapped more stain on the wood. Back where she started. Worse. Her mini escape had done nothing to lighten her mood, and now she felt foolish and foolhardy.

****

When the work session ended, Laura made her way to a seat in the orchestra section to view the rest of the rehearsal. Ranks of old church pews sloped up the barn's second story. Burgundy carpeting covered the aisle floors, but the rustic charm of the building's origin glowed elsewhere in the bare boards and beams. The theater's quaint and bucolic atmosphere welcomed and warmed her.

Among the orchestra seats, scattered knots of people chatted or pored over scripts. No tall, dark-haired male arrested her gaze. No compelling blue eyes drew her. Cole must still be backstage. Taking a seat toward the rear, she allowed herself a sigh. But was it of relief or disappointment?

A moment later he came up the aisle toward her, a cell phone at his ear. As he sidled down the row of seats toward her, he spoke into the receiver in gentle, coaxing tones—in Spanish. She recognized one word, *querida*, sweetheart. Then he said in English, "Gotta go," and disconnected.

Impressed at his facility in the language and eaten alive with curiosity, she knew better than to ask. An intelligence operative would have a cover story. But she couldn't help wondering if the person on the other end was a woman he'd met in Colombia.

"Tired?" He sat beside her, too warm, too large, and too close for comfort.

She turned, ready to do battle. Verbal duels kept the barriers up, kept conversation at a superficial level. A safer level. "No, but if you are, feel free to leave. I don't notice you doing much of a job of protecting me tonight."

His charcoal jeans and t-shirt revived the old bad-boy persona and heightened the aura of male potency. He offered her a smug curl of his lip. "You're covered.

Somebody has kept an eye on you since I left you."

"Someone was in the woods?" The rustlings, the shadows? That was an agent—um, officer—guarding her?

His gaze pinned her. He leaned against the bench seat, the thin cotton of his shirt stretched taut across powerful shoulder muscles.

She fought to control her erratic pulse. It was merely physical attraction. She could fight it. "What do you have set up? What are you doing in the theater? What—"

"Twenty Questions? That's an old game." The grooves in his cheeks deepened with the softening of his scowl. He covered her hands where she gripped the seat back in front of her. "Take it easy. We're working this one out. I won't keep you in the dark."

The warmth of his hands slid more heat to a part of her body she'd rather ignore. She ought to pull away, but remained still, savoring the contact. "Sorry. I'm a little spooked."

"Good one. Spooked." He grinned. "By the way, I checked your cabin's gas connections. The outside tank valve was tight. The safety valve on the heater itself must be broken. Hard to say if it's by design or accident. Damned unreliable method for murder, though."

"The valve's probably defective. I'll speak to Stan."

"Don't just speak to him. Get it fixed." He leaned back and propped one ankle on the opposite knee. "Now what's this damn play about?"

He was trying to divert her, calm her nerves. He was right. This wasn't the time or place for plotting. But his thoughtfulness and sincerity shouldn't surprise her.

Once he'd wrapped her in his leather jacket to keep her warm on his motorcycle. At an arcade he threw Ping-

Pong balls for an hour to win her a gold charm in the shape of a crown because he said Midas's daughter should have a crown. It was with the few things she'd been able to bring away with her when she ran from the hospital.

"The play?" he prompted.

"*Diner*'s a murder mystery, as you may have surmised from the title."

"*Death at the Diner*. A dead giveaway."

She groaned and smiled back, too aware of him.

He sat with his hands splayed on his knees. How large and masculine the fingers looked, with black hairs curling above the knuckles. As she remembered those fingers sliding across her skin, flames flicked through her veins.

"Unusual assortment of characters." He jerked a nod toward the stage.

She dismissed the spell cast by his nearness. "*Diner*'s on the order of an Agatha Christie story. It involves a group of disparate people brought together in one place."

"In this case, a diner."

"A snowstorm traps them. One by one, they're murdered, and the remaining characters have to solve the mystery before they too are killed."

"How well do you know these people? Has anyone joined the troupe in the past few days?"

"You mean, besides you?"

He cut her a calculating look.

Sarcasm was no more shield from his persistence than from his sensuality. She sighed. "You can't seriously suspect any of these people. Most of the actors and stage crew are regular guests or employees. Nearly everyone arrived at the resort long before Markos was spotted in Boston."

"I suspect everybody. Markos can pay big bucks for your scalp. Can you be certain nobody here would accept money to set you up?"

His soft tone didn't remove the sting from his words.

A frisson, like walking into a spider web, crawled over her skin. How could she fear any of these people, whom she considered friends? But she had no choice. "All right. What do you need?"

"Just connect names with faces for me. I have a list for background checks." He leaned forward as though absorbed in the scene. "And, Laura, don't go downstairs again without me."

At the image of Markos's thug Kovar leaping out at her from a rack of costumes, she flinched. Did she have the strength to place herself in jeopardy?

She had to if she wanted her life back.

A young man rolled on stage on a bicycle, followed by a perky young blonde, a trench-coated man, and another woman. "That's Burt Elwell, a local boy. He's our only handyman since his uncle Jake hurt his back."

"Ah, the young dude with the hots for you."

Surprised he remembered Burt's waving to her, she gave him a disgusted look. "I don't know why I'm even responding to that idiotic observation. He's twenty. He has the hots for all females between fifteen and forty."

Cole snorted.

She wouldn't consider jealousy as his motive for his attitude. No, his surliness stemmed from his protective mode. But her heart fluttered anyway.

"That's supposed to be a motorcycle," she whispered, "but we don't have one yet. He plays a rebel biker."

"The mountain bike suits the kid better," he growled.

"You must've met the owner, Stan Hart, when you arrived. There he is in the cook's apron behind the diner counter. Martin Rhodes, a retired dentist, is the detective, and a local teenager named Heidi plays his daughter. The elderly woman with the orange bouffant is Doris Van Tassel. She and her sister Bea were the leads in the last play, *Arsenic and Old Lace*. They come here every summer. You probably suspect them too." This was getting ridiculous.

When he didn't respond, she moved on to the observers in the front row of seats.

"I've met the stage crew," he said, when she pointed out Vanessa and the stage manager seated beside her.

The director, white-haired and regal, strode to the stage apron. "Let's get this blocking right, people."

"Rudy Damon once directed several plays on Broadway. He's a college professor now. He and Stan renovated this old barn for summer productions about five years ago." Laura pointed at the solid beams and gracefully curved gambrel roof. "This and the inn are the only structures left of what was a prosperous farm a hundred years ago."

"I see somebody trying to get your attention. Who's that at the edge of the stage? In that big yellow drapey thing, she looks like a ripe melon."

A laugh bubbled up. He did always make her laugh. His incisive wit had been one of the first things to attract her. "Oh dear, you're right. My father the diplomat calls that type of bosomy woman a powder-puff pigeon. And the drapey thing is called a caftan."

She waved back to the older woman, whose choices in fashion often didn't suit her short, plump stature. "That's Bea Van Tassel, Doris's sister. She's doing publicity and some light stage crew work."

Bea tripped down the steps from the stage and swept up the aisle toward them as they left their seating row. "Yoo-hoo, Laura, did you like the chowder I left for you?"

Laura smiled and patted the woman's arm. "Oh, yes, Bea, thank you. It was delicious. I'd love the recipe."

The woman wagged a parchment-skinned finger at her. "Sorry, dear, it's a family secret." Her modulated stage voice belied her eighty-plus years. "But I'll bring you something else later in the week."

She looked brightly up at Cole. "You've just joined us, I believe, young man."

Laura's stomach clenched. She didn't know how he was explaining his presence. Leaving it to him, she introduced them.

"I understand you and your sister wowed them in the last production." He took her proffered hand gently.

Clear blue eyes twinkling, Bea smiled. "You'll do, young man. And you'll love it here. This is such a beautiful place. And not a bad little theater for its location. These productions give me a chance to relive my glorious youth."

"Bea and her sister used to perform on Broadway," Laura put in. "They started out in the chorus line and eventually had starring roles."

"We had a good run," the other woman said. "Of course, that was decades ago. We retired before Rudy Damon's day."

"This director?" Cole asked. "I've never heard of

him, but I'm no theater expert."

"Oh, yes, he was in demand a few years ago. The white hair makes him look older. Unlike some people." She beamed and patted her sausage curls, as black as shoe polish. "He had a hot streak before his last two plays bombed. No producer would take a chance on him after that."

Laura patted Bea's shoulder. "That's a sad story. If it's any consolation, it looks like he'll have a hit with *Death at the Diner*."

"How could he not, with Doris up there?" She waved a hand at the stage, then gazed at Cole with interest. "What sort of work do you do?"

Laura could hardly wait for his answer.

"I'm a travel writer." His gaze was contemplative. Laura tried and failed to picture an authorial pipe dangling from his mouth. "I pen those articles in the travel section of the Sunday paper and on *Travel Tips* online about the latest vacation hot spot."

Bea's smile widened. "Stan must hope you'll write an article about Hart's Inn Resort."

"You never know." He gave her a boyish grin.

"Are you ready to go?" he said to Laura. His warm hand against her lower back urged her to movement.

When they hit the cool night topped with a dome of stars, he dropped his hand and walked at her side.

So much for distance. Sitting beside him in the darkened theater had heightened her consciousness of him to the point that now she felt bereft at the loss of his touch. And he made her laugh. Like old times.

Double whammy.

Chapter Seven

LAURA'S FURROWED BROW probably meant suspicion and worry at what he planned to do. Cole had caught a glimpse of her amazement at his cover story. Good. Let her stew a moment.

He was stewing too, itching to touch her again. Walking in the dark was too reminiscent of stolen kisses and a stolen weekend.

They left the theater barn behind and crossed the empty parking lot. When they came abreast of the three-story clapboard inn, Laura spoke, her amused gaze heating him another degree. "Travel writer?"

He shrugged. "It's a good cover. But Hart will wait a long time for any article of mine. The armpits of the world I usually visit end up in classified reports, not the travel section of a newspaper or blog."

She cocked her head, looking as if she wanted to ask more, but kept her silence.

"What was that about the chowder?"

She laughed, a lighthearted peal that belied her deep fears. "Bea thinks I'm thin. She's trying to fatten me up."

"You look good. Not skinny." Ripe curves and a golden tan, Midas's daughter all grown up. He could picture every millimeter of that creamy skin. The memory heated his blood and pissed him off for remembering.

"Thanks." She smiled at him as they approached her

cabin.

All it took was to be near her, and his cool resolve flew away like dust beneath his spinning wheels. Clearing up most of the past didn't chill the slow burn inside him. He had questions that needed answers. Answers about her choices back then. Answers that might drive away the demon voice of his old man. *You'll never amount to nothing, boy. You're just like me. No-account.*

He gave himself a mental shake. He was no good at understanding their so-called relationship, but he had to try. "Look, Laura, I've been thinking."

She turned from unlocking her door. "Always a dangerous thing."

Dangerous, maybe. He'd see if it was fatal. "Ten years is a long time to hold a grudge. But I can't let go of this ache in my gut until the past is totally settled."

She gaped at him, her eyes as big as pie plates. Even in the dim outdoor lighting, he could see her face go chalky. "What do you mean?"

"What do you think I mean? Why were you so quick to believe Valesko's lies?"

Color seeped back, and crimson daubed her cheekbones. How did he spook her so?

"I'd heard… rumors about you and another girl. I saw you together outside the college. People said she was your next conquest. I think her name was Mona."

He scrubbed a hand across his chin. "Mona was Valesko's ex-girlfriend. I helped her get away from him after he beat her up for the third time. That was all."

She gave him a rueful smile. "Of course you would help someone that way. I'm sorry I didn't ask you about her."

"Then later you never even asked about me. It was like we'd never been together. Like I'd never existed. I was in the Marines, but I had word from some of the guys. When you came back from Europe, you didn't try to find me. Then you didn't return to Penn. You went off to some new college out west."

Laura shivered and hugged herself. She stood rigid, transmuted into unyielding metal.

Her silence struck flint to the low flame inside him. "I used to feel we connected, that you knew *me*, not just the bum everyone else saw. Was I wrong? Were you just a rich girl slumming?"

Her chin shot up. She stood toe-to-toe with him, glaring at him. "You have no idea what I went through. Yes, we connected. I felt you were the other half of me. My world was turned upside down when I believed you'd tossed me away like a rusted motorcycle part. I had to put the pain behind me and find a new world."

The harsh belief he'd held all these years curled at the edges, ignited new questions. But finding the right words to ask her taxed him more than negotiations in Spanish or Pashto.

"During that damn weekend, we had plans to be together, dreams of a future. You were going to transfer to Georgetown. Finally I had attainable dreams. Education, job, and then kids. You knew how I felt about a family. How the hell could you mow down those dreams?"

Grief and sadness shadowed her face. She looked at him with overflowing eyes. "I'm sorry I wasn't there for you, so you felt you had to leave and join the service."

"Don't be sorry for me in that respect." Giving in to impulse, he hugged her to him. "No regrets here about joining up. My interests in politics and history paid off. Without the Marines, I wouldn't be a government officer today."

"Then you're fortunate. As for the rest, fate and our immaturity conspired against us back then. Let's leave the answer at that."

He shook his head. "It's not enough."

She wrenched from his embrace and moved to the door. Her mouth and shoulders firmed. "It's all I have to offer."

The tears brimming over glistened in the arc cast by the outside light. His gut instinct nagged him that she was still holding something back. If it wasn't their biker-and-princess differences, what could it be?

Damn. He was an idiot. Her tears were due to the shock of revisiting old wounds. Add to that her recent visit to hell. Witnessing a murder, nearly becoming the next victim. Going underground and living in fear. Then today's brake failure. Another near miss.

He'd pushed her as far as he should today. But he would eventually find out what she'd left unsaid. "Let's go inside." He tucked her behind him and finished unlocking the door for her. "You're a target out here."

"For mosquitoes, definitely." She swatted one on her arm. Her voice was thick with emotion, but not humor. "What on earth are you doing?"

He saw she was staring at the small Glock he'd drawn from his ankle holster. "I'm going in to check out the cabin. Stay out here until I call you."

Pushing the door in slowly, he slipped into the darkened cabin and skirted the great room. He gagged at the alien odor.

Gas.

The chemical odorant the gas company added to the odorless gas was a precaution he was damned thankful for. The lousy heater was still leaking. If there was a hit man inside, he was dead to the world. Or dead period.

After a quick tour of the rest of the cabin, he slipped the 9mm into its holster. No killer, sleeping or otherwise.

He located the heater and quickly shut off the valve. Fixing it might not be the answer. Not worn threads, but a human hand had loosened it. He'd notify the others to surveil the cabin full-time.

Shoving open windows to help clear the air, he called for Laura to enter. She was frightened enough for tonight without his laying the latest on her. "But don't turn on the light just yet. Even a small spark would be enough to blow us clear to New Hampshire."

She entered the kitchen and stood by the table, shivering. No longer angry, she looked small and fragile and grief stricken. "I'll see Stan tomorrow about getting that fixed."

Cole edged to the door, gazing out at the shadows beneath the trees. He braced his palms on the door frame.

Laura watched him. Sooner or later she'd have to tell him. How much did he know already? "Turnabout is fair play. Did you ever go back to Potomac to learn the truth? Did you look for me later?"

His back stiffened, and he turned slowly. "I went back one more time after basic. For my dad's funeral. He drove with a snootful one too many times and plowed his car into a highway abutment." His eyes were as bleak and bitter cold as winter.

She started to go to him, to put her arms around his big shoulders. He'd been all alone, far away, and no one comforted him then. Or since, she supposed. But she was too vulnerable to him as it was.

So she clutched the kitchen chair and stayed put. "Cole, I'm so sorry. I had no idea."

Hands fisted at his sides, he stared past her into the dark corners of the room. "I was celebrating the end of basic training on my first pass. A bunch of us guys just got back from a local bar after tossing down more than a few beers. When the cops phoned the base to give me the sorry-for-your-loss speech, I was drunk. Like him."

Her heart aching for him, Laura pushed the chair aside and crossed to him. His rigid shoulders didn't invite cuddling, but she pried open his hand, lacing her fingers with his larger ones. She longed to press her other hand to his whisker-roughened cheek, to trace the groove that had deepened with his emotion. But she didn't. "You couldn't have known. And you had a right to celebrate."

"A right to celebrate." He shook his head, then eased his hand away and opened the door. "I knew then I didn't want to end up like him. I haven't touched alcohol since."

Alcoholism ran in families, so his was a wise decision. Compassion and admiration for him were the last emotions she expected to feel tonight. "Always a clear head, then, cowboy?"

He barked a laugh. As she'd hoped, her light comment had lifted his dark mood a notch. "Not always, but at least my head's not pickled."

Hell, in the long run, I did leave him. When he said she did earlier, she wondered about the bitterness coloring his words. Now she understood. "Instead you've taken a long guilt trip. It wasn't your fault, you know. The drink would've killed him one way or another even if you'd been there."

"I know."

"Do you? Do you really?"

"Hell, woman. You know me too well. His liver was a sieve. Doctors said he didn't have long to live anyway."

"So let the guilt and regrets go."

"And you?"

His gaze and pointed question kicked her in the chest. Somehow the topic had changed. He'd turned her probing back on her. But she wasn't ready to delve into their mutual past again so soon. She merely shook her head and shrugged.

With that, he left the cottage and melted into the night.

She closed—and locked—the door and checked the gas valve again in the dark. Tight. Of course he'd made it secure.

She turned on lights in the bedroom and bath and got ready for bed. As she washed her face, she felt the day's tension and weariness deep in her bones. She barely had the strength to brush her teeth.

A pounding on the door jarred her awake from dozing on her feet.

The monster clawed at her. Trapped. Cole had left her, and she didn't know how to contact him. But would a hit man knock at the door? She nearly giggled at the notion. Dousing the bathroom light, she squinted at the kitchen door. Through the glass, she saw a familiar profile.

Cole. With a small duffel over his shoulder. An overnight bag.

She didn't know whether to be relieved or angry or terrified. But her first thought up on the mountain had been correct.

No escape.

****

Gasping for breath, Laura surged to a sitting position. She shivered. Sweat beaded her brow and chest.

Three a.m. The dial of her bedside clock cast the only light in the small bedroom. Outside, trees blocked the moonlight from the window. A sleepy chirp was the only disturbance in the night. She lifted the damp hair sticking to her neck.

The old nightmare.

She rubbed her eyes to rid her vision of the terrifying kaleidoscope—the spinning car, the screech of metal against metal, the rag doll that wasn't a rag doll. The blood.

Oh, God. A thunderstorm of memories crashed around her. She fought to control the anguish that churned like an egg-beater in her stomach.

Breathe. Count of four in… hold, then eight out. Four in. Eight out.

The techniques she'd learned from counseling were holding her together now, just barely. Breath control, visualization. She knew what to do, whatever the cause of panic.

After the attempt on her life, knives and tiny claws and crimson darkness had monopolized the prime-time nightmare slot, and then tapered off. Tonight by popular demand the old rerun returned.

In the dark she fumbled her way out of the clammy sheets. She was calmer now, but her parched throat needed water. She pressed her sweat-damp forehead against the closed door. The coolness of the solid wood recalled her to the present.

Her dead son's father lay out there asleep on her

sofa.

Drat the man. He was the cause of the dream's return. The cause of all her anguish. Tears leaked from her squeezed eyelids. How could she have any left?

Following the roller-coaster ride that had totaled her car, the day had continued its downhill slide. A wary Cole in military mode stayed close, a wolf on lookout. They cleared up past misunderstandings, but his not knowing the rest was a guillotine hanging over her head. If he kept badgering her, eventually she'd have to tell him.

At least part of the story.

Her emotions were too raw, and she feared breaching the dam if she explained now. She didn't owe him all of it. No, that was her private, lonely hell.

His reentry into her life had dumped her into a new level of the Inferno. The man was much more than the boy, a man to make her long for impossible dreams. Every minute with him burned that into her soul. He still knew her too well for her to dissemble for long. How long could she last?

Seeing pity and rejection in other people's eyes had cut her deeply. Seeing them in his would kill her. She would endure his suspicions. He knew she hadn't given him the whole story. She'd had two serious relationships after Cole, and both ended after her admission.

He'd left the cabin, grim-faced and strung tight. A while later, he reappeared. No more bivouacs in the woods, he said, plopping his duffel on her living room floor. By tacit consent, they avoided any further mention of the past.

And now he was snoring on her sofa.

The bathroom faucet sometimes shrieked like a

teakettle. So if she wanted water, could she sneak by him to the kitchen without waking him?

Awareness of his presence kept her so tense that her muscles and her temple ached. When he'd showered, she tried to think of anything but his fit, muscular body dripping with soap—her soap. After he settled down, she tried not to listen to every creak of the wooden frame, tried not to wonder if he slept in his underwear. Or in nothing at all.

Surely he slept soundly. Didn't spies and soldiers, like doctors, learn to sleep anywhere, anytime?

He slept, but she lay awake until exhaustion finally overtook her. Then the nightmare had strobed her mind's screen and woken her.

Her waking memories were no less torturous.

She didn't usually close her bedroom door, so she didn't know if it squeaked. Drawing a deep breath, she twisted the flimsy metal knob slowly.

Silence.

She pulled the door open.

Silence.

Relaxing a bit, she eased barefoot across the threadbare carpet into the living room.

"Are you okay?" He clicked on the table lamp.

Chapter Eight

SHE STARTED, AT his sexy, sleep-thickened voice as much as at the bulb's glare through the stained paper shade. His liquid drawl tempted her to curl up with him on the couch.

He was propped on his elbows, his bare chest above the sheet and light blanket. Whorls of dark curling hair sprinkled the muscled planes of his chest. Denser than in his youth, but not so heavy a woman's fingers couldn't reach the firm, warm flesh beneath. On his flat stomach, the ebony hair arrowed downward, disappearing beneath the thin coverlet.

She couldn't swallow. Her mouth was the Sahara. "I'm fine. Just thirsty." Drat. All she wore was a t-shirt and sleep shorts. She scooted sideways to stand behind the only upholstered chair. Not much cover, but most of the room lay in shadows.

"You sure? I heard groans. It'd be a miracle if you didn't have nightmares. The murder attack or the car crash?"

She reeled from the pain of his perception. How did he—

But of course he meant this morning's crash. Not the other one. He didn't know about that one. She hoped.

She exhaled slowly, aiming for nonchalance. "All my disasters seem to involve vehicles. Maybe in a previous life I was a race driver."

"Or a bad mechanic." He cocked his head at her. "When this is over, you might want some help with PTSD."

Post-traumatic stress disorder. She knew much more about PTSD than he imagined.

"You a psychologist now?" She shouldn't let him see her irritation at his bull's-eye. She was handling the stress just fine.

Except for the nightmares. And the odd panic attack.

She fluttered a hand. "I'm sorry. You're right."

A smile flickered and vanished. "You getting water?"

Tugging the t-shirt down to cover as much as she could, she hustled to the sink. "Would you like some?"

"Sure, if you're buying."

The warm resonance of his voice flip-flopped her stomach. Her unwanted reaction was a warning. She mustn't let down her protective barriers. She had to fight the attraction. Trying not to stare at his chest, she handed him a glass and turned to go.

"Sit down. You're not going to sleep anyway. We need to talk about your extreme driving... adventure."

Cole sprawled, one arm stretched along the back, the other propping the glass on his flat belly. Rumpled and heavy-lidded, he looked sensual and decadent. *Replace the jelly glass with a wine goblet and bring on the Roman orgy.*

Grabbing one of the pillows he'd kicked onto the floor, she held it in front of her bare legs. She sat in the chair that had hidden her from his burning gaze.

"Impressive control up there, babe. Worthy of NASCAR. How'd you learn those moves?"

She shrugged. "I took a defensive driving course a

few years ago." Her counselor had suggested it might cure her fear of driving after the accident. It helped.

"Being on the street for months, you must have developed a sixth sense for danger. Wasn't there a brake fluid warning light on the dashboard? I drove you home once because you ignored the low-gas indicator."

A heated flush crept up her cheeks at his reminder of her infamous neglect. But this time was different.

"I bought the car third or fourth-hand in New Jersey at Trusty Tom's, a shark's den where neither buyer nor seller asks many questions. I barely made it to Maine. I'd been having trouble with the dashboard lights, but repairs cost money I don't have."

He swallowed the rest of his water in one gulp. Her pulse quickened at the sight of the Adam's apple moving in his strong throat.

"I can't get over you living underground like this. How'd you get to Jersey?"

"I hitched." His brows shot northward at that. Enjoying his reaction, she went on. The topic was a safe one. "Truckers were very helpful. Sometimes I took the bus."

"Winter must've been tough in Maine."

He was fishing now. He had no idea where she'd been before Passabec Lake. Unaccountably, that pleased her. "I spent the winter in Myrtle Beach, South Carolina, delivering pizza and hooking plastic covers on dry cleaning."

"New skills for the anthropologist." He saluted her with his empty glass.

"Survival skills. I learned a lot about people. Most were kind. A pawnshop owner in Trenton helped me change the name on my driver's license from Rossiter to

Murphy."

"'Most were kind.' Not all. Guys hassle you?"

A shiver quaked her shoulders as his question triggered a memory. "Some men were pretty crude. I left the dry cleaners because the boss had wandering hands. But there was only one time when I was in real danger. I was on the way to buy the car, all my savings in cash in my purse. Two men came out of an alley and tried to mug me."

He leaned forward, forearms on his knees. "You got away?" The blanket slipped to show the black waistband of his briefs. Equally black hairs continued their journey downward beneath the edge.

Cheeks heating, she smiled at the appropriateness of black briefs on Cole, but she averted her gaze to her glass. "They were drunk and not too steady on their feet. I knocked a couple of trash cans over in front of them and ran."

In shock or in tribute, he gave a low whistle. His face somber, he set the empty water glass down on the low table between them. "Your toughness amazes me."

"I did what—"

"What you had to do. I know. Blows me away."

Desire burned in his eyes, tempting her to forget all caution. She imagined she could feel his body heat on her skin, but she was probably still warm from her battle with her nightmare demons. She swallowed.

Before she allowed his magnetism to erode her resistance further, she should put the bedroom door between them. She could survive his presence for the night.

He'd be out of her cabin tomorrow. He had to be.

The questions she'd wanted to pose earlier glued her

to her seat. "So, my junker from Trusty Tom is kaput. I have no transportation. It seems Markos has found me, and DARK has agreed to use me. I have nowhere to run to and no way to run. What's next?"

The vulnerability of her falsely light tone stung Cole like salt in a wound. He wished to God he had a different answer to her question. Wished he could win her confidence, draw out what she was still reluctant to share.

He bent forward, catching her scent. Were those her nipples he glimpsed through the thin cotton, or only shadows? Hell. He was too damned susceptible to her, to her courage and determination, to the gentleness in her eyes and the curve of her mouth.

And to the livid scars above the t-shirt neck.

"You don't have to do this. No one will force you to be a target. We can go on with the plan of a safe house." He'd hide her himself if DARK wouldn't go along. The hell with protocol. Fear for her was eating him up.

She squared her shoulders. "No. The trap is the best idea. If it helps catch Markos and finds New Dawn's leader, I'll paint that bull's-eye on my back."

The steel in her words punched him in the heart. He'd seen this mission as another step up in DARK, but the personal side of it outweighed whatever its success— or failure, but he wouldn't consider that— meant to his career. Setting their rock-strewn history aside, he would protect this courageous woman with his life.

Leave the past out of it. Leave the personal crap out of it.

"What's next, you ask?" Hell, he had nowhere to run, either. Run to me, he wanted to say. "My bivouac on your couch is permanent."

Her scowl could have curdled milk. "What do you mean?"

"I'm moving in permanently, Laura. As far as everyone's concerned, you and I are lovers."

****

Cole stood to one side as she locked her door the next morning. She smelled of sunscreen and insect repellant, and underneath, Laura. "How many kids are in this sailing thing?"

She stuffed her key in her shorts pocket and picked up the travel mug she'd parked on the step. "Eight, most about eleven years old. Kay is thirteen going on twenty-five."

He fell into step with her. "You never used to drink coffee." He clinked his mug with hers, then drank.

She sipped from her mug. "It's an acquired taste."

She looked down her elegant nose at him like he was a taste she'd resist acquiring. Yesterday he'd pushed her too hard. No one ever accused him of diplomacy, but he'd learned patience in his work. Doing his job of protecting her meant waiting to find out more about the past.

And, if he was honest, more about the woman she was today. Was the chasm of their differing backgrounds still between them or was it something else? The craving to know more warred with his fear of knowing and tightened his chest.

Her comment about wanting justice for the man who'd died at Markos's hands came back to him. And as wary of him as she was, she'd offered him comfort about his old man. In the midst of danger and her own grief, she thought of others. Compassion flowed automatically, part of her nature. Regardless of the past, protecting her was personal as well as duty.

And regardless of the present, he longed to taste her skin. To bury himself inside her until the rekindled passion burned all the lost years to oblivion.

But to do his job and remain alert he needed emotional distance. Neutrality. Guarding Laura would be more torture than the New Dawn Warriors could dream up.

"The class is held over on the east shore of Passabec Lake." She pointed toward a cluster of rambling outbuildings that included a bathhouse and boat shed. All gave a good view of the rental and private cabins on the west side.

They continued past the beach to the docks and the boat shed, about the size of a one-car garage.

"The boat shed's really an equipment building." She shoved the old-fashioned door. The heavy wood squeaked in protest on its metal runner, but yielded and slid to the right. "And before you ask, no, we don't keep it locked. This is Maine, not D.C. or New York."

He nodded, chalking up one more spot a killer could hide. Or a DARK officer for surveillance. Knowing he had backup downshifted the pressure to manageable.

Only the sunlight streaming inside illuminated the boating gear. Oars, odds and ends of lines and ropes, sail bags, and life vests lined the walls of the musty interior. A Coleman lantern and its fuel can sat atop a wooden stool, and an old rowboat lay in a corner beside a motor and red plastic gasoline containers.

He whistled softly. "You'd better hope a big storm doesn't come along and blow this shed away. Rotten boards all around."

She darted about the cluttered space, sorting sail

bags and life vests. The sway of her hips and the silken fall of her hair snagged his gaze. "The regular handyman was going to repair it, but he hurt his back."

"I hope this place doesn't get struck by lightning." The stuffing from a pile of discarded life vests bled through ragged holes onto the dirt floor. Busy mice.

"Eliminating the junk would help." Laura prodded a fist-size hole in the white dinghy's bottom. "I'd like this out of here too. It's identical to mine. A guest ran it up on the rocks last summer. Jake was fixing it with fiberglass. With him out of commission, Burt has his hands full with all the normal maintenance and gardening."

Heat fired in his gut. Must be concern at an unknown factor like that kid. Cole had no real reason to resent him. Relieved he'd kept his anger spike to himself, he swallowed the rest of his coffee. He set the mug on the floor when she shoved an armload of life vests at him.

"Here, make yourself useful. Put these out on the dock." She picked up a couple of sail bags and headed outside.

He followed into the brilliant sunshine as the novice sailors began arriving. Some wore t-shirts over swimsuits, others shorts over their swimsuits.

No chance of missing the going-on-twenty-five Kay. Wearing makeup heavy enough to require a neck brace and a cutoff t-shirt that displayed her budding attributes, she was dressed for a street corner rather than a sailboat. She gyrated onto the dock to the beat from whatever was playing in her earbuds. A chunky boy, likely her younger brother, trailed behind.

Six more youngsters trooped onto the dock chattering and laughing. Wreathed in smiles, they eyed him with curiosity.

"None of the kids I've been around lately looked this well fed or well kept," Cole said, struck by the openness he saw. "They were ragged and thin, wary of the Americans asking questions. Or big-eyed orphans desperate for affection."

Laura's gaze skittered away. "Did you... come in contact with many children? Orphans?"

"People are so poor in Colombia that some abandon children they can't feed. My unit picked up a baby in a field and took her to an orphanage just north of Medellín." The children's sad souls had reached right into his chest. He'd wanted to offer the attention denied him as a child.

"Thank God. But most of them aren't so lucky?"

"I wouldn't want to guess how many." Best not to get into that. "Anyway, the little kids at the orphanage liked my hokey coin tricks."

She tilted her head as if she wanted to ask more, but only smiled. She dropped her sail bags beside the life vests and turned toward the students. "Okay, swabbies, this is Mr. Stratton. He's going to watch today."

Saying their names, she tapped each child on the shoulder by way of introduction. Besides Kay and her brother, there were dark-haired twin girls. One peeked at him shyly from behind her sister. The last four were freckle-faced brothers sporting transfer tattoos of wrestling stars, a Chinese-American boy with the unlikely name of Butch, and a Mohawk-haired boy who eyed Cole with suspicion.

"Someone needs to bring out the rest of the sail bags," Laura continued. "First captain ready gets choice of crew."

The mad scramble for equipment had Cole's head whirling.

She waved at someone beyond the beach. It was the cocky young handyman. He waved back

Cole's friendly grin for the children warped into a scowl.

Hefting a sail bag, the older girl Kay called, "Hey, Burt, how about a ride on your sailboard sometime?"

Burt's reply would remain a mystery. When he spotted his employer and the play director sauntering along the path, he roared away on the mower.

Kay shrugged and continued rigging her sails.

Good riddance. The guy was too old for her.

When he turned back, Laura was checking the sailing dinghies bobbing on the calm water. The water mirrored their slender masts along with the few wispy clouds.

Mohawk-top remained standing there, gaze fixed solemnly on Cole. He stuffed a small camera in his pocket. "Are you a spy?"

Cole gaped at the boy. What the hell? How in blazes could this kid— But the boy probably had his own agenda. "Um, what do you mean?"

"The East Pond kids want to beat us bad enough to send spies. Are you here to scout for them?"

Cole laughed. "Nope. I'm a Passabec fan all the way. I'm just here to pick up a few pointers about sailing." And to keep an eye on the teacher.

But no hands. No touching.

"Pointers, huh? You keep your eyes on my boat. Me and Butch are the best. We skunk 'em every time." With a swagger, the wiry boy ambled down the dock, where his partner was finishing rigging the sails.

"Hey, mister," yelled one of the twins, paired with the older girl Kay. "Come watch us. We can come up into the wind better than yucky old Zach."

Cole strolled along the dock, commenting as kids vied for his attention. He lost track of Laura momentarily until he heard the putt-putt of an outboard. She was scudding away from the dock in a white skiff.

Damn. He hadn't realized she'd be alone in the middle of the lake, not a staked-out goat but a damn sitting duck. How could you protect a woman like that?

A few minutes later, the sailing dinghies, little bigger than Laura's skiff, glided toward the triangular course she was setting up with orange buoys.

The practice race came off smoothly. Two boats dunked their occupants, but the kids righted them and sailed away.

Hearing only snatches of Laura's instructions, Cole liked the gentle way she guided and encouraged the kids. He watched the shore for suspicious activity, but kept returning to her sunlit hair as she zipped around in the little outboard.

Sailing. Another sport too rich for him. Like the horseback riding. That last summer, Laura was the only rider who'd spoken to him. Maybe she shouldn't have.

When the morning's races and practice ended and the kids left, he helped her stow the sail bags and life vests. They were alone. Now was a good time to bring up reducing risk. Like eliminating solo jaunts on the lake.

Before he could speak, a small whirlwind blew into the shed. "Sailing is awesome, Laura! I've never had so much fun." One of the twin girls. The child's voice was chirpy, like words popping out of a bubble machine. She threw her arms around Laura's waist.

Laura knelt to return the bear hug. "I'm so glad, kiddo, but I knew you'd have a good time."

"I didn't even mind falling in the water. It didn't matter." She pantomimed lifting the mast out of the water. "Me 'n my sister can't wait 'til the race!" She shoved her team's sail bag at Laura, then dashed away.

Her cheeks flushed, Laura rose and swiped moisture from her eyes.

He cleared his throat. "I watched that little girl out there on the lake. She had a blast. Her shy sister too."

Blowing her nose into a tissue, she shook her head. "That *was* the shy sister. When she came in, I was afraid she wanted to quit. She's so timid, I didn't know how she felt. Talking to me like that must have taken all her courage."

He picked up his mug and helped her stack the sails.

These kids were middle-class and comfortable, rich compared to the San Sebastiano orphans in Rio Placido. But they needed nurturing every bit as much.

So many facets to her. She kept him guessing. Elegance and painstaking control in the face of danger. Slicing him to ribbons with her tongue one minute, nurturing and caring with her students the next.

She dusted her hands together. Placing them on her hips, she cocked her head at him. "Now are you ready for *your* sailing lesson?"

Chapter Nine

LAURA FUMED AS she entered the inn dining room on Friday morning. Cole had proposed they spend her day off together, which would foster the illusion of their intimacy. He gave her no choice in the matter, but she would protect her heart and her secrets. When this trap or whatever it was ended, when it was clear she'd never see him again, she'd tell him no more than what she owed him. She couldn't bear to rip the rest from her soul.

They'd strolled over together from her cabin, but she drew the line at holding hands. When Stan waylaid Cole with a request about the play, she welcomed the chance for respite from his intimidating maleness and take-charge competence.

Or was it her susceptibility putting her to flight?

Like a kid, he'd enjoyed their sail in one of the larger rental sloops. At first, nerves brought out his temper. The quintessential engine guy didn't like having no motor for backup. Then in spite of his fuming about privilege and leisure sports, he turned his face to the wind and took a turn at the tiller.

Anxiety about how he'd deal with the sailing class had aroused the butterfly colony in her stomach. But he charmed them. And her. He listened seriously to their shameless bragging, asked questions, cheered them on, and coaxed a giggle from the shy twin by producing a quarter from her ear.

The wistful hunger in his blue eyes had wrenched her heart. Hunger for children of his own he could take boating.

"Yoo-hoo, Laura," a high-pitched voice called from one of the tables by the window. "Come join us."

Laura smiled as she wove between tables toward the two elderly ladies in flounced, gauzy dresses and draped scarves. The Van Tassel sisters enjoyed to the fullest their stature as doyennes of the resort theater.

She chose her words with care. "Thank you, but I'm with someone."

Bea patted her shiny black curls. "Oh, is it that nice young man you introduced me to last evening?"

"Oh, dearie, what a hunk." Her sister Doris's teacup hovered in midair. Her wispy, teased hairdo matched her apricot-blushed cheeks. Neon-blue eye shadow completed the theatrical effect. "We observed the sailing class from beneath our beach umbrella. He is most attentive."

"Well, yes, he… that is, he and I…" Her tongue simply could not cope. Laura Markham Rossiter, two courses and a dissertation away from a Ph.D. in cultural anthropology, couldn't put words together to say she was having breakfast with a man.

With that particular man.

Bea fluttered the fringed edge of her paisley shawl at Laura. "And here he is."

"Good morning, ladies." Cole nodded to the beaming women as he placed both hands on Laura's shoulders.

Her cheeks as hot as toast, she at last found her voice and introduced him to Doris.

He bowed over the ladies' hands as he inquired what breakfast delights they recommended. In his charcoal polo shirt and khakis, he looked for all the world as if he belonged in the proper inn dining room with its white linen and polished wood. Only the scars on his face hinted at his rough edges.

How could he be so rested and look so gorgeous after two nights on the lumpy couch?

Tittering and blushing like the ingénues they'd once been, the Van Tassels sent them off with a recommendation for the blueberry pancakes.

Laura allowed Cole to usher her to a table in a private corner. Usher wasn't quite the right word. The warm hand at the small of her back felt like an electric prod. She scurried ahead of his touch.

"Put a smile on that pretty mouth, babe, or no one will believe we're a pair of lovebirds."

"And why should they?" As she sat opposite him, she stretched her lips into a facsimile of a smile. She hated being so bitchy, but she had little defense against her feelings. "I don't see what this… arrangement has to do with catching Markos's man. Won't he just back off?"

He covered and held her hand as she clutched at the flimsy anchor of her linen napkin. His heat and scent invaded her senses.

The elderly Van Tassels gaped at them. Teacups clattered and tea sloshed onto saucers.

"Maybe, but that will give us time to check employees and guests' identities," he said. "A call last night gave me more info. An FBI informant reported seeing a man known only as Janus meeting with Markos in Boston. He's a paid assassin the Bureau would like to nail."

"Two for the price of one." When he nodded, she said, "So do you have a description?"

"Not enough to go on. Average height, average build. Fits half the men in America."

"I see." She perused the menu as the waitress headed toward them with coffee.

Other diners entering glanced their way. She forced herself to smile and wave at Rudy Damon. The man's bristly white eyebrows shot up into his hairline.

Apparently their appearing together at play rehearsals hadn't cemented the relationship in people's minds as would having breakfast together. Drat Cole for being right. Word of her liaison would spread like jam on the scones she planned to order.

After they'd placed their orders—his the blueberry pancakes, hers a crabmeat omelet—she searched for something *im*personal to talk about. "What did Stan want?"

He smiled. The crinkling of the creases in his cheeks sent a surge of heat through her. "He wants to use my Bad Boy in the play."

"Your motorcycle? You call it Bad Boy." She grinned.

He shrugged, as if the irony of it hadn't occurred to him before. "I didn't name the damn thing. Bad Boy's the Harley model. A classic. They don't make them anymore."

A sudden thought pleated her forehead. "Were you planning to drive me to a safe house God knows where on your motorcycle?"

"I'd stow it in the truck bed. Figured we'd look more like tourists."

"I don't buy it. You just like having the motorcycle."

Drat, he was charming her in spite of her resolve. She retrieved her hand and held her coffee with both hands. "They must need the bike for Cliff Trigger."

"Cliff Trigger? The part the kid plays?" A sneer quirked his hard mouth. "The playwright's a fan of old Westerns, or the name's a sexual reference. Either way, our young stud isn't up to the challenge."

"I agree he's not much of an actor. He wanted the role because of the motorcycle." She narrowed her eyes, remembering the teenaged Cole. "The character is a disaffected biker, the ultimate outsider who wants no involvement. He's a rogue, a—"

"Cowboy?" His eyes mocked her, and his rumble of a laugh flickered her pulse. "I get the feeling we're no longer talking about a character in the play."

"Old resentments die hard." The waitress arriving with their orders saved her from further blunders.

Feeling the glow in her face, she attacked her omelet as if the crab in it had menaced her with its claws. She buttered the lightly toasted scone. If she couldn't sleep, at least her precarious situation wasn't affecting her appetite.

"Stan had some other news" He poured maple syrup on his pancakes. "Even our genial host can get angry. Guests have reported things missing from their cabins."

"Missing? Like stolen? What kinds of things?"

"Cameras, binoculars, CDs, small electronics. Easy-to-hock items." His cynical expression told her what he thought of the rural Maine custom of unlocked doors.

Distressed, she put down her fork. "How terrible. Has he called the police?"

He nodded. "I hope having the local boys in blue here won't interfere with our operation."

She wasn't sure what to say to that, although talking to him was easy, even after her embarrassing outburst. Talking to him was always easy, as were shared silences. How safe she'd felt—how safe she still felt—in his arms, how different he was from everyone else. He was so complex, his subtle sense of humor, his quiet strength, his sensuality. Even that hint of danger, of controlled power excited her.

But recapturing past magic was impossible. Dangerous. They had no future because she had nothing to offer him but disappointment. She couldn't let down her guard.

Later when they strolled out into the clear, sunny day, a sailing-class parent stopped Laura to chat.

Cole shook his head. She was doing it to him again. She knew how to make him crazy, certifiable. With her innuendos about contempt for commitment. With the total absorption in eating her eggs. Seeing her pink tongue lick the jam off the edge of her scone nearly had him climbing over the table.

Hell, she made him nuts just standing there in her buttoned-up green shirt and flowered pants that ended inches below the knee. He didn't see the point of revealing only part of a shapely athletic calf.

So delectable.

So out of reach.

That lone wolf and commitment bit was more about the differences between them than anything he'd done or not done. The truth was out. Or was it?

After their long-ago weekend together, they'd made plans for him to meet her family. Now that was a laugh. As if her society parents would've admitted him to their house, him a biker bum with overlong hair, the son of another bum embalmed in cheap booze.

You're just like me, boy... no way outta the gutter.

His old man was right. Laura was right. Anything long-term between them made as much sense as sailing his Bad Boy on Passabec Lake. The old differences still separated them.

She wouldn't admit those differences, even kept trying to minimize them. Had even roped him into sailing yesterday morning. Sailing wasn't so bad. Ah hell, it was the most fun he'd had in years. Whatever that signified.

When Laura joined him on the porch steps, he filed away his muddled thoughts. "So what do you usually do on your day off?" he asked as they headed back to her cabin.

"You don't have to—"

"Yes. I do. 24/7." He relaxed his fists and smiled at her. She was too pale. Fear of Markos or fear of him?

Dew glistened on the grass beside the gravel path. Birds chirped and dragonflies darted in the peaceful morning's freshness. The danger of an assassin seemed remote.

She sighed, apparently resigned. "I drive around. That is, I did when I had a car."

"Sightseeing. Finest kind, as they say here in Maine." He slapped on sunglasses. "I can put some miles on the bike before I have to give it up to Broadway on Passabec. There's a lighthouse near Rockland I want to see."

Alarm darkened her eyes. "But how is that safe? Markos's agent, this Janus, could follow us."

He nudged her toward the black-and-silver bike in the totaled junker's parking spot. "We'll be out in public the entire time. You won't see them, but we'll have backup. Let Janus follow. If he does, he's mine."

"I have no helmet."

She was stalling. "No problem." He produced two helmets from his saddlebag and held up a gold-colored one. "Not exactly a crown, but it'll do in a pinch."

He slid one hand down the sleeve of her cotton shirt, along the cool skin of her arm until he closed her fingers around the helmet's strap. "And you'll be warm enough in that fleece-lined windbreaker I saw hanging in your cabin."

She stood with the helmet in one hand and her house key in the other. He could see her brain spinning this one. Should she shut herself in the cabin or go with him? About when he was sure she'd run inside and lock him out, she said, "I'll just get my jacket then."

Tension drained from his shoulders, but he didn't relax completely until she returned and mounted the bike behind him.

"Is that the same helmet? The stolen one?"

The memory slapped him hard enough to rattle his cage. He was a fool to think he could relegate their past and his simmering emotions to a back file until this was over. Every image from the past was a reminder that she still had secrets. For now, he needed her more recent secrets. Ones without emotional pitfalls for him.

Digging out the details about Markos and the attack on her filled the bill.

He replied mildly, "No. But this one's custom-made too. State-of-the-art. Ready?"

Chapter Ten

WITH HIS WHOLE being, Cole felt Laura holding on as they roared to the coast, then via Route One through the center of Camden and on south. Her knees and thighs rode against his hips, and her hands rested lightly on his ribs. As he turned and accelerated along the coastal road, he sensed every flexed muscle, the heat and scent of her against his back.

He glanced behind them from time to time. Vehicles came and went. No one but their backup was following them.

He checked on her as well, to reassure himself that she was really there. Wisps of her hair floated out from the edge of the helmet like licks of golden fire.

He slowed the bike through the busy streets of Rockland, then sped up again on Route 73 out of town. The narrow route skirted the harbor, filled with both fishing and pleasure boats. Laura tapped his shoulder and pointed at a white ferry, its broad bow plowing up foaming waves as it motored in from the island of Vinal Haven.

Grinning behind his visor, he aimed the front tire at a shallow pothole. When the bike lurched, she emitted a squeak and wound her arms more tightly around his middle.

Where he wanted them.

They had no future together, but he couldn't resist

making the most of what time they did have. If all he could do was touch her occasionally, that would have to do. He squeezed her hands with his elbows and accelerated up the hill into Owls Head.

On a high point, the white lighthouse tower commanded a view of both the outer islands and the Rockland lighthouse at the end of its mile-long granite breakwater. A light breeze fluttered the laundry hanging on a clothesline behind the white clapboarded keeper's house.

"Most of these lighthouses are automated now," she said. "I wonder who lives in the keeper's house."

They climbed the steep steps to the tower. The high point provided a clear view of the trails around the light and the beach. A pair of hand-holding teens meandered through the pines, and a family with a toddler and a baby picnicked on a blanket. No one suspicious.

No one who could be Janus.

He watched Laura with satisfaction when she practically purred at the view. She tried to remain so cool and collected, but her sensual nature betrayed her. He enjoyed her pleasure at such simple things as the sun on her face or the salt-tangy scent of the ocean. The way she'd gobbled up her breakfast turned him on.

His body's reaction made him glad he wore roomy jeans.

He cleared his throat. "On a day like this, I bet you can see all the way to Mount Desert Island." He covered her shoulder with one hand and pointed with the other. "You can follow some of the harbors and peninsulas, but I don't know their names."

"I read about the history of this coast." Her voice was husky. "Before Europeans came to Maine in the sixteen hundreds, the Abenakis inhabited the area. They lived inland during the winters, but fished here during the summers. In some places, you can find middens, piles of shells they left behind."

"Spoken like a true anthropologist. Anthropology, a practical application of history. It suits you. How did a major in anthropology lead to museum work?"

She eased from beneath his hand. "It seemed a natural after summer interning at the Smithsonian. The human side of history intrigues me, the culture and art of ancient peoples."

He leaned against the building to look at her instead of at the broad bay. He wasn't certain what he wanted, but trust would be a start, would make protecting her easier. "Come on. Let's hit the beach down there."

They picked their way down the hill along a dirt track. At one point it narrowed, and he placed his hand on the small of her back to guide her ahead of him, but she strode ahead out of reach.

They left the path for the sandy beach. He skipped stones in the receding tide, while she sank down against a log. She tossed her jacket to the side and tilted her face to the sun.

With her, he drank in the peace of the setting. The warmth of the sun and the slap of water on the shore intoxicated him nearly as much being with the woman he—

Waylaying the ambushing thought, he stretched out, one elbow propped beside her on the log. "I hate to disturb your nap, but I need to know how it went down with Markos."

At his voice so close to her ear, Laura's eyes flew open. Her gaze dropped to his mouth. She drew in a sharp breath. "Don't you have a report on all that?"

"A report, yes, but I'd like to hear the details from you. In case they missed some little fact that would help us. Were you in love with him?" Damn, why did he ask that?

She smiled wistfully, her gaze roaming his face. Her index finger traced the length of the two white scars, first at his temple, then on his chin. "It seems we both have scars. How did you get these?"

Her cool fingers stabbed heat in the center of his body. He covered her hand with his, trapping it against his chin. When she struggled, he dropped a kiss on her palm and released her. He sat up and edged away a foot. If he didn't watch himself, he'd scare her off.

"Nothing as life-threatening as the way you got yours, I promise. This one—" he pointed to his temple "—was in the jungle. I swear every plant in South America has thorns, some as big as switchblades. And the other was in Afghanistan. We were behind some rocks—that country's all rocks—and gunfire kicked up splinters. One caught me on the chin."

Tenderness softened her eyes. "Both sound dangerous to me. Your sense of justice has set your life course. You put yourself in harm's way regularly. You could have been killed."

"I wasn't."

She levered up to sit on the log. "You were in the Marines then? Or that alphabet-soup agency?"

"We were talking about D.C. and Markos, remember?"

"I see. That's all you can tell me."

She turned to straddle the log so she faced him. The cropped pants rode up to her knees, giving him a better view of her legs. Too bad he'd made that no-touch rule. "Now I'll answer your question. I was not in love with Alexei Markos. I met him at an embassy cocktail party and saw him again at the museum where I worked. The Silk Road exhibit I'd just organized impressed him."

"Silk Road. That was an ancient trade route."

She nodded. A smile played on her lips. "'From Istanbul to Beijing, from the second century BC through 1100 AD, trade on the Silk Road brought about the first international cross-pollination of goods, knowledge, and cultures.'"

"Is that a quote from the museum guide?"

She grinned. "If so, I'm only quoting myself."

"I'm impressed." He wasn't kidding. "Go on. Markos?"

The grin flattened, and she looked away.

He started to take her hand, to offer a defense against the painful memories. But better sense stopped him. Besides, what he'd said to her was true. She was tougher than him.

Behind them at the lighthouse, children shrieked laughter as they raced up the hill.

"He asked me out," she continued. "He was charming and took me to all the society parties. From the first I knew he coveted my expertise, not my body or my charm."

Cole heaved a mental sigh of relief. Professional mode, he reminded himself. "What sort of stuff did he pay you to authenticate?"

"As you'd expect, a lot of Middle Eastern art and artifacts, some Chinese. Many were valuable antiques. He had me come to the office at his shop to examine them. Then I did my research and gave him a report."

"Were they legit? Paperwork and all?"

"All of the pieces had provenance. I had doubts, but no proof of black-market dealings. Values ranged from a thousand dollars to more than a million. I remember a seventh-century Aegean amphora, very beautiful. And a carved Syrian chest. A centuries-year-old cypress-wood altar from Anhui province in China. Priceless. Several pieces from Iran, including a two-hundred-year-old brass vase."

"And the Persian mummy that drove him to murder."

"The mummy excited him more than any other item. If it had been authentic, an auction might have yielded millions." Her eyes grew enormous. "Oh, thank God it wasn't real."

"The New Dawn Warriors would have had a bundle."

"And Markos. But I doubt the man who brought it was with the terrorists. Markos would've shown more restraint."

"Only an unfortunate intermediary. And how did you know the mummy was a fake?"

Eyes bright, she bent closer to him. "Although more than a few cultures attempted mummification, the ancient Persians were not among them. The Egyptians were the only ones with such elaborate knowledge and rituals for mummification. This mummy purported to be Persian, a princess from the court of King Xerxes, more than two thousand years old. She was wearing a gold crown and mask in the Persian style, with an inscription on the breastplate that named her as the king's daughter."

He should remain objective, take mental notes. Admiration for her expertise wasn't helping that effort.

"What else?"

"Tests revealed Egyptian techniques. Removing the internal organs, embalming, wrapping. The Persian Empire was far-flung enough that Egyptian embalmers might have traveled to his palace. Someone did a great deal of research. The ruse might've worked, except for a few miscalculations."

"Which you uncovered?"

"Not I alone." The excitement in her face dimmed.

A seagull soared overhead. Its raucous complaint pierced the calm air.

"You see, this wasn't the first Persian mummy to be offered for sale. A few years ago, a Karachi museum curator examined one from the Pakistani desert region. She noticed grammatical errors in the inscription. And she knew that the ancient Persians buried their dead above ground. They believed that a corpse would defile the earth. After forensic experts conducted tests, that mummy turned out to be a modern woman with a broken neck."

"Murder?"

"Apparently. And not just one. There is evidence of a sort of mummy factory in the northern hills of Iran."

"Gruesome. So you were suspicious from the get-go."

"This mummified princess had a broken neck too. More tests placed her in the present century."

He pictured the refined and cultured importer's jaw dropping. A laugh burst from his lips. In spite of the mummy's grisly origins, he couldn't help it. "I'd have paid money to see Markos's face when you told him."

A wry smile quirked her mouth, but didn't lift the pain from her eyes. When she spoke again, her voice caught. "I wish I could forget it. I've never seen someone so enraged."

He clasped her hands. So much for his rule. But this time she didn't pull away. "I'm sorry. Laughing was thoughtless. Can you go on?"

"Talking about it helps. I've had no one to share it with for eight months." She stood and brushed off her seat. "Let's walk along the beach."

Towering spruce trees and pink beach roses edged the pebbly beach, a blooming wall of privacy.

Again she didn't object when he held her hand as they walked. "So you were in his office when you told him about the mummy," he prompted.

"We were in the shop. It was night, after hours. I thought at the time we were alone, but the mummy dealer was in the office." She gave a small shudder. "I handed Markos the report and left. When I reached my car, I realized I'd been in such a rush to escape his temper that I left my purse behind."

She plucked a blossom from a nearby bush. He could barely hear her shaky whisper above the breeze's rustling of leaves. "I went to the office to tell him the shop door was still unlocked. I heard him shouting at someone inside. The door was ajar. Then I saw him. *Them.*"

She dropped the crushed rose blossom and covered her eyes with a trembling hand.

"And you made it as far as the shop door before he caught you." Cole had witnessed brutalities most people wouldn't believe were possible for one human to do to another. To think what this gentle woman saw and was forced to endure—

"Cole, you're hurting me."

He relaxed his fingers. "Sorry. Guess I thought it was Markos's neck."

Laura massaged her mangled fingers, but managed a smile. "Thank you for caring." She stepped closer.

So much for avoiding emotional pitfalls.

"I don't want to put you through any more now. You can tell me the rest later." Unable to resist, he bracketed her face between his hands. Gently this time.

Desire hovered between them, dancing like the butterflies in the roses beside them. Waves lapped the rocks. The breeze picked up, blocking out other noises and mingling the contrasting scents of flowers and the sea.

He cupped her nape and covered her mouth with his. She sighed as he brushed her lips with his, from one side to the other. He teased her mouth, first with his lips, then tongue. Her lips parted, offering the taste that he craved, and her arms crept around his neck.

He'd loved and made love with the girl, reveled in her willowy body and innocent heat. The woman surpassed the promises of that girl—with her curves and gentle yet tenacious nature. Holding her like this uncurled something soft and warm within him, something he'd forgotten existed.

With his tongue, he traced the raised ridges of the reddened scars at her throat. She flinched at first, but when he held her fast, sighed and allowed his tender exploration. She was so brave, so resourceful.

And so vulnerable.

She leaned into him. Through her thin cotton blouse, her peaked nipples pressed into his chest. The world tilting and his head spinning, he thought of nothing but her intoxicating scent and the hot, sleek moistness of her lips and tongue, joining his with demand.

Chapter Eleven

LAURA LOVED THE primal smell of him, the heat and security of his arms around her. She loved his fierce pride and even the dangerous side, the mysterious side.

She'd loved the reckless boy. She couldn't love the determined, controlled man. He tempted her with his sensuality and strength, with his gentle protectiveness, but danger and heartache lay ahead if she yielded.

As she stiffened and pulled back, he raised his head, eyes heavy-lidded. He held on to her hands and rubbed the backs with the pads of his thumbs. "Don't be afraid of me. I won't hurt you."

Worse. We'll hurt each other.

He released her, and she turned toward the lighthouse. "I think we'd better get back."

When she held on to his waist for the return ride, the heat of him seemed to burn her hands. She couldn't succumb. Every little bit of herself she revealed to him, recent or past, opened cracks in her defenses.

She didn't want to hurt him. By protecting herself from loving him again, she protected her secret. She protected them both from new heartbreak.

Didn't she?

****

When they returned from Owls Head, they found a pan of lasagna on Laura's doorstep. "From Bea," she said, as she carried it inside to the refrigerator.

Cole did a quick check of the cabin before returning to his to pack. After that searing kiss, both needed space.

In his more spacious guest cabin, he dragged his suitcase from the luggage stand and threw it onto the bed. Thinking they'd be on their way west, he hadn't really unpacked.

He could kick himself for kissing her when she was so exposed. For starting something that they shouldn't finish. That shouldn't happen again.

After slamming a few items from the bureau into the bag, he headed to the bathroom. Hell. She'd suffered so much. Time and time again. More than she'd divulged so far. And her expertise with the ancient cultures astounded him. He had to scrap his princess image of her and replace it with the successful cultural anthropologist.

But he couldn't quite scrap how he felt about her long-ago desertion. She'd believed that rat Valesko's every word and threw Cole away like the trash she thought he was. She denied his background made any difference, but it did. He dragged those leg irons with every step. He saw his old man's leering mug, haunting him. He relaxed his fist before he squeezed out the whole tube of toothpaste, closed top or not.

If he could only feel indifference toward her, the damn job of protecting her and catching killers would be tolerable. But around her, his control extended only so far. Either his hands ached to touch her, to hold her, or they itched to pound the wall. Nothing in between.

At a tap on the bedroom window, he gripped his 9mm. He moved to the wall beside the window and peered out. When he recognized one of his team, he unlocked the window and pushed up the screen. "Byrne, get in here."

DARK Officer Simon Byrne hoisted himself up and through the opening. "You just had a hot beach date with the lovely lady, Stratton. That should've set you up. What the hell's got you in a twist?" He pulled down the window sash.

"Not the lady's fault. And not yours." Cole dug fingers into his hair. "This gig's not going down as planned. It's all on the fly."

"And up in the air. Hell, aren't you spook types used to winging it? Changing on the fly with a subject that turns squirrely? Or phantom?" Grinning, Byrne helped himself to water in the kitchenette. He was about Cole's height, six feet, with a cocky attitude, a ready smirk and a nose that had seen knuckles at close range. A diamond earring winked through his shaggy brown hair.

DARK united special talents from various intelligence agencies, but the old rivalries cropped up, usually in the form of good-natured kidding. In spite of his mood, one side of Cole's mouth quirked up. The cocky nonconformist reminded him of his younger self. "I suppose you DEA humps always know who your subject is."

"Affirmative. Not usually a phantom. This Janus is a real piece of work. No clue as to his real identity so far." Byrne hiked a hip on the oak dining table and downed the glass in one swig. "The Feebs identified his MO in half a dozen hits from Tampa to L.A. Execution-style. Those guys never knew what hit them. Word has it he can be subtle too. Makes it harder to pin down an MO. People have mysterious accidents—falling down stairs or into traffic."

"Or down a mountain with punctured brake lines." Cole zipped up his toiletries. "Local police show today?"

"They flat-footed all over the place looking for stashed loot from the cabins, but struck out. They did grill the handyman. No surprise, since he has a juvie record. Small-town cops are no threat to Janus. I doubt they'll be in our way."

Cole had expected that. "Are we all set?"

"Ward has the inside covered. Furnished us with a map of the resort and who's in each cabin. The others are in place. We start our new jobs this afternoon. No sweat."

Cole zipped his bag and lifted it. He didn't like to leave Laura alone for long, even with Isaacs on surveillance duty.

"Man, Ward may be the Confessor, but you're Lockjaw." Byrne tugged at his studded earlobe. "You wouldn't spill what's eating at you if the President himself asked. It's the babe, isn't it?"

Busted. Cole's gut churned. He wanted to deck Byrne with his duffel. "What makes you such a damn expert?"

"Hope you don't play much poker, Stratton." The undercover officer unlocked the window and prepared to depart the same way he'd entered.

"Hell, Laura and I may have a history, but it won't stop me from doing my job."

"One reason the director picked you was because you *do* know her. Word in the agency says you're cool, one of the best. You take care of her. The rest of us'll have this place covered like fleas on a beagle. If Janus is here, we'll get him." He slipped out the window and into the trees.

Birds sang in the afternoon sun. Squirrels raced and argued in the pine branches overhead. No sign of anyone watching. And no more sign of Byrne.

Cole closed and locked the screen and window. His fellow officers might trust him. Laura seemed to trust him to keep her safe. But could he trust himself? He stowed his emotions like he stowed his luggage, but being close to her blew that all to hell. Could he control his confused feelings enough to do the job?

He'd proven himself over the years. With every new mission, he kept striving to prove himself. Who for? Only himself.

Until now.

It was her life on the line, but protecting her, stopping an assassin, and nabbing Markos fit into his personal goal.

Hell, didn't that make him the selfish bastard she'd accused him of being?

****

That evening, the stage crew completed the last of the scenery for *Death at the Diner*.

Laura hung the curtains Stan's wife had sewed. Like the woven pattern in the yellow gingham, her feelings for Cole intertwined with her fear of Markos's hit man. Cole's arrival had ignited the flame of hope, that they'd catch the killer and Markos, and she could return home in safety.

But hope was her enemy as much as fear. Either could weaken her vigilance and send her screaming into Cole's arms.

After the kiss on the beach, she'd intended to think of him only as her bodyguard, nothing more. But where he was concerned, she had about as much willpower as a child with a bag of Halloween candy. How could she maintain a vow of indifference when her awareness of him overrode her good intentions? She mustn't leap into his arms as she did that afternoon.

She knew better than to try to persuade him to drop the hot-lover act. He intended to stay close. So emotional distance was the key. She'd fortify herself with a wall of indifference. She was strong. Hadn't she overcome challenges greater than her attraction to Cole Stratton?

She hurried forward to help Bea and him shove the counter-and-stools unit into place. "Careful, Bea, the paint's still a bit sticky."

The older woman accepted her tactful out to avoid moving the heavy scenery. Bea painted and decorated with enthusiasm, but she was eighty or older. "I'm sure this dear man would rather have you beside him," she replied with a wink.

"Put a little more hip into it, babe, and you'll move me along with the scenery." Cole grinned.

Laura rolled her eyes at his suggestive comment. "You do your part, and I'll do mine." Pushing together, they slid the unit onto its marks on stage left.

"The two booths and we're done." He strode into the wings.

"Ah, Stratton, you're a lifesaver," Rudy Damon said. Somewhere between forty and sixty, the director cultivated a bristling white moustache that forever fought gravity in an attempt to merge with his full head of white hair. "This bike is just what we need."

Parked beside the completed booths was the Harley-Davidson Bad Boy. Burt, in a leather jacket dripping with zippers, stood beside it. Running a hand over the leather seat, he drooled over the black-and-silver machine.

Laura grinned, noting Cole's compressed mouth.

"So this is the bike I use on stage? Way cool." Burt smoothed a hand over the black leather seat.

Rudy adjusted his ever present red silk scarf, this time tied in an elaborate overhand knot. "Cole has offered the use of his motorcycle. I feared we'd have to use a cardboard one."

Leaving the bike, Burt ambled over beside Laura. "I want the one with the CD player, fringes on the saddlebags, the works."

Cole's wolf eyes sharpened. "This is a Harley Softail. A cleaner look, not some poser garbage wagon."

Laura picked up a box of props. "Maybe the bike's too new to suit the play. We are back in the fifties, you know."

"No, no, we need it," the director said. "And I need to find my notes for the stage blocking. I'll leave you folks to setting up the scenery."

"Hey, I'll help with that." Burt rushed to Cole's aid.

The two bent to tip one booth onto a dolly. Eyeing each other across avocado-green upholstery like wrestlers on the mat instead of crew members, they nearly heaved the booth off the stage. Then had to drag it back into place.

The effort flexed powerful shoulder muscles beneath the black cotton of Cole's t-shirt. It strained the sinews in his arms and stretched the cargo pants' khaki fabric across his taut backside.

Laura forced her gaze away to the booth she and Vanessa were balancing.

Vanessa winked at her.

Busted.

****

When Cole and Laura left the theater, thin fog

hovered just above the lake surface. The disembodied masts of the sailing dinghies levitated in midair. The air was sharp with wood smoke from a bonfire on the beach.

The idea of what or whom the ghostly, gray scrim might obscure jittered her pulse. Seeming to notice her anxiety, he curved an arm around her shoulders. She should object, but welcomed the added shield of his heat and strength. She breathed in his scent and relaxed.

"What's the deal?" he asked as they drew near the fire.

"You remember my mentioning Jake Elwell?"

"The handyman."

"He still can't do any heavy work, but once a week he builds a bonfire for the guests. They roast marshmallows, and he tells stories."

His eyebrows scissored together. "What kind of stories?"

"Ghost stories mostly. Jake spins wonderful old Maine tales too. You know, the kind of stories you tell around a campfire." A suspicion, inchoate as the fog, invaded her consciousness.

She stopped, just beyond the congenial circle of adults and children, and faced him. "Have you ever done that? A bonfire, I mean, with tall tales and marshmallows?"

His eyes, midnight dark and brooding, focused on her warily. She had the impression of coiled energy, a wild creature that at any moment could either pounce or flee. "The stories Marines tell around campfires would singe your hair."

Something flickered behind the intensity in his eyes. Hurt and envy. They curled around her heart. "But as a boy, you never did this, did you?"

His lack of a reply told her he hadn't. He'd either had to work or deal with his father. If the old man wasn't already dead, she'd like to choke him for denying his son a childhood. In spite of Cole's achievements, he hadn't banished the feeling of inadequacy engendered by missing small joys like fun around a campfire. The hostile biker facade had been a guise. He still felt unworthy, an outsider.

"Then let's make up for lost time. I see room for us by the rock beyond the fire circle." She took his hand and began tugging him toward the spot she'd selected, apart, yet near enough to hear Jake and roast a marshmallow or two.

She might've tried to uproot a tree. He didn't pull away from her. He simply didn't budge.

His hard-hewn jaw was set. "You don't have to do this." He spoke in a low voice serrated by bitterness.

"No, but you do." She laced her fingers with his long, callused ones. "You can't undo injustices and fill in gaps, but you can move on by not denying yourself simple pleasures everyone should experience."

She bestowed on him her best come-hither smile and pulled again. The thickening fog formed a gray nimbus around the outdoor lights and left jewels of mist on her hair.

He cleared his throat. "We ought to get to the cabin. I need—"

She clutched his arm and whispered. "There's a strange man standing behind us. Look by the tree."

Chapter Twelve

"LET'S SEE. AVERAGE build, brown hair, closing in on forty?"

"You already checked him out?" Laura asked.

His lips nuzzled her ear as he whispered back, rocketing her pulse. "You can relax. He's DARK. Stan has hired two new groundskeepers. I thought you'd noticed him earlier in the theater. He's assisting with lighting."

She inhaled slowly and deeply, exhaled. "Stan knows?"

"Had to tell him. He wants to help you. Besides, the intrigue appealed to him like a three-act thriller."

She relaxed against him, secure and trusting he was protecting her. Brushing hungry mosquitoes away, she let him nudge her away from the happy campfire scene and to her cabin.

"You would've enjoyed toasting marshmallows and listening to Jake's stories," she said as they entered her cabin. "It would've been one less thing to complain about never doing."

He hung his windbreaker, damp with mist, on the back of a kitchen chair. "You can make a list and check off every item if you want—bonfire, sailing, horseback riding, a damned cotillion. It's not the same."

"Don't you think I know that?" She poured water into the kettle for some herbal tea. "Simple joys like roasting marshmallows as a child don't make a man who he is."

He turned off the gas heater. "Dammit, I smell gas. This was loose again. The pilot light's out."

"I don't understand. Stan told me at the theater that Burt fixed it today." At least the thing worked. In a few minutes they could relight it. A little heat would nip the evening chill brought on by the fog. And the sudden chill between them. "So you had a rough beginning. You turned yourself around."

"Bully for me." He growled like an unfed wolf.

"Don't you get all defensive on me, Cole Stratton." Hands on her hips, she glared at him. The man was all hard lines and uncompromising angles. A hard surface that one day would crack when the hidden fires beneath erupted.

He threw up his hands. "I know you mean well."

"Whining about what you never did makes you a martyr to no one but yourself. Don't tell me you didn't get a kick out of sailing. We can even find horses to ride if you want. Maybe we can invite Janus to come along." Horrified, she stopped.

The kettle shrieked, and she spun back to the stove.

He trailed after her as far as the refrigerator, where he'd stocked some root beer. "Speaking of Janus…"

"Ah, I was wondering when you'd get around to finishing our conversation of this afternoon. My story may rival some of Jake's more hair-raising tales. It's not for children." Describing the attack would be easier than walking this minefield between them.

She took her tea to a stool beside the heater, restored to giving warmth. "The weather was hot, one of those humid D.C. October nights, when the murder… when

107

everything happened, but telling it gives me chills."

Cole worried about her emotional state for relating this violent incident. He'd witnessed the havoc wreaked on war-torn villagers as they'd detailed atrocities committed by radicals on both sides of conflict.

Fixing his gaze on her, he sat cross-legged on the floor beside her. In the villages, family members had held and soothed hysterical victims. Laura might not want his support, physical or otherwise, but he was ready. "Tell me about Kovar."

She clasped her tea mug with both hands. "He's not very tall, but wide as a house, with dark eyes like iron pellets. I think he enjoyed hurting me. Markos ordered him to kill me, to dispose of me where no one would find me. The beating and... creative knife work were Kovar's idea."

She spoke with the toneless and disjointed remoteness of a computer-generated voice. Or as if she were reading a newspaper account of an unimportant event, not even a crime. Maybe the impersonal approach prevented the horror from overwhelming her.

"He took me to some dark place. I don't know where. An alley or warehouse. First he used his fists. Then he pulled out a switchblade. I knew what was coming. I remember the blade clicking into place."

She stared into the heater's small flame, as if it kept her warm and steady during the narration. A veneer of calm covered her, a fragile shield of courage. She continued, but with increasing tension in her voice as unseen blows pummeled her. Cole longed to wrap his arms around her, but feared his touch might snap her control.

"The pain was unbearable. Blow after blow on my

head, my neck, my ribs. His fists. The knife. I didn't know which. I screamed and screamed. No one came. I was dizzy and nauseous. And then I lost consciousness." Her shoulders stiffened as if prepared for another strike.

"Drink your tea." He forced the words past his constricted throat. His gut seethed. He lifted the cup to her lips. His hands shook almost as much as hers. "Its warmth will help."

As she swallowed the mint-scented drink, her shoulders relaxed. "When I opened my eyes again, the darkness, like the inside of a tomb. I couldn't tell where. I was so weak, but I could feel and smell. Humidity. Stale beer, blood, vomit—maybe mine—and the ammonia sting of animal droppings. I gagged at the stench." Tears flowed, but she didn't seem to know she was crying.

Cole's chest ached with the need to take her pain into himself. Unable to resist, he circled her hips with his arms, holding on as her anchor. Telling the story, getting it out, might stave off the nightmares that haunted her.

"I felt like a hollow shell. So much blood lost. I lay there, bleeding away, drifting. Dying. Then I heard a noise beside me. A chittering sound, like a bird. But not a bird. Something plucked at my sleeve. It plucked again. I felt pricks on my arm. Like needles in a cluster."

His eyes narrowed. A chill prickled his spine. He knew what was coming. He tightened his grip on her.

"I... reached out and touched—a rat." Laura's voice was cold as a January moon. "It was standing on my arm, licking at the blood soaking my blouse sleeve."

A shudder racked her slim body. Shivering like a hypothermia victim, she swayed, boneless, and nearly fell from the stool. But still the words came in that artificial monotone.

His insides roiling, he listened as she related the shock of touching the sinuous, furry body. Of realizing what the creature was doing. What it wanted.

"Oh God, oh God, I panicked. Fear and revulsion of that rat threw me to action. I flailed out with both arms."

"What happened?"

"The thing ran away. And then I scooted as far away from where it had been as I could. I came up against a curved wall. Nausea choked me. I lay there a while to gather strength. I don't know how long. I panicked again when I realized the foul creature might return. What if I was too weak to fight it off? What if more followed the smell of blood?"

Her knuckles shone white from her death grip on the tea mug. He kept his arms around her.

After a deep breath, she continued. "I knew if I stayed put, no one would find me. Panic would do me no good. I would not let Markos win. I was weak. I'd lost a lot of blood, but I was alive. And I did not want to die in that box.

"I realized was locked in a car trunk. An old car, without a trunk safety latch. If a rat could find an escape, so could I. I remembered reading somewhere about the seat back being a weak spot." She described how she rolled to it and found where the rats had gnawed a hole. Moving doubled, trebled the pain, as if her attacker was thrashing and slashing at her again.

If only he could protect her from the agony of remembering. His throat tightened at her bravery and willpower.

"Pain was good. Pain kept me alert. I scooted around so I braced my feet against the seat divider. I had no strength to kick, so my leather pumps couldn't budge the hard surface. I kept kicking until exhaustion put me to sleep. When I woke up—no telling how much later—I kicked again. And again. And again. Until finally the seat back collapsed and I saw light. And a hole big enough for a gang of rats."

She gave a bitter laugh, a laugh dragged up from the roots of her tortured soul. "Crawling through that hole meant squeezing and twisting slowly. It might have been hours later that I flopped out onto the ground."

"The report said you were in a junkyard. In a car slated to be crushed the next morning." Nearly as wrung out as she, he drew in a ragged breath, took the empty mug from her stiff and cold hands and covered them with his. "You got out just in time."

"I found the night watchman. He helped me and called the police. I'll never forget the poor man's shocked expression when I shuffled toward his trailer. He thought I wore a red shirt. It was my best cream silk blouse, but… the blood, I…" Her voice scraped, as if she'd swallowed nails.

"Hush, Laura, everything's all right. You're safe. I've got you." He kneaded at the knots in her hunched shoulders. "You're the bravest person I've ever known. Most people would have given up and died. But not you. You turned tragedy into triumph."

And then her nearness, her haunted eyes, live wires shooting sparks between them, robbed him of thought. He sieved his fingers through the hair at her nape. Twining his fingers in it, he traced her skin from ear to chin with his thumb before he released the curls. He touched his mouth to the salt trails on her cheeks and kissed away the remaining tears.

Each stroke zapped his nerve endings. He didn't

want to feel this voltage. He should keep their relationship professional. But need sapped his will.

"But I…" Her words died as the spark in her eyes heated to flame.

Caught in each other's stare, neither moved.

Laura let her gaze roam over his heated face and settle on his lips. His complete focus on her, his strength and support kept her from falling into an abyss while she relived that harrowing experience. She felt cleansed of the horror, its talons withdrawn and the pain soothed after holding it all in for so long. And now she had another need.

Cole.

He tugged on her hair, tilting her head back as he lowered his mouth. "I can't keep away."

Offering no gentle, exploratory kiss, his mouth plundered and devoured hers. While one hand cupped the back of her head, the other bracketed her body.

Her knees dissolved, and she could only clutch at his shirtfront as she slid from the stool onto his lap. His heart raced beneath her fingers. She fitted her lips to his, claiming his mouth as he did hers. He tasted of heat and hunger and something darker.

As the kiss deepened, she forgot everything—her fears about the past, about the present. Everything but the intoxication that reached deep into her soul. With no other man had she ever felt this intense rush of agony and pleasure, this piercing need, this spiraling fall, as if she'd tumbled off a precipice only to soar. No other man. Only Cole.

Too late. She'd fallen over that precipice into love with him.

If she'd ever stopped loving him.

Her heart stumbled and slammed against her ribs. The knowledge that loving him would bring only more pain to both of them suffocated her until she could barely breathe.

But it was Cole who ended the kiss. "Damn, I didn't mean to take advantage of you." Lifting his arms, he let her slide away. Desire dilated his pupils so there was almost no blue. "Wanting you is a fire in my blood. And you want me just as bad. You can't deny it."

Fearful her emotions played across her face, she could only shake her head as she pushed to her feet.

At her bedroom door, she turned. "No, Cole, I can't deny it, but I can refuse. What we had is over. It's too late now. Nothing can change what happened. We're not the same people."

"Of course we're not the same. No one is. But—"

"We have no future together. Our lives are different." When more questions furrowed his brow, she knew the time had come.

She owed him the truth, the simple part.

Chapter Thirteen

SHE DREW A deep breath, steeling herself. "You need to know something I've kept from you. I didn't tell you before because I wasn't prepared. Because it was, *is* painful. We were still half angry with each other, and—"

"It's okay." Cole was on his feet, arms at his sides, his hands flexing. The wary wolf. "Tell me."

Aching at the pain on his face, she held the doorknob for support. Her throat was so dry she could barely speak. "After our weekend together, I was pregnant."

He reeled backward as though she'd slugged him. His tanned cheeks paled. "Pregnant. A baby. But…"

Tears burned her eyes, and she blinked furiously, but the dam burst. "I had an… a miscarriage."

"Oh God. What a hell of a thing." Scrubbing his knuckles across a day's growth of dark stubble, he started toward her, but stopped two steps away. Distrustful, or did he perceive her invisible barrier? "Damn, there were a couple of times that weekend we didn't use protection. I'm sorry. I should've known better."

She swiped the tears off her cheeks and gulped down the lump in her throat. She closed her mind to the images of the lost baby and others that could never be. A boy with Cole's eyes. A little girl with his dark curly hair.

Her chest ached with tension and regrets. She

resisted running into his arms. "We both should have. I admit I blamed you at first. I hated you for the pregnancy, for deserting me, for everything. But later I realized you were the easy target. I was responsible too."

"I have to know. Can you tell me how it happened, the miscarriage?" His voice throbbed with anguish.

"Not now." Every cell in her body slumped with exhaustion. She'd tell him about the accident, but another time.

"Aw, hell, of course. I already put you through the wringer." Clearly, desperation to know more tensed his whole body. "Enough for one night. I can wait."

Nodding, she escaped to her bedroom.

****

Crows cawing reveille, dragging Cole from a fitful sleep. He couldn't blame the damn couch. Half the cushions sagged nearly to the floor with his weight, and springs in the rest bayoneted his back. Lumpy as it was, he'd sacked out on worse. Not discomfort but awareness of the woman sleeping in the bedroom had kept him on edge.

He blinked at the window, hazy with sunlight seeping through the fog. Raking a hand through his hair, he headed to the shower. The hot water pelted his head like a waterfall, but couldn't wash away last night's images. She'd opened her soul to him by relating her painful escape from death. Afterward she clung to him, and they kissed until both were aflame.

And then he pushed her into revealing what she kept secret for so long. A baby. His heart twisted. Had he slipped up on purpose? Had he wanted her so much that he risked a pregnancy to bind her to him? What a farce. As if her parents would've allowed it.

115

He tried to picture her round with his baby growing in her belly. Turning his gritty face up to the shower spray, he allowed a small grin before the rest of what she'd said flattened it. Miscarriage.

Was it a boy or a girl? What caused the loss? So many questions peppered his brain that he felt as wired as if he were dodging an AK-47 volley from an Afghan cave.

Laura had been right to call a halt last night. They had more hurdles before the path smoothed out. But he wished she'd at least let him hold her and comfort her—and himself, if he was honest—when she was so clearly in pain. She suffered more over the years than he'd imagined.

Yet comforting would've for sure led to more. He kept imagining lying with her in that double bed. The damn iron frame creaked with her every toss and turn. Ten times he threw back the covers to go to her, and ten times he called himself a fool.

The scent of her shampoo perfumed the bathroom. Spitting out creative expletives in two languages, he dialed the shower all the way to cold.

****

As soon as the rushing shower masked other sounds, Laura stepped into her swimsuit, shorts and secondhand boat shoes. She tiptoed from her bedroom and out the door.

The rising sun was dispersing most of the fog. Over the grass, only cotton balls of mist drifted here and there, but an amorphous swirl curtained the cooler lake surface. From the far shore floated a loon's eerie tremolo.

Yes, her solo outing was risky, but she needed time alone. She headed for the boat shed. Having Cole under

116

her roof—holding her when she was vulnerable enough to succumb, tempting her—held far more risk. Acknowledgment of her doomed love for him added exquisite torture to an already untenable situation.

Revealing the pregnancy and miscarriage would inevitably lead to more confessions. Including one that she might never be ready to broach.

His constant hovering was only dragging out the ordeal. If evading his presence invited the killer to try something, so be it. She desperately needed a break from being cooped up with him in that tiny cabin.

It was more likely the hour was so early that no self-respecting hit man would be up and about. No one knew she was out here, and the fog would conceal her. The two DARK men had to be around somewhere, but she saw only Burt mowing by the tennis courts.

The air was cool against her bare arms, and the smudge of the smoldering beach bonfire hung in the still air. She hurried along the path. There. She was out in the open. A target. Her pulse pounded in her ears and her stomach clenched. Her steps hurried as she neared the docks. Shrouded with fog, they isolated her from view. She'd be fine.

The little regatta between Passabec Lake and East Pond wouldn't begin until nearly eleven or when the breeze came up. She didn't need to prepare so early, but aside from everything else, setting up the markers with no one on the calm waters appealed to her.

The fog curtain muffled the only other sounds, Burt's mower and some too cheerful songbirds. She would appreciate the solitude. Something she'd grown accustomed to during the past months, but had little of the last few days.

After sliding aside the door to the shed, she hesitated in the opening. Shadows lurked in every corner. She was as skittish as a child seeing bogeymen under the bed. Shaking her head, she marched in to get the marker buoys. Afterward she climbed into her small outboard skiff. The low and steady putt-putt of the motor reassured her as she steered to a point fifty yards out. The sun's rays were shredding the fog, parting the curtain as if to aid her in placing the buoys. No need to be afraid. No harm could come to her with not even a fisherman on the lake. She idled the motor as she placed the orange marker, one of three tethered to a weight that rested on the lake's muddy bottom.

Was the fog thick enough to shield her from a sniper? In movies, a telltale glint warned of a rifle. She saw nothing out of the ordinary on shore, but the fine hairs on her nape lifted. She hunched lower in the boat.

To give the young sailors a challenge, she motored farther down the lake, nearly half a mile, to place the next buoy in the triangle-shaped course. She'd neglected to wear a life vest, something she drilled into her students. Rummaging beneath the seat rewarded her with only a paint-smeared hand.

Wet paint? That was odd, and now her feet were wet. A few inches of water sloshed over her shoes. Oh great, what now? She reached farther beneath the seat.

No bailer. Not even the sponge she normally kept there.

She bailed with her hands, but water poured through a hole in the bottom faster than she could scoop. Water fountained in like a bathtub filling from the bottom. Hand bailing was futile. Her mouth tightened.

Stupid, stupid. No life vest. No bailer.

She was a strong swimmer, but through the wispy fog the shore loomed light-years from the middle of the lake. No help in sight, and she had one more marker buoy to set. It bobbed to the surface an unreachable distance away. At the absurdity of attempting to place it now, she couldn't stop a giggle.

With a loud glug, the outboard motor pulled the stern down. The boat followed, and she splashed into the water. Comprehension flooded her. Her stomach wound into a tight knot. Someone had done this to her, with deliberation and premeditation.

And she knew how.

The water felt warmer than the morning air, but it would soon chill her. She had to get out. She lunged for the orange marker that had plopped out along with her. It would help support her until she could decide which way to swim.

Something stopped her short of the buoy. A steel grip held her right ankle fast. A torrent of adrenaline coursed through her. Her heart hammered.

No! She'd beaten death twice before. She fought too hard to let drowning be her fate. She kicked and splashed. No give. She yelled for help, but hadn't enough breath for volume.

Adrenaline fueling her muscles, she jackknifed down to look. Her captor wasn't a hired killer. It wasn't even human. The painter, the mooring line, was looped around her ankle. Eel grass and the frayed line had interwoven. The tangle imprisoned her as surely as a leg iron.

With the boat as anchor, she was a balloon on a string.

Blood roared in her ears. She peeled off her water-filled boat shoes, then heaved and pulled to free herself. The grip refused to yield.

She was going under with the sinking boat.

Chapter Fourteen

AS SOON AS Cole left the bathroom, yawning, he strode into the kitchen. No coffee. No Laura. Not even in the bedroom.

Where the hell was she? Did the woman have no care for her safety? He knew better. What was she up to then? As he stomped into his sandals, he peered out the front window.

Damn fog. And the trees. He could see nothing. He fitted his 9mm into his inside-the-waistband holster—easier to get to than an ankle holster—and pulled on a fresh t-shirt, leaving it out to cover the weapon. He hit the door.

Like him, she'd thrashed through the night. And this morning probably needed to get out or to get away from him. Probably went to the boat shed. The other officers were out there, but their job was to spot the killer.

Laura was Cole's responsibility.

Whether she liked it or not.

At the docks, the shed door stood open and her outboard was missing. He squinted across the lake. What he saw cleared his head and raced his heart faster than a vat of caffeine.

He pounded along the dock toward another outboard bobbing beside her empty spot. He jumped in the boat and released the tether. He yanked on the cord and the little engine roared to life. As he zoomed away, he was vaguely aware of people yelling and running along the dock behind him.

Too bad if he'd taken someone's skiff. He had no damn time for that. Thank God the fool had left the key in it.

Even as he searched the water's surface for any sign of her, recriminations writhed inside him. How could he have been so careless? Was he going to have to handcuff her to the bed to keep her safe? Where the hell was she?

At first, she was splashing wildly, fighting something or someone in the water. Then as he took off, he saw only her pale head at water level.

Now, nothing but ripples. And the orange markers.

He willed the boat to go faster, but full throttle didn't get him much. The spot he'd last seen her was so far away. The boat slogged through mud.

At last he reached the buoy. He cut the engine.

Laura popped to the surface.

Thank God! His heart could start again. "Laura, here!" He reached for her.

She sucked in air and coughed as she flailed at the water. "Boat … sank…. Leg … caught …line."

He clasped one hand, and she gripped the life preserver he extended with the other. "Hang on. I'll get it."

He stripped off his shirt and shoes. Leaving behind his 9mm with the clothing, he opened his multi-tool to the serrated blade and slipped over the side.

Following her leg downward, he found the fouled rope. In two swipes, the sharp blade freed her so she could kick upward. He followed and helped her into the outboard, heaving himself in after her.

"You have no idea how scared I was, seeing you go

under like that. You used up another of old Murphy's lives."

She sat in the bow, facing him, her hair plastered to her shoulders and dripping around her pale face. Shivering, she gave him a soggy smile. "I should've known you'd understand why I used the stable cat's name."

He was about to head back to the dock, but she insisted on placing the third buoy for the race. She'd only have to come out again later, she told him haltingly as she recovered her breath.

They motored to the third point in the racecourse. "What the hell happened? Was that an accident?"

"I think the boat sinking was deliberate. I'll know for sure when we get back to the boat shed. But no one could have rigged the painter to get fouled in grass."

"Thank God it didn't sink in deeper water." He shuddered at the thought. She'd had just enough leeway to reach the surface. She might've drowned anyway if exhaustion or hypothermia overtook her before help arrived. "If the boat was sabotaged, it was a damned inept murder attempt. If you hadn't gotten tangled, you could've swum to shore."

"Maybe to make it look like an accident?" she said.

By the time they reached the dock, the sun had burned away the last remnants of fog and mist. A small group of anxious spectators clustered.

Burt Elwell snatched the painter. "Laura, are you okay? I saw what was happening and ran to my boat here, but Stratton beat me to it."

"Your boat, is it? Thanks, then. You helped after all." Calm and collected as if she hadn't nearly drowned, Laura bestowed a beatific smile on the fawning jerk.

Cole nearly pushed her back in the water. The kid too.

"Easy, buddy. Don't forget your clothes." A grinning Kent Isaacs, in his groundskeeper's green work duds, handed Cole his shirt, with the gun concealed in its folds.

"Thanks." He slipped the sidearm into his shorts pocket and yanked on the shirt. He tamped down his anger. Every time he saw how the kid looked at her, his testosterone spiked.

He'd check later with the DARK officer to learn what he might've seen. For now he hot-footed it to catch up with Laura and the kid, who were headed to the boat shed.

****

Laura barely heard Burt squawking like a seagull behind her. Her heart sprinted. She needed to see the damaged skiff, to know if what she suspected was true.

"Me and one of the new guys cleaned this place up yesterday while you was gone," Burt said. "See, everything's organized. I threw away the old junk."

Inside, she weaved through equipment to the overturned skiff. A paint rag lay loosely draped over where the gouged hole should be.

"What do you think, Laura?" he said, eager as a puppy.

She jerked away the cloth.

No hole.

"What do I think?" She turned as Cole and the DARK *gardener* named Isaacs entered the shed. "I think that *this* is my skiff. Someone switched boats so I got stuck out in the middle of the lake in a skiff with a badly patched hole. And whoever did it made sure I had no bailer or life vest. I bet mine is still tucked under the seat of this one."

"What do you know about this, Burt?" Cole's eyes had that cold, assessing look as he prowled around the shed examining everything.

Sure enough, the shed was neat. Gear was organized, more hooks hung on the walls, a cleared aisle for walking.

A puzzled frown on his forehead, Burt scratched his chin. "Geezum, I dunno. Me 'n Isaacs spent a couple hours in here, but we didn't touch the skiff."

"We didn't have time for repairs," Isaacs added. "We were in here together."

She understood. He was telling Cole that Burt didn't have the opportunity to switch skiffs. And why would he? Someone wanted her dead, but Burt couldn't be involved. He was no Ph.D., maybe not even a G.E.D., but he meant well.

"After that we was working on the other side of the lake, by the campground. Anybody coulda come in here and carried out the skiff," the young handyman added.

"He's right," she said on a sigh. "The shed's never locked."

Knowing the how didn't deflate her anxiety, but only ballooned it. Knowing the *who* was the important issue. Who was the hired killer, this Janus? What kind of fiend could take money to kill people, innocent people?

To kill *her?*

How foolhardy she'd been. She'd waved the red flag—herself—at the bull, but all the bull had to do was wait. Rather than avoiding her killer, she'd fallen into his trap. Her pulse stammered, and her breathing turned shallow. She curled a hand into a fist and put it to her mouth as she sought calm.

When Cole's arm came around her, she leaned into him, accepting his strength and protection. In spite of her fears about their relationship, she needed him. She knew that now.

No, not *him*.

She wouldn't let herself need him. Just his protection. His hard-eyed federal officer competence. Not him.

"Prob'ly some kids fooling around," Burt said. "Got the two boats mixed up. Who would want to hurt you, Laura?"

"Who indeed?" Cole said as he ushered her out.

****

Later that morning, Cole and the East Pond Camp sailing instructor carried the last of four sailing dinghies down the boat ramp and slid it into Passabec Lake.

"Thanks for your help." The instructor, a shaven-headed teenager in baggy shorts, shook Cole's hand.

He held the dark-blue boat for one of his students, who paddled it to the dock where the other East Pond boats danced on the light chop, bobbing and weaving as if warming up for the race.

"Glad to help." Cole was telling the plain truth. The physical exercise of moving the boats and equipment worked off some of the hyper-drive pumping through his veins.

Mopping his forehead with the paper towel he carried as a handkerchief, he strode around the lakeshore and sat in the shade. From there, he had a clear view of the beach, the lake and the sailing groups. Laden with binoculars and picnic baskets, families of the young sailors cluttered the sand beach. More spectators putted and paddled around the racecourse. Among them were two DARK officers, in case Janus had more plans for the race. His gut knotted at the possibility the killer would endanger children to hit his intended victim. Shit, hadn't he told Laura the kids wouldn't be in danger?

After leaving the boat shed earlier, every nerve ending he possessed had twitched to quiz Laura about her solo defection. But she insisted on first telling Stan about the sunken skiff. At the inn, Joyce clucked over her and wrapped her in towels and a terry cloth robe.

Cole assured them his team would investigate, but Stan insisted that the owner should investigate a boating accident on his property. He relished the task like a starring role. Cole expected to see him skulking about in a deerstalker hat.

Bea, bearing a pot of chicken soup, and Vanessa met them at the cabin. Once the solicitous friends had departed, he raged at Laura like a wounded buffalo in the middle of the living room. Chin up and eyes calm, she listened to his rant. Then surprisingly, she apologized, admitting her move had been foolish. She had promised not to do it again and then went to shower. He'd gaped at her retreating back.

Now, he angled his body toward the clusters of chattering kids, Laura in their midst. She'd clamped her hair back. In her polo with the collar turned up and her khaki shorts, she was the princess—except for her overt and genuine warmth with the kids.

Who would guess the deadly danger she'd faced earlier?

She and the gangly East Pond leader were conducting some kind of icebreaker with the youngsters, so they got to know each other. Damn, but she was good with them. Her eight loved her, hugging her in relief she was safe and begging for the story of her adventure.

Right now he didn't want to hug her. He wanted to strangle her. She'd give him gray hair. An ulcer. A heart attack. Janus and anyone else that slime Markos hired to kill her would have to get in line. Still, she had his admiration that she refused to be a victim. She charged into the boat shed, demanding answers. But that admirable courage placed her in unnecessary danger.

If she'd let him accompany her, he'd have freed her ankle and they could've swum to safety together. He swiped at his brow, new sweat not from exertion. In the boat shed, he'd seen the aftermath catch up to her, the pastiness and hitched breathing that meant panic attack. The ache to protect her ignited a flame in his chest, but his arm around her didn't seem enough of a shield. Hell, his attempt at protection in general was a near bust. First the car brakes, now a sabotaged boat. He didn't detect or stop either. She was still alive and unharmed. Thanks mostly to her own ingenuity and fortitude.

Pride in success at his missions was part of who he had become. Necessary to his identity and his self-respect. This time that inner drive took a back seat. Failure didn't enter the equation for a different reason entirely. Laura. The only woman he'd ever loved. Her life was at stake. He couldn't fail her again.

He wouldn't.

A commotion among the jumble of children yanked his attention back to the present. The East Pond leader dragged a yowling blond boy aside while Laura headed Cole's way with the Mohawk-styled boy in hand.

Anger pinched his face into a bulldog snarl. "I don't care," he growled. "Somebody done it, and they gotta pay."

Laura drew him to a halt beside the shrub where Cole sat. "I know you meant well, but whoever switched boats, it wasn't one of the East Pond sailors." Softening, she placed both hands on the boy's shoulders and beamed him one of her million-megawatt smiles. "Zach, I appreciate your caring, but accusing a person without cause achieves nothing."

Giving Cole a questioning look, she continued, "Now I want you to sit here by Mr. Stratton and think about this until we're ready to start."

Cole gave her a nod.

"You're still gonna let me race?" Zach lifted bleak eyes that glinted with hope.

"After you apologize to that boy and his instructor."

The spy hunter slumped to a cross-legged position beside Cole. Even his normally rigid Mohawk sagged. He glared at the only adult within range. "Told you there were spies."

"That you did." Cole nodded morosely. "I screwed up too. Why do you think we're sitting over here together?"

"This whole day sucks. My camera's missing."

Cole sat straighter. The burglaries. He'd nearly forgotten. "How'd that happen?"

Zach shrugged. "Mom said I prob'ly left it somewhere, but I didn't. Kay's iPod's gone. With her fave tunes. Spies or burglars, I dunno." He slumped deeper, chin on his fists.

Cole said nothing, grabbing time to think.

The boy heaved a sigh. "That stupid dork shouldn't have laughed about her boat sinking."

Cole lobbed a pebble into the water. "You think a

lot of her."

"She listens to a guy. And she makes the sailing class fun." Zach found his own pebble and copied Cole's action. "Without sailing, I don't got much to do but hang at the beach."

"Your folks over there watching the race today?"

"Nah, my parents are divorced. Divorce sucks. Mom and Dad take turns at our cabin. This is Mom's month, but she works in Alderport. She's at work today, so I'm on my own."

Cole could relate to that. For most of his childhood, he'd had only the one parent, such as he was. He came home from school more than once to find an empty fridge and his old man passed out on the floor. "That's a rough deal. What did you do yesterday, when you had a day off from sailing?"

The Mohawk perked up as Zach's eyebrows shot north. "Yesterday was sweet. Butch's dad took me and him to a Sea Dogs game in Portland. They won, nine to five. And two of the Red Sox players were there. I got their new pitcher's autograph."

"Very cool. I'd like to see that sometime." Cole heaved an exaggerated sigh. "Too bad you weren't on the beach, though. Maybe someone as observant as you would have noticed a spy messing with the boats."

Zach scooted closer. "I been asking around. Chuck—that's Kay's brother—said they were on the beach, except his sister kept hanging out at the boat docks." He rolled his eyes. "Prob'ly looking for that dumb guy she likes."

He cautioned the boy to keep his ears open, but not to confront anyone again. "I have to make it up to her, too, big guy. So if you tell me whatever you find out, we'll both hit her A list." What had he come to, running an eleven-year-old agent? "If you put yourself in danger, you'll only worry her. You leave any interrogations to me. Agreed?"

He pointed toward the sailing group, where Laura was beckoning to Zach.

"You got it." The boy grinned, leaping to his feet. "Geezum, I guess I have to apologize now, huh?"

"It's the right thing to do. The honorable thing." Cole bumped fists with him before he raced off.

The handyman again, he mused, remembering Kay flirting with Burt Elwell. Maybe he'd have a talk with Miss Hot-to-Trot Kay. For more than one reason.

Chapter Fifteen

"NO AFTER-EFFECTS from your dunking?" Vanessa asked when Laura and Cole arrived at the theater that evening. Her red-blond hair was piled on top her head in a froth of cognac curls. She gave Laura a comforting hug. "What a terrible thing. You're sure you feel all right?"

"I'm fine." She'd been more shaken up by the brake incident. After today she was more determined than ever to trap Janus. Tonight she and Cole would try to find out what anyone in the theatrical troupe knew about the boat sinking. "Of course, having my sailing class win the regatta against East Pond later perked me up considerably."

"Congratulations," said the other woman. "I'll be downstairs doing makeup. Come keep me company if you get a chance."

Bea walked by with a stack of programs. She made a clucking sound. "Two accidents in a matter of days. You should be careful, dear."

Laura forced a casual smile. "You're absolutely right. And thanks for the chicken soup. Having something good and hot in my stomach made me feel much better."

Tonight the elderly actress wore a velvet turban spangled with tiny mirrors. She whisked off in a flutter of paisley shawl and gauze muumuu.

Laura answered Cole's surreptitious prodding and made her way backstage, where they were to help with props during the first act.

"Chicken soup?" he whispered, a glower knitting his brow. "I saw the pot. You sure as hell didn't offer me any. I didn't get any of her lasagna, either."

She ducked around a tied-back curtain and skirted the old upright piano that was part of the set. "Anyone would think you were starving." They'd cooked steaks and potatoes on an outdoor grill. "And you should thank me for not sharing. Bea's sweet and generous, but she's a terrible cook. I poured out the soup."

His reaction could be described only as a classic double take. His head jerked back as if on springs. Mouth quirking up and eyes glittering with humor, he sputtered, "The powder-puff pigeon is cuisine challenged." Humor rumbled from his chest and burst from his mouth in a Falstaffian guffaw that crinkled his eyes and dimpled the grooves in his cheeks. His shoulders shook, and he slapped his thigh.

Seeing such a rarity as Cole laughing with uninhibited glee was worth a near drowning. Laura covered her mouth as she joined in his mirth. "Bea's cooking is a bit like her fashion sense, extravagant."

He frowned. "A little of this, a little of that?"

"A lot, not a little. The Van Tassels' cabin porch is covered with pots of herbs. I think she dumps some of each in it—tarragon, basil, oregano, thyme, sage, you name it."

Still chuckling, Cole looped an arm around her shoulders. "The Van Tassel sisters starred in the last play, I remember. Lucky they're such good souls. With all the danger around you, I might worry they got ideas from—"

"*Arsenic and Old Lace*?"

They gaped at each other. Shook their heads.

Both erupted in a fit of laughter. People surrounded them—actors rehearsing lines, other stage crew carrying props, the director checking the lights. The ozone odor of hot lighting mingled with greasepaint. Laura buried her face in Cole's shirtfront. Better if the others thought the reason for their merriment a private, romantic joke.

His other arm came around her, and his laughter reverberated in her, spiking sensation deep inside.

"Laura." His voice was husky, but not from laughing.

She raised her gaze to his burning one. His masculine scent and the naked hunger in his face scoured heat through her and banished their surroundings.

"Cole, Laura, you're just the ones I need to see."

They jumped apart as Stan Hart approached.

The resort owner was tying his character Cookie's white apron around his stocky body. "Haven't got any leads yet," he said behind a hand. He clearly loved considering himself a coconspirator. "A lot of folks are on those docks all the time."

"And no one pays attention to what others are doing," she said. "Some kids in my sailing class were on the beach. None of them saw anything unusual."

"I put a padlock on the boat shed this afternoon. Stop by tomorrow for a key." He started toward the stairwell. "You sure it wasn't like Burt said, kids mixing up the boats?"

Storm clouds couldn't loom darker than Cole's expression. "Whoever shuffled those boats went to a hell of a lot of trouble to transfer the outboard motor to the damaged boat and to conceal the bottom of the good one. No accident."

Stan nodded glumly. "I'll keep checking. Gotta go. Vanessa's expecting me in makeup." He raised an arm in a dramatic pose. "The show must go on!"

After Laura finished helping set up the diner props, she whispered to Cole that she was going to the makeup room to talk to Vanessa, who'd been kayaking on the lake that morning. "Maybe she went out yesterday too."

Cole's eyes snapped as he readied a warning. The male potency in his pale eyes took her breath away.

"I know." She countered with a sweet smile before he could open his mouth. "Don't go off by myself. It's a crush down there. I'll be surrounded at all times."

"You got it, babe. Stick with Vanessa." He tilted his head toward a trio of kids in the wings. "I got... a tip to ask Kay about what she saw yesterday."

Laura scrutinized the girl as Cole threaded his way through the milling crowd. Kay, in Rock-Star-Barbie mode with a boatload of mascara and a halter top that hugged her budding breasts, was gabbing with the girl who played Debbie and flirting with Burt.

Maybe a talk with her parents was in order.

She paused at the top of the narrow staircase leading to the lower level. In spite of his good humor about Bea's cooking, all day Cole had brooded and hovered like a hawk, especially after her apology. Apprehension about what might happen next twisted her stomach in knots, but she wouldn't let fear rule her.

Was worry for her the cause of his lowered brow and hard mouth?

She had secrets, and so apparently did he. She'd overheard two more phone conversations in Spanish, one with someone named Marisol. Whatever relationship he had with other women shouldn't affect her. Acknowledging her resurrected love for him didn't mean he reciprocated. She didn't want him to love her. He *mustn't* love her. There was no future in it. And he deserved a future.

Whatever he'd said to Zach put the sunshine back in the boy's disposition. Cole was a natural with kids. He'd make a terrific father. He needed more than she could offer.

Renewing her resolve ought to bolster her, but it only scraped at her heart.

****

After their first-act duties ended, Cole and Laura searched for seats in the house. On Thursday, *Death at the Diner* had opened to a sparse house, but tonight the only seats left were in the last row.

"Good," Cole murmured, "we can make out."

His good humor over Bea's culinary disasters was making him bold. Or was it his conversation with Kay? Laura elbowed him in the ribs. "Behave."

"What did Vanessa have to say?" His warm breath tickled her ear. Angled toward her, he practically nuzzled her neck. His scent, mingled with soap and charcoal smoke from their cookout, fuzzed her brain.

Making out, indeed. This had to be part of his act as her lover. They both knew love between them had less chance of being real than a Persian mummy.

She cleared her throat. "She stayed in the inn yesterday with sunburn, so my detection was a bust." She ought to scoot aside so he didn't loom over her, but the man on her other side was too close. "And Kay?"

"Later. The play's starting." A wink, and he adjusted

136

his position toward the stage. Placing his hands on his knees, he focused on the rising curtain.

When she realized what the action was at the start of the second act, she swallowed hard and edged away from him. Never mind her other neighbor's bony elbow.

The couple, Debbie and Cliff, were just returning from searching for an exit, and a romantic evening drive on the motorcycle. Debbie swung off the back of the bike and leaned over to press her lips to Cliff's.

Laura waited nervously for Cole's reaction. This scene came too close for comfort to the first time they had kissed. Maybe he wouldn't see the similarity. Or remember. Maybe her stomach was tied in a half hitch for nothing.

Long ago, Cole and she had left the graduation party crowd to return to her car. Like the play character, she delivered a quick kiss, but even that brief contact stunned her with its heat and power.

Debbie walked to the diner entrance, away from Cliff.

Cole shifted in his seat, stretched an arm along the seat back behind her, his gaze on the performance. His scent caressed her, ensnared her so she scarcely knew what was memory and what was now. She had to resist the urge to snuggle into his hard strength.

Onstage, the couple kissed a second, longer time.

Laura had no awareness of what Cliff said to Debbie, but Cole's words were branded on her heart. Even now, the memory of his mouth on hers evoked enough heat to speed her pulse and make her tug at her sweatshirt neck.

She forced herself to concentrate on the action as the young couple entered the diner for the discovery of a murder. Cliff and Debbie were to find the waitress Daisy Rae prone behind the diner counter. One by one, the others would arrive for dinner, only to become witnesses. Laura liked the scene, which brought all the principals onstage together.

Cole's breath feathered across her temple. "Remember?"

She jumped as if her seat prodded her with an electric charge. Oh God, he did remember what she'd said. *"Wondered what that would be like, cowboy."* She'd tried to walk away, like Debbie, but the intensity in his eyes had held her as surely as his embrace. "Remember what?"

"I could've written that bit. Better. I had a better line. *I wondered too, babe. I still do.* Well?"

"Yes, all right, yes, I remember." If she scooted farther away, she'd land in her neighbor's lap. "Although Cliff Trigger's an improvement over the original. He's certainly more civilized."

Appalled at her snippy outburst, she scrambled to her feet and out of the theater.

****

"I didn't mean to push your buttons," Cole said to Laura's bedroom door. Damned clear why the reminiscence had upset her. Any memories of that time carried more emotional baggage than Maine had mosquitoes. "The scene brought back graduation night. I have great memories of that party."

He'd followed her out of the theater and back to the cabin, where she retreated to her bedroom. To escape him? Or the memories? First they laughed together. Then sitting close to her in the darkened theater, with that scene… If she hadn't run out, he'd have kissed her.

He was an ass. She'd have run out then sure as hell. Faster.

The door opened.

Laura stood in the gap, shadows beneath her eyes, the sparkling remnants of tears on her lashes. How she could look regal and perfect in a sweatshirt and jeans, he didn't get "I'm sorry I overreacted. The business with the skiff must be affecting me. I shouldn't have snapped at you."

"You had a big day. Truce." He held out his hand.

"Truce." She placed her hand in his, but slipped it away before he could savor the touch. She headed toward the couch, but veered to the chair, as if afraid to sit on what had become his bed. "You were going to tell me about your conversation with Kay."

"Ah, Kay. Yes. She spent some time yesterday afternoon on the finger docks. Some of it sunning herself in Burt's outboard."

"The boat that you commandeered."

"The very one. She was waiting for him, hoping he'd give her a ride. And not just on the boat."

"I see." A stripe of color spread across her cheeks. "Maybe I should talk to her about the dangers of chasing after older boys."

"Especially older boys with police records. Definitely jail bait. Did you know that our Cliff Trigger spent some time in the county jail?"

"Of course." She tossed her head with haughty assurance.

"How? I doubt he'd brag about being a jailbird."

"Stan told me a long time ago. Burt and some other boys stole an outboard motor from a marina in Alderport. He spent a few days behind bars. He was a teenager then." She cocked her head at him. "Did you tell that to Kay?"

He worked his jaw, chewing his decision again. "I started to, but I asked her only about yesterday. You saw her tonight. All tarted up. Hard to tell how young she really is. And I remember my teenage years enough to know that warning her off him might have the opposite effect, kinda like your folks warning you about the biker."

Laura's blush deepened at that. "Maybe I'll have a talk with her dad. Or with Burt. You don't suspect he's in league with Janus? Not Burt."

Cole scrubbed at the scar on his chin, about as effective as trying to remove nagging doubts about the boy. The underlying suspicion came from his confused feelings, nothing concrete. "I don't know what I suspect. The kid's up to something. Isaacs said after they went to the other side of the lake to work, he lost track of Burt. But Kay said he didn't come to the docks either. More likely he's the resort burglar. He has keys and opportunity."

"I can't believe he'd betray his uncle and Stan that way. He was probably goofing off, taking a nap or something. He's not a self-starter. As distractible as a puppy. Stan has mentioned frustration at Burt's occasional, shall we say, unauthorized absences."

"More puppy stuff. Geared for fun rather than work."

She yawned and pushed to her feet. "I'm going to need a nap soon myself. A long one. But since we're here and not at the play, I have brownies to bake. I promised the sailing class a celebration tomorrow."

He enjoyed the sway of her hips as she sauntered to

the kitchen. "You could call on Bea."

She laughed, music that warmed him to his toes. "The kids would never forgive me." She rummaged in the refrigerator.

"They'd forgive you anything." He shared his conversation with Zach. He joined her in the kitchen and leaned against the wall to watch her as she measured and mixed ingredients Joyce Hart had supplied.

"Poor kid. I knew his mom was away at work a lot, but I didn't realize how much he was at loose ends." She stirred cocoa into the mixture. "I'll ask Stan if he can fit Zach into an archery class."

She cared deeply about her young charges in both the tennis and sailing classes. The dunking had deterred her not a bit from the responsibility of the regatta. Nurturing and mothering came to her as naturally as breathing. Years ago, they'd dreamed of having the family both wanted. Neither ever married. In spite of the past, and with danger facing them, he was falling for her again.

Hard. The realization staggered him.

They communicated like before. Better than before. With more honesty. She knew him better than anyone. He thought he knew her, except for the pain that shadowed her eyes.

She kept telling him to toss the chip off his shoulder. If his rough background wasn't the barrier, did it have to be too late for them? She wanted him. And he sure as hell wanted her. So why did she deny her feelings?

If they could get through his questions about the baby…

If he could get past that wall she kept around her…

Chapter Sixteen

WHEN LAURA TURNED from placing the brownie pan in the oven and setting the timer, Cole was gazing at her solemnly.

He pushed a hand through his hair, then scrubbed knuckles across his jaw, a habit of deep thought. At the confusion and questions she saw in his eyes, her pulse scrambled, and heat rose in her cheeks. She braced herself for the questions she feared.

"If there had been a baby, would you have told me?"

His words came out measured and slow and laden with anguish, dredged from his soul, tightening a band around her chest. He suffered too.

But relief at his question eased her anxiety about what else to tell him. "I tried before... before I lost the baby."

"How? I was at Parris Island."

"I phoned your dad from Boulder, from the university."

"He had my address. Was he drunk?" His hard mask once again in place, he pivoted away to the doorway and looked out through the screening.

"I don't know. He didn't say anything about the Marines, but he promised to get back to me with your address. I called again, but the phone was disconnected. I—"

"That must've been after he died. Too late."

The pain in his forced ironic tone squeezed her chest. "I'm so sorry. I should've tried harder to find you."

He shook his head. "It wasn't your fault. I didn't want to be found." He returned and gripped the chair back the same way she had. "How were your folks about the pregnancy?"

A wistful memory lifted her lips. "That was the one bright spot in those dark days. Mom and Dad were great, very supportive, aside from wanting to keep it secret. I guess I wanted to hide too. At first I was too angry at you to tell you about the baby. I blamed you. I wasn't ready."

"Yeah, I know. You were right." His voice broke, and he cleared his throat. "How did it happen? The miscarriage."

Oh God, how to begin. How to tell it without revealing everything. She could hardly breathe, let alone speak. "It was December, Christmas vacation."

"December." As realization dawned, horror roughened his voice. "You were six months pregnant."

She continued, on automatic, the only way she could get through the tale. "My family went to Colorado, so they could hide my pregnancy from anyone at home. My cousin Angela and I were driving back to the cabin after skiing at Steamboat Springs."

"Angela's the one you went to Europe with?"

She nodded, a lump the size of France in her throat. "Actually, Angela skied, and I relaxed. I'm a fair skier, but being pregnant put me off balance. But during the drive, the car hit ice. Black ice. Invisible. My sportscar spun out of control. It slammed into the guardrail. It... burst into flame. The seatbelt was too uncomfortable on my belly, so I wasn't wearing it. I was thrown out.

Angela didn't make it."

Tears stung her eyes again, but she set her chin and blinked them away. She could still see in slow motion the other cars, the shocked faces of drivers as the sportscar spun around and around, faster and faster toward the metal guardrail.

She could hear the shriek of rubber on asphalt and ice.

She could hear Angela's horrified gasps.

She could feel the sickening carnival-ride whirl.

And the rush of air when the door swung open and an invisible hand flung her like a rag doll from the careening automobile. Then red-hot shards of pain in her side and in her belly.

"That must have been horrible." She didn't know when he moved, but he stood beside her. His hands on her waist seemed to be the only force keeping her on her feet. The anguish in his eyes must have mirrored hers.

"I'm all right." She plucked a paper towel from the kitchen counter and blew her nose. "I was pretty depressed for a while. Counseling helped, so I could move on. Talking about the accident brings back all the anger and sorrow."

"Can you go on?" The warm support in his voice offered a cushion for her pain.

She nodded. "I tried to struggle to my feet, to go to Angela, but my legs didn't work. People held me down, wrapped me in a blanket. And then I must have passed out."

"And you… lost our baby?" His voice was so gentle, so full of pain it made her chest ache.

He placed the flat of his hand on her stomach. She felt the imprint of every finger, of the palm and of his heat. She allowed the gesture to comfort her. As long as he couldn't see the scar beneath his hand.

"When I woke up in the hospital, I was no longer pregnant. He was too premature and too damaged in the crash to survive." Cole's body went rigid, but she didn't stop. "The surgeon brought him to me only because I pitched a fit they could hear in the next county. He'd been cleaned up and swaddled in a soft blue blanket, but he was so tiny, like a doll. So perfect. So still."

"A son." His voice grated like ground glass on sandpaper. "We would've had a son."

She raised her head to gaze at him. His eyes were as opaque and bleak as winter frost. "I named him David Cole Rossiter."

"David. It's a good name. Thank you for the Cole." His tight mouth tilted at one corner. "A son. Laura, if only I'd… known…" His voice broke, and he squeezed shut his eyes.

"He's buried in the family plot beside Angela. She died on impact." In her own way, Laura had died too. The whole experience had left her scarred inside and out. And empty.

But no emptier than she felt at this moment. Emptier than when she was bleeding in that car trunk. Empty down to her soul. Drained of all energy and hope. A hollow shell.

His fingers smoothed her hair back from her face. "You couldn't have saved Angela. You'd have only endangered yourself." He pulled her into his arms.

A sob choked her voice. "The ice… the car wasn't good in winter weather. I shouldn't—"

"Stop. Blame the ice, not yourself."

"I know." She cried against his chest. He smelled so

good, sunshine and life and strength. She didn't want him to be her anchor, but she needed him at that moment. "They call it survivor's guilt. I wasn't even driving. Angela was. She'd insisted we take the sportcar because she loved driving it. She wanted to buy it from me. Aunt Emily, Angela's mother, has hated me ever since. If only I hadn't given in, she might be alive. And our baby might have survived."

Our only baby.

His arms tightened around her, and he murmured, "You couldn't have known. The accident wasn't your fault."

"Oh, Cole, I wanted our baby. Every day I talked to him and sang to him. I could feel him move, and I saw the sonogram images. They showed his tiny fingers and toes. He..." Sobs racked her, and she could say no more.

"Hush, I said it before. No if-onlys. Thank God you're alive. You could've died too."

Blinking away her tears, she leaned back and gazed at his dear, dear face. He'd donned a defensive mask devoid of emotion, but moisture beaded his lashes.

Yes, the truth hurt him, but no more than rejection for no reason. She'd been wrong to keep it from him. But not wrong to keep her renewed love to herself. Neither of them needed more heartbreak. She knew love again, but her scars would never heal, and the ghost of what could never be would separate them again. Forever. Her love for him was only a dream she could hug to herself during the long, cold, barren winters to come.

He smoothed a hand down the side of her face. She savored the roughness of his skin, absorbed it into her memory. "I understand why you went into a depression afterward. You had a lot of grief to work through."

After her body had healed from the accident and the surgery, grief and loss threw her into a self-destructive spiral. Maybe telling it would be enough to drive him away. He'd think her unstable and unbalanced

"My body healed, and I went back to school, but I couldn't sleep or eat or concentrate on my studies. I skipped classes and slept. Too much. But it kept my mind off the baby and off what happened to Angela." *And off the rest.*

"Then you got some help?"

"Not soon enough. I couldn't tolerate anyone touching me. I felt dirty, but I hadn't the energy to wash. I could barely tolerate me." She gave a mirthless laugh, expecting him to move away from her. "Shocking, isn't it? I shocked myself."

His chin rested on the top of her head. "You weren't yourself."

Both touched and stymied that he wasn't repulsed, she rested her cheek on the steady beat of his heart. "Finally my roommates dragged me to a counselor. She hooked me up with other grieving women who'd had miscarriages."

"A group."

"We had little in common except losing babies. Some of the women had lost more than one. Hearing their stories was wrenching but also healing. We shared our stories, we hugged, we held hands and wrote poems and made small memorials."

"And you healed each other," he finished for her.

"Their support helped me stop my downward spin. I focused on my studies again. I relearned the comfort of human touch through holding hands with my group and later with my roommates. But I didn't have another date the rest of my college career."

Later she immersed herself in her work and teaching tennis to inner-city youngsters. "Some of us in the group keep in touch by email and grief chat rooms. I've missed them terribly since I've been in hiding."

"No wonder you hated me. I caused you all that pain with my carelessness." His voice sounded as choked as hers.

She closed her eyes against the pain of a new realization. If she'd told him about the pregnancy, he'd have stood by her. She should've remembered his integrity and sense of responsibility. She shouldn't have believed Valesko or the rumors. If only she'd been thinking clearly and not through a haze of anger and resentment. There would've been no accident, no miscarriage. They would've had a son. And possibly more babies. Regret washed over her, choking her with pain.

When she could breathe again, she raised her head to gaze into his eyes, dark with fierce determination. "Never say that you caused all my pain. You didn't cause the miscarriage, and both of us made the baby."

His big hands massaged her shoulders. She hadn't realized how stiffly she was hunching them until he eased the tension. "Now I know even better why you chose Murphy the cat's name. Nine lives, but three or four have expired. I promise you I'll get Alexei Markos and whoever he's hired. You'll be safe this time."

She watched his eyes kindle with a laser-blue flame. Years had passed since she felt the heat of desire. Not since that single weekend with Cole. During her brief relationships later, she went through the motions.

She didn't burn.

Until now. With him.

She traced the grooves tracking down his cheeks. "I can't tell you how sorry I am that I concealed the truth this long, but…" Surely she had more to say, but his heated gaze blurred her mind and seared her body.

She was finished talking.

Clearly, so was he.

The hard ridge of his arousal pressed against her belly. Her confession had shocked him, but he still wanted her. Shaking with love and need, she turned her mind away from the shadow still between them. She needed an affirmation of the love that once produced a small ephemeral life. She needed a flesh-and-blood memory to accompany the dream.

He slanted his mouth to fit hers. Heart racing, she met his tongue hungrily with her own. Her eyes closed as his lips devoured hers. As his fingers molded her body, her skin heated and her bones melted like butter. She burrowed into his neck, kissing and murmuring her need into his throbbing pulse points. Her body remembered his. The feel of his hands, the texture and salty scent of his skin.

She felt herself lifted to the counter behind her, her sweatshirt tugged up and her bra roughly pushed aside. He spread her legs and ground his hard body against her as he sucked on one nipple and then the other, shooting sparks of need along her nerves directly to the core of her passion. From somewhere far off she heard a whimper and was startled to recognize her own voice.

Dropping hot kisses around the shell of her ear, he whispered in a voice smoky with desire, "Laura, you make me crazy." He tore off his t-shirt, shucked down his jeans. "Say you want this, you want me."

"Yes, Cole, yes," She popped the snap of her own jeans and wrestled with them. He slid them and her panties down and away. She heard a groan escape him when her hand closed over him.

"Wait," he rasped out, "I want to protect you." He stepped away to slip a foil packet from his toiletry kit.

He didn't need it, but she couldn't tell him.

The air between them seemed to heat as he came to her, sliding his hands over her thighs and up her hips. A wave of need coursed through her. She had to have him inside her, to fill the emptiness, if only temporarily.

She wrapped her legs around him and dug her fingers into the bunched steel of his shoulders. He lifted her easily and lowered her onto himself. The impact of his entry jolted her entire being. It had been so long. *So long.*

Uttering guttural sounds of pleasure and control, he held himself still inside her as she adjusted to him. The magnetic tides that pulled them together stirred and pulsed inside her.

"Cole! Please…"

His eyes met hers, and lightning flared between them, searing her to her very core. She strained against him as he drove into her with the same uncontrollable need that raced through her. His thrusts rolled waves of pleasure through her and beckoned her closer to delirious oblivion.

Tongues of flame licked through her body. When he reached between them to stroke her sensitive center, heat spread relentlessly through her body, and as he followed, they were catapulted into the heart of the fire itself.

Chapter Seventeen

LONG MOMENTS LATER, Cole dragged himself to awareness. His lungs heaved and his heart pounded. He reeled from the emotional and physical tumult. He couldn't believe he'd been so rough, so fierce in his need, slamming into her like a wild animal. He was a selfish bastard, taking advantage of the emotional maelstrom. But he'd needed her to fill up the fissures of new grief.

The swell of her breasts, the curve of her cheek, the sweetness of her lips, he drank nectar from each, shaking with lust. He lost himself with her. With no one else had he ever felt such frenzy. In a raging fever, his body burned. He had to be inside her or expire. With her, only with her, passion burned away the reins of control. His whole body erupted with his release. Sex with Laura was earthshaking, a force of nature. Even more, a union of their hearts and spirits.

Was this time out of time all they had? She said they had no future. When the danger ended, she claimed they would go back to their separate lives.

Not if he could help it.

She had so much pain to overcome, but not alone. She was so brave, so strong. With his support, she could move on to a future they would build together. With more children.

He kissed her mouth gently and held her close, wanting, needing to keep their bodies connected a while longer, linking them in the only way he could. For now.

He felt her raise her head and shift position. She sighed, clearly still dazed. Then she leaned forward and lightly kissed his chest. The brush of her lips triggered heat in his loins again. A blush colored her cheeks, and her hand went automatically to her throat to close her collar, but the sweatshirt she still wore had none.

"Don't hide from me," he said softly. He traced the highest scar with a finger, soothing the reddened ridge that formed a jagged arc up the side of her neck. "You've survived more than any one person should ever have to endure. Those scars are badges of courage."

"Scars, yes…" Her eyes widened in what seemed to be fear, and she tugged down her sweatshirt, twisted and bunched up under her arms, to cover herself. "It's late."

A jarring dinging noise turned their heads around.

"The brownies," she said. "I have to get down." The rich aroma of baking chocolate filled the room, masking the scent and aura of their loving.

She kept her eyes averted as he lifted her down, separating their bodies. She yanked on her jeans and tugged her sweatshirt down as if to conceal her entire body.

He made a quick trip to the bathroom. When he returned, she had slid the brownies from the oven.

Once she set down the hot pan on a burner to cool, he pivoted her to him. He cupped her chin and nailed her with a challenging stare. "You can't pretend it didn't happen. We burned each other up. Whatever else time has erased, we still have that. You were right there with me."

She shook her head, her skin waxen. Exhaustion probably. "I know. But it was just because of the emotion of the moment. It can't happen again. We can't go back."

His gut clenched. After so many years, he hoped he again understood her. If he didn't, if he couldn't reach her, and they had no chance. "Not back. Forward." He crossed mental fingers and toes. "Your survivor's guilt is talking. And guilt for more than the car crash that took our baby. You urged me to let go my guilt about my father. Take your own advice, sweetheart."

Suspicion crinkling her eyes, she paused from wrapping foil over the brownie pan. "What do you mean?"

"You've forgiven me for the carelessness that made you pregnant, but have you forgiven yourself for that same carelessness?"

"You don't understand. There's too much pain. There's…." Shaking her head, she fled to the bedroom.

Letting her go hurt him, but he ought to give her time to think.

For him, their loving meant more than the emotion of the moment. Sex could never be simple between them. Gentle and kind, courageous and vulnerable, she never backed down. She challenged him to be the man he'd made himself, not the bitter biker with a chip on his shoulder as big as a Humvee.

Or was he only kidding himself? Maybe she wanted no more from him than a *wham bam thank you ma'am*. Did she need him only so long as she was in danger? To her was he still a Harley hoodlum? Doubt's long stinger pierced his chest. Rubbing his chest, he shuffled to the couch and spread the covers. He might as well rest, but he wouldn't sleep. More turmoil spun in his mind.

A son. David. They'd made a son.

His chest ached. He felt like Prometheus who stole

fire from the gods. Cole had dared to steal love, another heavenly fire. Having his guts chewed over and over by a vulture was the Greek's punishment. Grieving for his lost son chewed Cole to shreds. The loss would gnaw at him every day from now on.

Laura had suffered that torture for the last ten years. She'd nurtured their child within her, loved him, and wanted him. The accident that took him from her almost killed her. After the brake line sabotage caused another accident, she clutched her belly and murmured. Her disjointed, mumbled words coalesced in his mind.

My baby... my baby.

Thank God she'd survived. She'd overcome death over and over. He had to keep her safe this time.

His hands trembled. So she was right to reject him. Sex between them would complicate matters too much. Complicate and maybe compromise protecting her and finding the scumbag hit man Janus.

He clicked off the light. His first decision had been the right one. Stuff his hormones and his emotions in his Harley saddlebags and do the job.

****

Dawn crept in with a cool, misty summer rain that veiled the world and kept most vacationers indoors.

Laura would teach no sailing or tennis that day. The sailing-race celebration would have to wait, so she stowed the brownies in the refrigerator. Puttering about, cleaning and straightening, she worked around Cole, who tapped away on his laptop at the table. Instead of using the landline, he set up a miniature satellite receiver. He said ordinary wireless would be too easily compromised.

Using a torn t-shirt, she dusted the small tables

around the couch, the funny little one made from a power company spool and the other low one of bamboo-like plastic. She smiled. Until a few months ago, she would have turned up her nose at such tacky furniture. Now she counted herself lucky to have a roof over her head.

At his mumbled curse, she glanced up. He was utterly focused on the screen, his back to her.

Being cooped up with him in her cabin had her grinding her teeth. After their lovemaking last night, her every molecule was tuned to his frequency. He sat quietly working, but didn't merely occupy space. He controlled it. He dominated the entire room. The scent of his soap and shampoo seemed to follow her. His wide back looked too sexy and touchable. She longed to run her hands across his shoulders, down the ridge of bone covered with thick muscle that shifted and flexed with his every movement. Even the tapping sound of his fingers on the keys aroused her senses.

Yes, she had a memory to tuck away for later, a memory of heated passion and emotions on overload, but at this moment the memory tormented her with the desire for more.

More would be a disaster.

In their frenzy to possess each other, she'd forgotten her other scar, the surgical one on her abdomen. Since she'd remained partially clothed, he didn't notice. She made sure of that afterward. She would conceal her sad secret if she could, but she wouldn't lie to him. If she succumbed again, he would see the scar and surely ask. And she would have to answer. Seeing rejection in his eyes was what she expected, but pity or sympathy would tear her apart. So she needed to resist temptation.

Finished with the dusting, she wandered to the

kitchen, sidling past him at the table. Over his shoulder, she glimpsed the name Marisol in an email.

Just what she needed to quell her libido. And ignite her temper.

After making love with her, how dare he exchange notes with another woman! She slammed the neglected brownie pan to soak into the sink and twisted on the faucet full force. She attacked the baked-on cake bits with steel wool.

"You find Alexei Markos in that sink? Or something else grinding your gears?"

Her hand fluttered to her collar, then to her burning cheek. She had no right to be jealous. Hadn't she told herself a hundred times they had no future? Add to that she'd been snooping.

How to explain the fit of uncharacteristic temper? "Sorry. It's just being cooped up." *With you.* "I'm used to being active, to being outdoors." She rinsed the pan and deposited it in the dish drainer.

Drying her hands, she turned and shrugged. "I enjoy cooking, but I've discovered that I hate cleaning. I'd rather scrape paint off a boat hull or pick up seventy-five tennis balls or catalog the cross-references for third-century Aegean pottery than clean house."

He tilted the chair back on its rear legs and folded his arms. "The domestic type you're not. The maternal type is more like it. You're damn good with those kids." His eyes softened, and he held out his right hand.

She wanted to accept it, to let him fold her into his arms, to tell him she loved him. But she couldn't. If she did, she'd have to tell him the rest. Heart thumping painfully, she skirted the table and sat opposite him.

The laptop lid suited her as a wall. "Are there any

reports on Markos?"

His canted chair clacked down to four on the floor. "He seems to have vanished again. The operatives tracking him must have their heads up their asses." He scratched his jaw and frowned. "I've been going through the background checks on guests and employees."

"And?"

"And zip." He slapped the laptop closed. At least the table remained between them. "Everybody's cleaner than that pan you reamed out. Nobody who could be Janus, but some folks who need money. Who doesn't? Even Stan. Look at the employee cabins and the furnishings. This resort is in hock to the bank for the next forty years."

She clucked her tongue. "You can't suspect Stan Hart!"

"Wouldn't have confided in him if DARK wasn't sure of him. Just making a point."

"Anyone else?"

He tapped a pencil on his computer lid as he ticked them off. "The Van Tassel sisters are living on a small pension. Rudy Damon is soliciting funds to buy into a Broadway play. Martin Rhodes's dental practice is mortgaged to a casino in Connecticut. How's that for boring, solid citizens?"

She chuckled. "I'll remember not to go to Dr. Rhodes for any fillings. But you don't suspect any of them?"

"Except for our boy Burt. There's too much that doesn't fit."

"What do you mean?"

"Whoever has arranged some of your *accidents* has been damned clumsy. The brake line tampering might have worked. But the boat switch wasn't surefire. Not professional."

"I see what you mean. So if Markos hasn't found me, hasn't sent this Janus here, who *has* been trying to kill me?"

"That's the million-dollar question." He reached across the table, palm up, an invitation she should resist. When she kept her hands in her lap, he scowled and withdrew his hand. "My money's on Burt for the boat switch. Who else would have known about the damaged boat or known what to do?"

"But why?" She shoved her chair back and crossed to the window beside the door. She gazed out at the drizzle. Rejecting him stabbed her, but she had to keep distance between them. "Why would Burt want to harm me? He seems to like me."

"He likes expensive toys. His outboard. A windsurfer. Remember that Harley he's saving for? Same reason he might've done the burglaries." The scrape of his chair told her he'd stood up.

She sensed his body heat at her back and breathed in his scent. This cabin was way too confining. How could she resist him if he persisted in pursuing her?

Then his words sank in. "You said something once about selling me out. Is that what you think? That Janus or Markos paid Burt or someone else here to—" She couldn't bring herself to utter the words.

"To off you?" He curled his big hands around her shoulders. One hand fingered her hair where she'd fastened it at her nape. "It's possible. But the kid? He'd pilfer cameras and CDs. Maybe he did the boat sabotage, had his boat ready, thinking he'd zip to your rescue and impress you. But murder? I doubt it. And I've even checked and eliminated my DARK team."

She suppressed a shiver of awareness at his touch. "Um, what about fingerprints on the remaining boat?"

He flipped her hair aside and began rubbing her neck. "Nothing. Clean as a brand-new set of porker pipes. If Burt's prints were there, it would prove nothing. He was in the boat shed yesterday, remember? They didn't touch the skiff in there. The switch could've happened before that."

With the gentle rotation of his massaging hand, the tension melted from her shoulders, and a different tension invaded. Her skin heated, and her knees grew weak. She could focus only on his touch and the rumble of his voice, not on what he was saying. If she turned to face him, he'd kiss her. And that would lead…

A vision formed in the dappled droplets on the window-pane—the two of them tangled in the sheets on her iron-framed bed. A rainy day and nowhere to go. Except to Cole.

She was in big trouble.

Chapter Eighteen

COLE BREATHED DEEPLY to ease the tight band of fear for her in his chest. The fragility of the bones and warm flesh beneath his hands underscored her vulnerability. Being so near to her kept him in a constant state of semi-arousal that their lovemaking last night had only increased.

He cared for her again, more than he'd realized. More than he should. They had their past—and a lost baby—in common. They'd now rediscovered the friendship and understanding that had once bound them. And sex. Past and present fused with the joining of their bodies and souls to sear away pain and brand them only with ecstasy.

But was it enough in the face of so much remembered pain?

She'd learned to survive on the street. She gave up luxury and a closet full of designer clothes. She was tough and smart, but still too classy, too generous, too everything for him. She needed him now because he could protect her, but as soon as she was safe, she'd go back to her high-society life. She wouldn't need him then.

Outta your league, boy.

He had to remember that. Last night's revelations and passionate aftermath had inflated his hopes. Rather than let passion blind him to the facts, he'd better back off. Which he'd already told himself earlier, dammit.

He dropped his hands from her shoulders and stepped aside. He cleared his throat. "It's too wet for a walk, but how about a drive? The truck hasn't been on the road for a few days."

What he took for relief whooshed from her like air from a punctured tire. Laura snatched her windbreaker from the hook by the door. "Let's go."

Cole called Isaacs and Byrne to alert them to their plan.

"The phone surprises me," she remarked. "You have that little satellite receiver. So why not high-tech communicators?"

He climbed into the driver's seat. "Talking into a lapel would attract more attention than yakking in a phone. Everyone has one of these pressed to their ears. The DARK phones contain security software."

They made it as far as the inn before Stan waved them down with a request for the resort barbecue.

"Tuesday is the Alderport Founder's Day celebration." Laura tucked the grocery list in her jacket pocket as they drove away. "In the village, there's a parade with floats, high school bands, and craft sales, followed by fireworks. Tuesday I'll have to help with the cooking for the barbecue that the Harts provide for guests and employees on Wednesday."

"That ought to put you out of harm's way for a while." And out of temptation's reach.

The brief curve of her lips suggested she welcomed the same relief.

He wished to God DARK would roll up Markos or that Byrne would spot someone suspicious or the others would ID Janus, so this fiasco could end. He wished his time with Laura would end.

That was a crock. He wished his time with Laura would never end.

Hell.

****

Out of harm's way, Laura mused as she put away the tennis ball machine on Monday afternoon. When would it end? When would Markos be caught and her life return to normal? She was so used to looking over her shoulder that it seemed the norm.

Yesterday's outing to town and the supermarket had refocused her on different priorities, but didn't solve her dilemma about Cole. From being cooped up in the cabin, they went to a closed, moving vehicle. The sheer domesticity of grocery shopping threw in her face the future she'd never have. And their outing showed her a new side of Cole.

He shook his head at the bountiful produce heaped into tempting displays as he described the deprivation in the resurgence of the Taliban. What open-air markets they didn't destroy offered only overripe fruit and nuts and a few elderly, stringy goats. Barefoot children scavenged in the ruins and begged in the streets. Along with ferreting out plots, Cole and his fellow intelligence officers had directed food and medicine drops.

Compassion and charity in the midst of danger and destruction. Love edged aside resolve and burrowed deeper into her heart. Beside the empty part.

When he met her after she left the tennis court, seeing him gave her pulse such a kick that she bit her tongue. If she missed him this much after two hours, how would she cope with the next decade? And longer?

Emitting small rumbles of satisfaction, he

surrounded her with his arms and held her. Longer than was necessary to demonstrate their lover status. But objecting wasn't in her. The evening loomed ahead. No performance of *Diner* to occupy them. Only the long night. In the small cabin.

Alone. Together.

So when he suggested dinner out, she agreed with alacrity. They'd be out in public, he assured her, and one of the other officers would provide backup for the outing.

After a dinner of blackened Atlantic salmon with a side of buttery new potatoes and followed by blueberry pie, they went to the blues club in Rockland.

From a handkerchief-size table in a dark corner, they listened to the guitar riffs and cigarette voices of Sammy McKee and the Smokehouse Band from somewhere in the Midwest. The five-piece group borrowed songs and styles from a mix of genres, ranging from the Texas swing tune "Blues for Dixie" to "She Gotta Thing Goin' On," that was pure Chicago.

"I'd forgotten you liked the Blues," Laura said at the band's break.

"I didn't know you did." He covered her hand with his and held it gently but firmly, his hard gaze daring her to object.

The server delivered their refills, Chardonnay for her, cola for him. A steady parade of more-or-less sober patrons jostled past them, on the way to the restrooms or to the bar. Their passage swirled the odors of hops and smoke. She and Cole were the young ones in this mostly middle-aged crowd filling the dance floor. One man boogied in a kilt and matching plaid socks. Another man sporting a white handlebar mustache danced with every unattached woman in the place.

Laura smiled and relaxed. "I know you don't drink because of your dad, but there's a lot I don't know about recent years. Can you tell me more about Afghanistan?"

"You understand I can't give specifics." When she nodded, he continued, "But here's a story I can share. I can't say where, but my partner and I were scouting a cave."

"Alone?"

"No." He offered no explanation.

"Ah. That means you were with a Special Forces unit. Muscle to accompany the intelligence officers. I thought all that was declassified by now, but never mind."

He shook his head. "Laura, you would've made one hell of an intelligence officer. Nobody's secrets would be safe from you."

"Why thank you, sir. I think. Do go on with your story."

"Our Afghan escort lagged behind, but he suddenly caught up to us yelling, *'Samla! Samla!'*"

"*Samla.* What does it mean?"

"I'll get to that." His boyish grin started a pulse beating low in her body. "That was early days for me in that wild country, and I was still learning the language. Both of us turned. I thought he was just calling for us to wait, not to leave him behind."

"But he wasn't?"

He shook his head. "When gunfire erupted behind us and he dived behind a boulder, I caught on quick. He was warning us of an ambush. *Samla* means *Get down.*"

"The man risked his life to warn you. Was he all right?"

Cole's eyes darkened. "He took a bullet in the leg.

164

But he lived."

"And so did you." With her free hand, she traced the webbed scar on his chin. "Is that when you got this?"

"I learned to duck lower and faster after that." His reaction to her caress, a rumble deep within, sounded suspiciously like a purr. "You must have had some adventures as an anthropologist? Or am I thinking archeologist?"

She laughed. "No digs or aboriginal burial sites. A few trips to Egypt and China. I even spent time in Iraq after the war, where looting destroyed many ancient treasures. Seven thousand years of Mesopotamian history." She shook her head sadly. "But my most eye-opening adventures were at home. In D.C."

"From your expression, I'm guessing you don't mean the one that sent you on the road."

"No, I'm referring to my volunteer work at the Sojourner Truth Community Center."

"Work with kids?" Interest lighting his eyes, he leaned forward, probably to hear her better over the canned music.

To fill the break, a deejay spun tunes by New Orleans songwriter Tab Benoit, the next week's performer.

Laura tapped her foot to the Cajun beat as she began. "I do—did—tutoring and tennis lessons with a group of four teenaged girls who'd been in trouble with the law."

"I'd sooner shoot it out with Colombian drug lords. What were these kids like?"

"Pretty amazing. Strong, resilient. At least one is ambitious. I miss them as much as my support group. I enjoy the kids at Passabec, but most of them don't tug at my heart the way those girls did."

His brows beetled as though he were trying to picture her, the privileged princess, with ghetto kids. "Go on."

"Jamila's gang member brother dragged her into some of their dealings. Desirée's quiet, sometimes too quiet. She was sleeping on the street some nights because one of her mother's boyfriends tried to climb into her bed." The image of her narrow little face, pinched with fear, twisted pain in her chest. "And Missy was headed down the road— should say street—to prostitution, under her older sister's tutelage."

"I see they got to you. Who's the ambitious one?"

"Tanisha. Now she's a piece of work." Laura smiled, remembering the girl quivering with intensity, bells jangling on her many braids. "She's a cross between Queen Latifah and Serena Williams."

"Big mouth and big swing?"

She chuckled at his perception. "Exactly. She thinks tennis is her ticket out of the ghetto. She has talent, but I'm no expert tennis coach. I wonder what's happened to them, whether the center found someone to replace me."

He brought her hand to his lips. Her skin tingled. "Nobody could replace you. Not with your combination of guts and talent. You'll make it back to them. I'll see to it."

"I want to believe you." The heat of his gaze shimmered into her body, and she needed him to keep talking, to give her time to bolster her resistance. "You mentioned Colombian drug lords. Was that duty as dangerous as Afghanistan?"

He shrugged. "Colombia was more intelligence coordination and less combat potential. Locals were less suspicious of us."

"Who is Marisol?" Her cheeks warmed. Drat. The words escaped her mouth before she could stop them. Her heart betrayed her every time she tried to resist him. "I couldn't help seeing the name on your laptop screen."

Sadness infused his eyes. Affection canted his half smile. "Marisol is an orphan. She's four years old."

He might have yanked her chair from beneath her. Her brain could barely process the words. "A child." *Marisol is a small child.*

"At the San Sebastiano Orphanage. I mentioned it before."

He'd mentioned the orphanage the first day of sailing class. "You did coin tricks for the kids. And you said something about finding a baby."

"Another operative and I found Marisol when she was only eighteen months old. Her family had abandoned her in a field. She was hungry and dirty and screeching louder than a parrot."

Tears burned her throat at the thought of a mere baby alone and frightened. "Abandoned her? You said that before, but it didn't sink in."

"Colombia is improving, but there are so many orphans from all the conflict and poverty. Desperate mothers who can't feed their children feel they have no recourse. And Marisol has a deformed foot, so she probably was seen as too big a burden."

Her throat tightened. "And in San Sebastiano?"

He smiled more broadly. "The nuns take good care of her, but she's still too thin. She needs an operation to rebuild her foot. I'm acting as intermediary to arrange that at Johns Hopkins. The specialist will do it for free, but I have to get her there."

She sat back, speechless. All those phone calls and

emails were to help a small child have a chance at a full, productive life. No voluptuous señorita at all. And the tragedy of it for him scraped at her heart. This proud man who so longed for his own family had only a long-distance, substitute one. She was grateful when the band's next set stifled further conversation.

When the musicians began a softer ballad, Cole murmured in her ear, "I wonder if country music is just Blues from an Anglo-Saxon background."

"Now who's thinking like an anthropologist?" Seeing other couples fill the dance floor, she stood and tugged on his arm. "This song isn't country, but it calls to me. Their singer even sounds like Maria Muldaur. Dance with me."

And dancing was a legitimate excuse for being in his arms. She swayed her hips to the dreamy beat of "Meet Me at Midnight."

Cole didn't budge. When his jaw clenched and one eyebrow shot up, she knew. "Oh, no, you're not going to get out of this by claiming you can't dance. Anyone can dance to this."

With a crooked grin, he set down his glass and followed her to the dance floor.

"See, you just hold me and let the rhythm take you." She nudged his right arm around her and clasped his left hand.

"With you in my arms, babe, I usually move to another natural rhythm." His arm tightened around her, sliding downward to her derriere, to press her against his solid planes. And a harder bulge.

Her inner flame flickered higher, shimmering heat along her veins. With each swaying step, their hips and thighs slid together. Oblivious to the press of other couples, they might have been the only dancers.

She slid her arms up to link her hands behind his neck, but resisted going up on tiptoe to run her tongue along the white scar. Tonight was another memory to carry with her. He didn't look dangerous to her now, only handsome and unbearably dear with his rugged face and square chin. His hair had grown a little longer, and she longed to run her fingers through the rich midnight waves.

On a groan, he pulled her hands from around his neck and dragged her from the dance floor. "Laura, we're playing with fire. Let's get out of here."

Chapter Nineteen

COLE SLAMMED MONEY on their table and hustled Laura out of the club so fast that their DARK cover nearly missed catching up to them. She appeared so shell-shocked by his rush that she didn't utter a word all the way home.

Or was she in the same desperate state as him?

His jaw clenched and his entire body taut with desire, he set a new land-speed record for the drive to Passabec Lake.

Was the woman mad? Didn't she know what holding him, grinding her hips against him like that did to him? He was a horny kid again, his craving for her ripping him apart. He could no more separate the job from his feelings for her than he could sever his bones from his body, and the thought it could lead to a screw-up scared the hell out of him.

But it wouldn't stop him from the inevitable tonight.

Once locked inside the cabin, he gathered her in his arms and kissed her. Deeply, as if it was the last time. Or the first time. He took possession with his mouth and tongue, staking a claim that seeped lava through his body. He felt the rapid thudding of her heart, in time with his. His tongue slid inside her mouth, caressing and reacquainting him with her taste, layered with tonight's wine. He burned with the press of her fingers on his biceps. He scooped her up and headed to the bedroom.

"Laura?"

Hesitation swirled in her eyes. But then the flame of desire burned the doubt away. "Hurry, Cole."

He laid her on the bed. "Where's the light?"

She clutched at his hand. "Leave it off. The light from the other room is enough. Come to me."

Damn, but she was as needy as he was. He stripped off her shirt, the peach ice cream one he liked, and her white cotton bra. Trembling, he tossed away his clothing so he could revel in the feel of her breasts against him.

A little friction from his chest hairs feathered her pink nipples to attention, and he tasted as she wriggled out of her short linen skirt and panties. Luscious as the apple lotion she smelled of. Ah, her breasts. He loved her breasts. He suckled hard, wanting more of her taste.

She writhed beneath him, moaning into his mouth. "Cole … please!"

His pelvis anchored her to the firm mattress as he hardened and pulsed against her. Her hand found him. He arched as she closed her fingers around him. Kissing his chest, she swirled her tongue over one nipple, then the other. A ragged gasp escaped him, and he brushed her hand away. He pulled back, his breath sawing in and out of his lungs like he'd run ten miles carrying a field pack.

"Easy, sweetheart. I want this to last more than a blink. I want to revel in every touch, every taste. I want to explore all your sensitive spots." *In case this is the last time.*

With his lips and tongue, he laid a moist path down her breasts and belly to her thighs. Kisses bathed the crease of her mound, and when his tongue flicked her intimately, she thrashed with urgency and called his name. To hear her cry her need, that he could make her need him with such desperation, and no one else, hardened him to stone. If only it didn't have to end... When she began to buck and arch, he penetrated her with one finger and laved a new trail up to her mouth. Tingling sensations tightened his butt. He was close to the edge. So was she. She tangled her hands behind his neck and pulled his mouth to hers. He kissed her, hard, and then reached for the foil packet beside him. When he was ready, she guided him to her. She squeezed her eyes shut, as if concentrating on the sensations. The slide of their skin. The feel of her tight nipples. He probed her, slid in partway.

"Laura!" he said in a hoarse whisper. "Open your eyes. Look at us. See how perfectly we fit." He clenched his jaw, and his mouth contorted with restraint. For all his much larger size, their bodies molded together perfectly. All denials evaporated like mist over the lake.

He loved her. He wanted her. He needed her.

Whatever happened afterward, she belonged to him tonight.

She opened her eyes. "Now, Cole!" She gripped his shoulders and fitted herself to him.

He drove home, deep inside her. His control cracked, and he gave a shout as he thrust again and again. When inner tremors convulsed her, the pressure jolted him, and he pulsed inside her, with her. When the aftershocks ceased, he cleaned up and then tugged the blanket over them. Curling her close, her backside tucked against him, he wrapped an arm around her so he could cup one breast. At last she was where she belonged. Here he could keep her safe. And he slept.

Laura did not.

Her mind and body still in a daze, she lay awake, a battle raging within her. Why had she let desire overrule her judgment? And what could she do now? If Cole saw the scar on her abdomen, he'd know or she'd have to tell him the rest of the truth. And then she'd have to watch him withdraw from her, from a woman with no means to give him what he needed.

The dam of her resistance had crumbled, but she could no more cope with the flood of passion and love than with the threat to her life. Love, like the fear, drained her, leaving her exhausted. Love and death were inexorably linked. Once Alexei Markos and his hit man were caught, she would never see Cole again.

Tears stung her eyes. She held still as they leaked out and trickled down her face. Why did he have to be so gentle and strong, so caring with her students, so generous with a vulnerable child, so protective. And even more than the proud, successful man she always knew he could become? He deserved the family she could never give him.

Why did she have to fall in love with him again?

And what was she going to do now?

****

Cole lounged in a beach chair as he waited for his phone. His contact should call soon with an update on Markos. Laura was safe in the inn kitchen with Joyce Hart and some other women, so he could damn well sit here staring at the lake and digging his toes in the warm sand until the hellish device chimed.

He scraped fingers across his jaw. Hell, he should've known sex would make no difference to her in their relationship. He shouldn't have been surprised that when he woke up, she was already in the shower. Hadn't he said it himself? She wanted nothing more from him but sex. He was only a reminder of her past mistakes and heartbreak.

"Take what you can get, buddy." But the acknowledgment twisted a knife in his chest.

"Who you talking to?" piped a laughing voice.

"Looks like he's talking to himself," said another.

Cole swung around, springing to his feet at the same time. Butch and Zach. The way this op was dragging out was making him too jumpy. "Hey, guys. You caught me."

He sat back down and the two boys sank onto the sand cross-legged before him. Both wore cargo shorts, Sea Dogs shirts, and sly grins.

"My dad talks to himself all the time," Butch offered. "Says it helps him think."

"Does he? Guess that's why I do it too." He glanced from one to the other. "So, what's up?"

Zach's grin transformed into a conspiratorial expression. "Remember you told me to look out for suspicious characters?"

Cole ran his tongue around his teeth. Damn, the kid might get in over his head in spite of their agreement. "You got something for me?"

"Me and Zach are going to see the fireworks in a while," Butch interjected. "My mom and dad are taking us. So we only got a few minutes. Go ahead, Zachy."

His friend nodded, the action bobbing his Mohawk do. "There's a guy in cabin twelve, you know the one with the little elves in the yard."

Cole nodded. "What about the guy?"

Zach scooted across the sand on his butt until he was nearly sitting on Cole's toes. He looked from one side to the other, on the outlook for eavesdroppers. Nobody was on the beach but them. "Well, the dude's weird, that's what."

"We call him Mr. Blow-Dry," Butch said. "On account of his hair. One of those comb-over jobs to hide a bald dome, but poofed up and fluffy."

Zach nodded. "He goes around with binoculars and stares at people. Like in their cabins. Or on the beach. He hides behind trees. This morning during class I saw him watching us. Watching Laura." He nodded his head twice for emphasis.

Butch added, his eyes narrowed for effect, "He's some kind of spy, for sure. Definitely up to something."

Could be the hit man. Or the burglar. Or merely a bird watcher or a sailing aficionado. The problem bore checking into. He leaned back in the wooden chair and placed his hands on his knees. "This Mr. Blow-Dry's mighty suspicious. I agree."

"So what do you think we ought to do?" Zach's wide eyes glittered with anticipation.

"You did good, bud. Both of you. Real smart spotting this character and keeping an eye on him. Laura will be proud of you, coming to me about this, like we agreed. But your part of the job is over. You go ahead to the fireworks, and I'll take it from here."

"But what if you need help? Um, like backup," Zach said, as intent and focused as a DARK officer.

Cole nodded thoughtfully. Clapped the boys on their shoulders. "If I can't handle this dude alone, I'll wait 'til tomorrow when you guys can back me up. In the meantime, don't say a word to anybody."

Zach appeared to be ready to object, but Butch's dad called to them. Pantomiming zipping his mouth closed,

175

Zach raced away with his friend.

Adrenaline revving his pulse, Cole tapped his phone. Maybe this was the break they'd been waiting for. To end the damn mission.

Discounting the punch to his heart, he punched numbers. "Byrne. Meet me in ten."

****

Laura yawned as she peeled vegetables in the inn's kitchen. Twilight had given way to semi-moonless dark, and she was tired. Little sleep and an undercurrent of fear and dread did that to a person.

But she was safe for now. Physically.

Between sailing and tennis, the time she spent slicing and dicing afforded her protection among a chatting group of kitchen volunteers.

And gave her respite from Cole's intensity. And her own weakness for him.

She pared another potato down to its white pith. The past few days had scraped away her protective hide and left only shaky resolve, mushier than a potato. Like peeling the layers of an onion, the togetherness with Cole was stripping away her secrets one by one, down to the last, the one hoarded for ten years in her soul.

These few hours of separation from each other provided no respite. This morning, hoping he hadn't noticed what lay on her bureau, she'd slipped the chain over her head and tucked the charm inside her shirt between her breasts. If he saw the little gold crown he'd given her so many years ago, she couldn't deny her feelings for him. As it was, he occupied her every thought when she ought to be worrying about an assassin.

His hovering didn't help. She didn't see him now,

but before sunset when he was supposedly relaxing on the beach, every time she looked out the window above the sink, he was prowling around, on patrol. She could almost hear him growl and grind his teeth.

Vanessa handed her a phone. "Call for you. It's Cole."

Laura blinked, then dried her hands on a dish towel. Cole? Why would he have Vanessa's number? What was going on? "Yes?"

"Laura, something's come up, and I can't meet you. I'll tell you about it later. Vanessa will escort you back to the cabin. You'll be safe with her. She's one of us."

"Va—"

"Don't say anything. You'll blow her cover. I gotta go. You can trust Officer Ward." With that he disconnected.

Had she already ruined their secrecy? But Joyce and Stan were conferring over the menu for the festivities. Bea and Doris Van Tassel and two of the regular kitchen staff were peeling boiled eggs and cutting up chickens. No one had apparently noticed her conversation.

The redheaded vacationer known as Vanessa, aka Officer Ward, nodded and smiled as she plucked her phone from Laura's nerveless fingers. "It's okay. We'll talk later."

She'd known there was another officer, but hadn't a clue as to who. The woman was open and gregarious, not a flinty-eyed warrior like Cole. Perhaps that made her suitable for undercover work. The notion that Vanessa had been looking out for her comforted her, but the reminder that she needed extra protection added another layer to her fear.

After the potato salad was mixed, the two women

walked toward Laura's cabin. Faint booms and crackles announced the distant Alderport fireworks, but the barrier of Deer Mountain kept them from view. The recent rain perfumed the air with scents of green grass and flowers. Sunset brought cool air and mosquitoes, and Laura shivered in her short-sleeved shirt as she flicked away a tiny marauder.

"Sorry to shock you like that," Vanessa said gently, "but we'd hoped my being undercover would help protect you as well as put me on the inside. The fewer people who knew, the safer for all of us."

"It's all right. I understand." Laura smiled. A memory puzzled her. "That night you found me downstairs at the theater, was that coincidence?"

The officer laughed. "Not a chance. Cole sent me to look for you. He was searching everywhere else. I've never seen the man panic before."

"Now your stealth makes sense. Can you tell me what he had to do that was so urgent? Is something breaking?"

"I can't say. He'll tell you when he returns." She smiled and patted Laura's forearm. "I know this is very hard for you. Cole's the best. And we're all doing everything we can."

"I know. And I'm grateful." She was. But if she had run to some new, anonymous spot, she could've stayed out of a killer's crosshairs. Would she have avoided new heartbreak? No, Cole would've been right with her, like now, 24/7. Yet she wouldn't give up this time out of time with him. "Maybe Markos will be caught soon, and we can all go back to our lives."

The other woman flipped her braid off her shoulder and laughed. "Not for me." She looked behind them and peered down the side path, her hand in her pants pocket. "Undercover is my life."

A gun, thought Laura. Vanessa must have a gun in her pocket. She'd had one that other night too. She'd had her hand in her pocket the same way. An automatic pistol like Cole's.

A small frisson prickled her spine. "Don't you get tired of being someone else? Of playing a role?"

"Sure I do," Vanessa said as they approached the cabin door. "And I'll give up fieldwork for a desk job one day, analysis or supervision. But for now, this works for me. For some reason people tell me their worries and secrets. The other officers call me the Confessor. I'm good at what I do."

Laura laughed, more at herself than at the other woman's words. "That you are. I certainly never suspected."

After the officer checked through the cabin, she said, "Isaacs is on outside surveillance tonight, and Cole should be back soon. He didn't ask me to, but I can stay if you want."

"I'll be fine. Go ahead. You must be as tired as I am."

Vanessa acknowledged her weariness and left after a reminder to lock up.

Before Laura closed the door, she spied a folded paper jammed in the screen.

Chapter Twenty

NEITHER WOMAN HAD noticed it. What was this? With trembling fingers, she plucked out the paper. After unfolding it, she sagged with relief.

Deep breaths slowed her pulse rate as she read the scrawled note: *"Meet me on the stage at 10:00 p.m. — C."*

Cole had returned. With that knowledge, she felt safer. But why did he want her to meet him on the stage? The theater was dark on Tuesdays. And why would he ask her to go alone if he'd had Vanessa escort her home? The handwriting meant nothing. She hadn't seen his handwriting for years, and the only writing he did here was on a keyboard.

But a darkened, empty theater? She frowned. Only the too-stupid-to-live movie heroine would go without a thought. Would endanger herself that way. She had to think through this logically, not with fear vising her stomach.

Her watch read nine-thirty. If she could reach him on his phone, she'd know. She hurried to the phone in the bedroom and keyed his number. When she placed the receiver to her ear, she heard only dead silence. The phone was dead. She dropped the instrument like a live scorpion.

If someone planned to trap her in the cottage, the first thing to do was eliminate the telephone, cut the line or something. She ought to have a cell phone, but she'd feared being traced.

The other cottages around her were unoccupied, and everyone else was in Alderport for the fireworks. Maybe that's why Cole wanted her to get out of there.

If he sent the note at all.

Whatever the case, staying alone in the cabin seemed like a bad idea. She made a quick circuit, closing blinds as she went. Her pulse pounded, and she forced her lungs to perform deep, calming breathing.

If she went to the inn, she could alert Vanessa, who would know what to do. Or they could go together. Laura stripped off her flowered capris in favor of dark jeans. She was stuck with white sneakers. She'd lost her only other shoes in the boat sinking.

One pair of shoes. Only one. Her closet back in D.C. had custom shelves filled with shoes. Flats, high heels, slides, running shoes, tennis shoes, sandals. Red, blue, black, white, puce. Chuckling at how unimportant that seemed, she tugged on a dark sweatshirt.

If she left through the back window, any would-be intruder would think she was still in the cabin. She could sneak through the woods around to the inn. She listened at the open window before lifting the screen and slipping outside.

She kept low, darting from tree to tree, shadow to shadow. The soft mulch of evergreen needles cushioned her steps and sent a reassuring pine fragrance to her senses. Occasional sleepy twittering and the eerie call of a hunting owl broke the silence.

Except for the porch light, the inn was dark and battened down. Guests had to use a key after nine o'clock, and their movement triggered lobby lighting.

Not much at the resort was locked, but security at the inn gave city dwellers the protection they expected, whether necessary or not.

But it meant Laura couldn't go inside. She didn't know Vanessa's room number anyway.

If she went to the theater, was she the ditzy blonde heading down the dark basement steps where the serial killer waited? Or was Cole waiting for her? She couldn't go back to the cabin. The note had to come from him. So…

Skeins of clouds played hide-and-seek with the half moon, a mocking smile in the night sky. The unreliable light decreased her confidence, but her feet insisted on taking her toward the theater. She swiped perspiration from her brow when the leviathan bulk of the barn loomed ahead. Quick steps brought her to the entrance.

No vehicle in the parking lot. That meant nothing. Cole could easily arrive on foot.

The backstage doors were kept locked, but not the lobby. She slipped inside. The only illumination came from the exit lights, enough to prevent her blundering into the Bad Boy, parked in the lobby as advertising until hoisted on stage.

"If only you could talk," she whispered to the motorcycle.

Her palms were clammy and her pulse clattered. Sooner or later, whoever had cut the phone line would catch on and search for her. If she waited for him on the stage, as the note directed, there were plenty of props to hide her. Or was she better off with lights?

But why on earth the stage? Did he find some evidence of Janus in the theater? Stomach clenched, she headed through the inner door, then left toward the technician's booth. She slapped the wall searching for the light switches.

The brilliance of the house lights cheered her like candles on a birthday cake. With a sure stride, she descended the aisle and mounted the stage.

Even if she said so herself, the stage crew had performed miracles in creating the *Diner* set. Two booths with gaudy plastic-topped tables, a lunch counter with metal stools upholstered in shiny red and behind the counter a swinging door through which the phony cook delivered meals and pithy comments. The central part of the floor rotated—a permanent installation—to reveal the other major set, the lobby of the next-door motel, complete with reception desk, couch, and the upright piano.

Laura perched on a diner stool. How long should she wait? The lobby clock had read exactly ten.

Darkness descended with the snap of the backstage control switch. Smothering blackness enveloped the theater.

Stifling a cry, she dropped to the floor. Her pulse thundered in her ears. She blinked, willing her eyes to adjust to the cave-like gloom.

Stupid, stupid. The note didn't come from Cole. Janus could've watched him leave. Not Cole, but the hit man waited here. By cutting her phone line, he'd ensured she'd leave the cabin's safety. She naively ran into his web.

Now she had to make certain she didn't become his victim.

Thank goodness she knew the theater as well as her own cabin. Even in the dark, she could use it to her advantage. Whoever flipped the switch waited in the wings stage right. All was silent. He couldn't know the layout as well as she did.

Leading with her outspread hands, she stood and placed one foot in front of the other. She prayed she hadn't gotten turned around. She felt the edge of the first booth. She had to head toward stage left, and the backstage stairs to the lower floor.

Closer. Closer. Almost there.

She fell, crashing to her knees, tangled with a folding metal chair at the edge of the curtain.

Heavy footsteps scraped across the floor from stage right. Going slow in the dark.

She pushed up and flung the chair toward the footfalls. When she heard a muffled cry of pain and rage, she continued to Braille her way to her escape hatch.

Silence reigned again. Except for her own panting breath and her hammering heart, nothing. Then a metallic squeaking and the rumble of a heavy object rolling across the floor.

A massive, flat bulk hurtled into her side. Pain hammered her hip. The impact thrust her across the room. Tinny notes jangled maniacally through the cavernous barn.

The piano.

Did he mean to crush her with it? She could hear him straining with the cumbersome instrument.

She shoved back.

Momentum favored her attacker. Farther and farther backward he pushed her.

She tried to sidestep.

He changed direction. The casters on the old upright shrieked in revolt.

In one desperate lunge to the side, her foot stepped

into air. The stairwell she'd been heading for.

She plummeted down.

Her knees hit the first steps with a sickening thump. A bolt of lightning hitting every bone in her body. The impact knocked the breath from her lungs in a great whoosh. Limp, out of control, she bounced down, her body pummeled by each of the ten wooden steps. In a welter of battered limbs, she slammed onto the cement floor.

Her head spun and she had no breath to move. Agony radiated into every part of her body, but she was conscious.

As if from a great distance, she heard a cacophonous crashing. A discordant clanging like the destruction of all the harps of heaven.

The piano was following her down through the opening.

****

Cole slowed as he turned the truck into the woods road that led to Laura's cabin. He rubbed his stiff neck.

Mr. Blow-Dry had been a dead end for DARK, but an arrest for the local cops. The interminable evening was ended.

He needed to see Laura. Anxiety about her had shortened his temper and cut his concentration. He wasn't used to interference with his cool control during a mission, and he damned well didn't like it.

At the cabin, he turned in and parked with a squeal of tires and a scattering of gravel. The cabin lights were still on, and all was quiet. Curtains drawn. Door buttoned up. Windows closed. All appeared normal.

Then why did he feel this prickling at his nape?

He reached for his 9mm.

Chapter Twenty-One

DISORIENTED, LAURA HUDDLED in a heap on the cold floor. How long she'd lain there she didn't know.

She opened her eyes. "You see stars after all."

After drawing shaky, deep breaths to reassure herself that she could, she sat up slowly. When she felt for injuries, her hand found the warm dampness of blood on her cheek and on her right knee.

Nothing broken, just scrapes and bruises. Enough for three people.

Gingerly, she pulled herself up on the railing. It fell away and clattered to the floor, and she stumbled. Sensing the presence of something overhead, she reached up. Her fingers brushed dangling wires, and an eerie twang echoed through the darkness.

So that was it. The piano was wedged upside down at an angle — effectively blocking the stairwell.

Shoving her down the steep stairs and crushing her beneath the piano, as heavy as a sarcophagus, had been her attacker's intent. He would've succeeded except for the stairwell's narrowness.

The acid-tasting nausea of horror swam in her throat. She bent over to clear her head, bracing her hands on her knees. Pain throbbed in the right one. It would quickly incapacitate her.

She could be trapped in the basement. The

realization sent her heart racing. Holding her breath, she listened for noises above her. Nothing. Not even the groan of a board. Did he leave, believing her to be dead?

Doubtful. A professional would want to make sure.

Damn you, Alexei Markos!

Her best chance was to escape through the lobby. Feeling her way, she proceeded down the hall. Ironic that the area Cole had warned her to avoid alone would be her escape route. Moments later, she bumped into the lobby exit and stopped for a breath and to listen.

Creaking. Someone stepping on a squeaky board or just the sounds of an old building settling? Was he listening for her?

Maybe he'd left through the stage door. He might not know about the lower-level egress to the lobby. If he waited outside, she hadn't a chance with her battered knee, puffy and swelling painfully in the tight denim. She couldn't run across the open parking lot or through the woods. She couldn't move fast at all. Unless…

A millimeter at a time, she opened the door. No one.

Biting her lip, she stepped out and approached the Harley, dozing on its kickstand in the exit light's red glow. She whispered, "Easy, boy. Are you like the cowboy's loyal horse that won't let anyone else ride him? Your owner won't mind, I promise."

If Cole hadn't changed his habits, she had a chance. She groped beneath a leather flap on the seat padding. Stomach clenched but heart triumphant, she extracted the key. Quietly, delicately, she loosened the catches on the double doors so all she had to do was push her way through.

After releasing the kickstand, she straddled the bike. At least it wasn't as enormous as his old one. If she could only remember how to drive the thing.

Feet pounded across the stage. *He heard me.*

Don't listen. Her heart drummed and her hands trembled like autumn leaves. *Think!* Like an incantation, she began a recital of the basics. Gear shift on the left footrest. Front brake lever on the right handle. Clutch on the left.

A thump told her he'd jumped from the stage.

The bike had an ignition button. Thank God. Her increasing stiffness wouldn't let her manage a kick-start. Praying that she'd remembered ten-year-old lessons and that the gas tank wasn't empty, she turned the key and pressed the button.

Charging footsteps. He was nearly at the end of the aisle. Closer. Coming to the lobby.

As the engine rumbled to life, heavy feet reached the swinging doors behind her.

Now or never. She let off the clutch and twisted the hand grip. With a whoop from her and an accelerating roar from the bike, Laura burst through the double doors.

She rolled down the handicap ramp and sped into the moonlit night and freedom.

No stealth for her, not on Harley-Davidson, a bike nicknamed rolling thunder.

****

As Cole approached the cabin door, headlights and a distinctive engine roar emerged from the footpath. The light swerved like a drunken locomotive. He stepped behind the tree.

The motorcyclist wobbled to a halt, doused the headlight and killed the engine.

At the sight of the golden fall of hair and the pale oval of her face, his jaw dropped. "What the hell?"

"Thank God it's you," Laura said, her voice quivery with emotion. "How do you work this damn kickstand?"

He toed the offending prop and helped her to dismount. When she weaved on unsteady legs, he pulled her close. He gently touched her bloodied cheek. "What—"

"You can have your horse back now, cowboy. He saved my life." She crumpled in his arms.

Cole scooped her up and jogged to the cabin door. He set her down and fished in his pocket for the key she'd given him.

"Wait. I've got a key in my jeans." She leaned, barely upright, against the door frame.

"Dammit, the one time we need to get inside fast. How bad did he hurt you?" He snatched the key. A wildfire detonated in him. He'd empty his 9mm into the bastard. Or rip his freaking head off.

At last inside, he laid her on the bed and stripped off her jeans. Wincing as he examined her swollen knee, he said, in what he hoped was a calm tone, "Tell me about it. Just what were you doing out alone this time of night? And where the hell is Vanessa? Didn't she—"

Her eyes snapped sparks at him. "Don't you yell at— Ouch, my cheek!" She accepted the cool washcloth he handed her and dabbed it on the lacerated cheek. "Vanessa walked me home, as requested. She even checked the cabin. Then she left. For all she knew, I was tucked in safely for the night. Except for your note. That I quickly learned wasn't your note."

"Laura!"

Closing her eyes, she lay back on the pillows.

He'd have to wait until she had enough strength to talk. He fetched a plastic bag of ice cubes from the kitchen. Kept his hands gentle as he placed the makeshift ice pack on her knee and wrapped a towel around it.

He sat on the bed beside her.

"Thank you." She managed a lopsided smile as she began her story.

He kept his gaze on her wounded cheek, while she explained about the note. He curled his hands into fists when she described the attack in the theater and her escape.

"There's the note, on the table where I left it."

Barely glancing at the printed words, he exploded with oaths that widened her exhaustion-smudged eyes. "I shouldn't have gone! I should've let Byrne and Isaacs take care of that piece of crap. Janus has just been biding his time, waiting until I left you unprotected." And why in hell did Grant Snow never spot the guy?

She frowned. "It looks that way. But maybe I'm just delirious." She rubbed one hand over her eyes. "Where did you go tonight? What happened?"

He didn't want her to worry about the boys' involvement, but Zach would probably bring it up. "Zach and Butch wanted to help catch the guy who switched your boat."

Eyes widening, she sat up. "Those little boys. Oh my God, what did they do? Are they all right?"

He pressed her back into the pillows. The feel of her shoulders beneath his palms reassured him. "They're fine. They did the right thing. Told me about a mysterious Mr. Blow-Dry. Said he was spying on you with binoculars."

"So you and the other officers went to check him out. Judging from my misadventure tonight, Mr. Blow-Dry isn't Janus. Or there are two killers after me."

"He's not a killer. But he is our local burglar. His cabin had all sorts of toys he'd liberated. Including Zach's camera. He'd used the binoculars to see who was away from their cabins. Byrne and I delivered him to the Alderport PD."

"But Zach and Butch are safe. They didn't talk to him."

"No, Zach came to me, as he'd promised."

Her shoulders quaked with a shudder. "So how—"

"No more discussion. You need rest, not conversation. Dr. Stratton insists."

She flopped back down, the touch of humor apparently convincing her. Careful not to irritate her injuries, he helped her put on the baggy T-shirt and shorts she slept in. Not what he'd fantasized, but on her as sexy as a negligee.

After locking up and dousing the lights, he stripped off his clothing and lay down beside her. He wasn't returning to the lumpy couch, and she didn't complain about his presence. Wouldn't have done her any good.

"Cole, hold me" She scooted closer to him.

It warmed him throughout that she wanted his comfort, but he feared hurting her. Sliding one arm around her shoulders, he gathered her close, carefully so he didn't touch her wounded cheek or knee. Her skin was cold, her body trembling. The aftermath of a terrible ordeal. Shock.

If he ever got his hands on the son of a bitch…

"One little question."

"All right." In spite of the knot in his chest, he couldn't help smiling into her fragrant hair. The woman had incredible courage. She was weary and hurting, but still curious and fighting.

"How did he know you were gone? I didn't know until you called. And how did he disable the phone?"

He kissed her temple. "Too many questions for someone as wasted as you. We'll sort through it in the morning."

If he knew the answer to her questions, he could lay his hands on the killer. A killer close enough to know Cole had left that night. A killer who was getting closer to accomplishing his goal.

And there was one piece of news he'd keep to himself. Laura had been through enough. When Cole's contact officer had finally called, he reported that they'd lost Markos again.

The importer had vanished.

Chapter Twenty-Two

WHEN COLE AWOKE the next morning, Laura had already left the bed.

How could she even think about going out alone after the beating last night? The woman didn't know when to quit.

He flung off the light blanket and was about to hit the floor when he heard water running in the bathroom. Swinging his legs back up, he lay back on the pillows.

Last night had been so hectic and she too upset and shocked to think clearly. But today he'd have to do damage control. Explain more to her. And to Stan.

He would let Stan think he'd driven the Harley out earlier and that vandals wrecked the old piano. Announcing this new attack on Laura would mean having to call in the cops for more than vandalism. He couldn't risk exposing the DARK team and blowing the trap, so they would keep mum. But it grated on him not to let Stan know the truth and not to hustle Laura somewhere safer.

A moment later, she appeared in the bedroom doorway, wearing only shorts and bruises. Varying shades of purple blotched her thighs and calves. Daring but so vulnerable, too much so, she made him feel he needed a sword and shield to defend her.

Heat pooled in his groin. Lust mingled with satisfaction that she'd had few lovers over the years.

She'd confessed a deep freeze ever since their disastrous weekend. That he'd been the one to reawaken her passion fed his ego.

The violet and purple on her legs, arms and back told the tale of her tumble down the stairs. She wasn't flaunting herself, but neither was she hiding her near nakedness. She'd stopped concealing the neck scars from him. A teasing smile tilting her full lips, she attempted a limping pirouette for him.

"I was checking out my war wounds. So what do you think?" she said. "Will these rainbow hues catch on fashion-wise?"

"I hope not, babe." He held out his arms, and she eased down with him on the rumpled sheets. Semi-prone against the pillows, he helped her to lie half across him, one leg thrown over his and her head on his shoulder, her breasts against his side. "How do you feel?"

She threaded her index finger through his chest hair. "Last night I felt as if I'd been pounded with hammers, then flattened by an upright piano, like Wile E. Coyote. I ache, but I'm reinflating."

He ran his palm over her hair, sexy and disheveled from sleep. Smudges beneath her eyes spoke of her pain, but a glint in the gold flecks had been missing last night. A tough cookie, she was more resilient than the cartoon coyote.

"Tell me what you found out last night. I know you got up after you thought I was asleep." Her fingers grew still on his skin, her gaze alight with intensity. Her hands were cool, but electric tingles spread from their touch.

Hating this sordid business, he gave a grunt of disgust. "Not much to tell. The phone cord wasn't cut, just unplugged outside."

"And who did you call?"

He grinned and smoothed a hand down the one shoulder with no bruises. She'd washed her face and smelled of soap and her apple lotion. In spite of her bruises, she felt supple and warm in his arms.

"You don't miss much, do you? I let the others know what happened. Mixed communications last night kept Isaacs from watching over you. He was posted outside Blow-Dry's cabin standing guard until the local cops could take over. Byrne was with me. Snow did his usual walk-around about nine-thirty and saw nobody."

"Interesting that Butch and Zach noticed this Mr. Blow-Dry and your men didn't."

"Apparently our friendly neighborhood thief put on a good bird-watching act. Snow talked to the guy a few times and thought he was clean. He even threw off suspicion by reporting a portable CD-player missing."

"You weren't too hard on Vanessa, I hope."

"Not me. When I told her, she nearly choked. She was ready to go out and hunt Janus herself. Alone."

"She shouldn't feel guilty. Everything seemed safe when she left." She propped herself up on one elbow, one leg bent beneath her, the other with the swollen knee stretched out before her.

"I told her that. And I'll get you a phone and set speed dial so you can reach me no matter what." It would also contain a GPS tracker. She should've been able to call for help. Hell, she wouldn't have needed help if Isaacs had done his job or Ward had stayed. But Cole couldn't blame the lapse on them. He was in charge.

He wished Laura would throw something over herself. No, he didn't. But she was too tempting, sitting there so open, her world-class legs within reach. Did she have any idea what she did to him? She would soon because his reaction was becoming acutely visible. *Down, boy, she's injured.*

Naked and on top of the covers, he had little means to hide his reaction to her. He raised one knee in partial concealment. "I saw Burt—" he couldn't help inflecting the name with disdain "—driving to Alderport for the fireworks."

"I doubt his involvement in this anyway. And we know he's not the thief." She tugged her hair behind her ears. The action lifted her breasts and drew his gaze.

He nearly groaned. "Protecting the little twerp?"

She batted her eyelashes at him. "Jealous, cowboy?"

Jealous? If that was the name for this tangle wrenching his gut. Hell, yes, he was jealous, murderously so of any other man who'd ever touched her. He felt like breaking faces. Straining for control, he schooled his features into detachment. "You do remember that someone—Markos's hit man—has tried to kill you? More than once? And he'll try again?"

"Right. But it's not Burt."

He plucked up her hand from the bed and brought it to his lips. Even the tennis calluses felt feminine. "Maybe now you'll let me take you to a safe house. We still have nothing concrete to ID this damn killer, and I want you to have more protection."

She shook her head vehemently. "That piano almost made dust out of me. Or made me part of the cellar floor. I considered a safe house, but no, I'm making my stand here." Arms folded, she appeared ready to duke it out if he disagreed. She'd win because he couldn't take his eyes off her body.

He kneaded the sheets instead of reaching for her.

"Providing you *can* still stand."

"Very funny. I'm better now. See, the swelling's down on my knee."

He nodded, dragging his gaze downward to the still puffy knee. "The ice packs helped."

"I know what would make me feel even better." Her throaty voice dropped to a heated honey-dripping tone that sent his heart whacking his ribs. She bent closer so that the hard peaks of her nipples tickled the sensitive skin on his torso. When her pink tongue moistened the hollow at the base of his throat, he shuddered.

Her caresses were stiffening him like the wrought-iron bedposts, but sex might chafe her injuries. He could wait. He wasn't some horny kid. Or maybe he was. A groan escaped his lips. "Another ice pack?"

Her husky chuckle doubled his aching need to nearly bursting. "No, but ice might decrease a certain other swelling. Interesting, that swelling looks hard, not puffy like my knee—"

"Fiend." As her fingers trailed down his belly, he gritted out the next words between clenched teeth. "I don't want to flatten you again, Wile E."

"You won't. And until you yield, I'll just keep you pumped up—like my knee." She gazed at him with enough heat to incinerate the bed. The pink tip of her tongue crept out to lick her full lower lip. "What was that Pashto word for get down?"

He groaned as she scored one fingernail down his belly toward the more than ready anatomy in question. "*Samla.*"

She smiled, a feline creature with her prey. "*Samla,* big boy, *samla.*"

Unable to withstand her torment any longer, Cole

rolled to his side, pulling her full against him, skin to skin. "Be gentle with me, Murphy."

In reply, she clasped her hands behind his neck and covered his mouth with hers. Her tongue swirled around the textures of his inner lips, the underside of his tongue. He reveled in the taste of her, mint toothpaste and Laura.

Sliding lower, he dropped kisses down the curve of her neck, along her breast bone, to one breast, where he closed his lips over the pink nipple. Sweet.

Her answering moan was one of pleasure, not pain.

His fingers found her. She was ready for him, hot and tight and slick with wanting. With his thumb, he massaged the key nerves that would unlock her passion.

When she arched off the bed and stripped away her shorts, he barely had time to reach for protection before covering her with his body and sliding into her welcoming heat. The throbbing ache of need instantly surged into a wave of pleasure. She clamped herself around him to complete their joining.

"Cole!" Tears trickled into her temples as she thrashed beneath him. "Please!"

He couldn't get enough of her. If sex was all they had, then he'd take it. And her. Only connected with her did he feel secure. Whole.

Home.

"Laura," he rasped out. You're mine. Mine."

When he felt her contractions begin, he could hold release back no longer. Uttering a shout of ecstasy, he poured himself into her in a scalding tide of completion.

****

Before the sailing class, Laura applied makeup, which nearly concealed the scrape on her cheek. A bit warm for long sleeves, but they and light-weight pants hid most of the bruises.

On the dock, she and Cole had a talk with Butch and Zach about the man who'd been arrested the night before. Cole explained that the man they called Mr. Blow-Dry was the thief who'd taken Zach's camera and Kay's iPod, but he probably hadn't switched Laura's skiff for the damaged one.

Laura hugged both boys. "You guys were great to go to Mr. Stratton with your sharp observations. You're my heroes."

They beamed. They blushed. Then they ran off, punching each other in the shoulder.

At Cole's tight mouth, she made a mental note to tell him later that he was her hero too. He'd rushed off thinking he'd be able to tie up the case only to find Mr. Blow-Dry was the wrong man and she'd faced a serious threat by herself. Clearly, he felt he'd failed her. Success for him was intertwined with his past and his need to prove himself. If he cared for her again, that was also part of his emotional stew.

Or maybe she should keep quiet. She didn't want him to care more than he already seemed to, didn't want him to think their relationship was more than sex and friendship. She'd initiated this morning's lovemaking out of a deep, fierce need for him that had made her wanton, made her burn for his touch, for his possession. He knew most of her body intimately, even the scars on her neck, but she'd concealed the most telling one along with her secret. Although he might've seen it this morning…

He believed that she disdained the hoodlum lurking within him, no matter what respect and stature he'd earned in his work and as an honorable, kind and generous man. He deserved to know the real reason she must leave him once this horrible situation ended. It was the same reason he would ultimately resent her and reject her.

But revealing the truth now would alter the way he looked at her and the way he thought of her, and she couldn't face it. Not yet. Not while they still had time together.

Cowardly of her. But there it was.

After the sailing class ended, she and Cole helped Stan and the two DARK officers masquerading as grounds crew set up tables for the afternoon barbecue. Her tennis class and any other regularly scheduled activities were canceled. Games and contests at the barbecue would take their place.

Once the tables were arranged, Cole hustled her to her cabin and made her rest her knee until the barbecue. He tossed her an ice pack and immersed himself in his laptop.

In his faded jeans that clung to his muscular thighs and a black Harley t-shirt, he looked so masculine and handsome her heart did a little flutter kick. As he worked, he grumbled to himself and occasionally ran his fingers through already disheveled hair.

"Damn thing!" He slammed the laptop cover shut. "Frozen again. I hope to hell the hard drive's not kaput." He stomped off to a corner chair with his phone.

He was concentrating so hard, he seemed to have walled her out. She picked up the Elizabeth Peters novel she'd started a week ago. The historical mystery, set in Egypt, would ordinarily suck her into its world, but today her mind and heart lingered with Cole. Something was wrong, but she didn't think it concerned her situation.

The feel of the phone he'd promised tucked in her pants pocket constantly reminded her of the danger she was in. God, she hoped she never had to use the speed dial, a smiley face on the touch screen.

Later they walked to the barbecue under a July sun floating high in the azure sky. The aromas of barbecued chicken and other traditional summer treats feathered to them on the freshening breeze, but couldn't dispel her concern. "Problems beyond the laptop crash?"

He heaved a sigh and curled a hand beneath her hair and around her nape. The gesture of familiarity and affection pleased her. "It's Marisol. The little girl in Colombia."

She gasped. "Has something happened to her?"

He gave her neck a gentle squeeze. "Nothing, no. Just glitches in the red tape. The State Department is balking at issuing her a visa. Something about no relatives or a sponsor. I can't be the sponsor. DARK already frowns on my connection to the San Sebastiano orphanage. Hell, I'm stymied. I've contacted everyone I know in D.C."

"I know a few people I could call. Old colleagues of Dad's."

He shook his head, his jaw firm, his mouth clamped. "No way. Too dangerous."

She stopped walking, wrapped her hand around his forearm. The tension in the muscles was electric. "But Markos already knows where I am. How can it hurt?"

Removing his hand from her nape, he kneaded his own. His eyes burned with intensity. "As far as all those people you know are concerned, you've vanished. If you start calling bigwigs in Washington, it would take about three seconds for the word to get out. The vampires—

news media to you—would descend and suck the life out of our op here. Janus and Markos would slip out of the trap, and we'd be back to square one."

Her heart twisted at the thought of that little girl not receiving the care she needed. Poor helpless little orphan. At least Laura had some defense against her enemy. "At least let me give you some names. You could call them."

He emitted an inarticulate rumble and strode ahead. "Same damn problem once I told them who gave me their name." His fists were clenched at his side.

"Mom and Dad could be her sponsor." She hobbled along to keep up. Her knee felt better, but she couldn't match his stride.

"Damn, I'm sorry, Laura." He slowed his pace to suit hers. "Thanks, but their being out of the country doesn't cut it. There's a short window here. The doc's got a date set for the surgery, a week from now. After that he goes to Africa for a year with Doctors Without Borders. This guy's a pediatric orthopedic specialist. I don't know if I can arrange the same deal with another surgeon. And the older Marisol gets, the chancier the repair job will be."

"And here you are, stuck with me."

He turned on his heel so fast her head spun. His mouth was hard, and his eyes drilled hers. "Don't ever think that way. Keeping you alive and safe is my mission. My only mission. You're not to worry about Marisol or any of that. I'm here to protect you with my life. I can deal with the surgery glitches once this mess is all over."

"And Markos is behind bars." She smiled to ease his tension. And hers. "Promise me that if there's any way I can help, you'll ask."

"You got it, sweetheart." He cupped her elbow, and they proceeded to the broad, sloping lawn between the inn and the beach. He cleared his throat, and a wry grin quirked his lips. "Don't think the irony has escaped me."

She widened her eyes in an innocent expression. "Why whatever do you mean?"

"The fact that for Marisol's sake I'm asking for the kind of connections I've always resented."

"I'm so proud. You got it." She poked him in the biceps with an index finger. "Not only that, but you're opening doors with your own credentials, your own influence."

"Like hell. I don't see a visa with Marisol's name on it dropping from heaven."

"You talked this orthopedic specialist into the surgery, didn't you?" When he merely sputtered and slapped on his sunglasses, she grinned. "I rest my case."

As soon as they neared the picnic tables, crowded with families and laden with food, Stan marched up and pumped Cole's hand. "I can't tell you how much I appreciate your handling that… situation last night," he said, his usually genial expression overlaid with distress.

"Glad I could help."

"I don't know what the world's coming to," continued the resort owner. "You try to make a family resort like this safe for folks."

"And it is safe. Look at all these families here."

Stan shook his head. "And there's the vandalism in the theater. Lucky you got your motorcycle out earlier. Looks like I'll have to button up every building from now on."

"I'm sure it was just teenagers fooling around," Laura put in. "An aberration. Still, locking up seems like a good idea."

"I hate to bring this up today, Stan," Cole said, "but the gas heater in Laura's cabin still leaks. Does Burt know what he's doing?"

Stan ran his fingers through his wispy hair. His morose expression exaggerated his horsy features. "That blasted kid. Too much of a slacker. I don't care if he is Jake's nephew. I'll send him to tackle it again. They say bad luck comes in threes. Lord knows what can happen next." Waving his arms in frustration, he hurried off toward the children's contests.

"Mr. Stratton, Mr. Stratton, you gotta help me." Zach dashed up to Cole, nearly barreling into him in his haste.

Chapter Twenty-Three

"HEY, BUDDY, WHAT'S up?" Cole frowned. "Not another suspicious character, I hope."

"No way." The boy danced a step back, steadying himself. "The three-legged race is about to start. Butch and his dad are ready to go. I wanna beat them, but my dad's not here. The prize is a watermelon—a *whole* watermelon!"

Cole leaned down, his hands planted on his knees. "And you need a partner. I'm your man, Zach." He glanced around and gave a barely perceptible nod to Vanessa.

"Suh-weet." Latching on to Cole's arm, the boy tugged him toward the racecourse beyond the picnic tables.

Laura's heart melted. She waved off Cole and quickly lost sight of the two in the milling throng of shorts-clad people.

Vanessa came to her side. "After my screw-up last night, I'm surprised he trusts me near you." The redhead carried a platter of fresh vegetables cut in curlicues and arranged in decorative swirls.

Laura helped herself to a carrot curl. "We both know none of last night's disaster was your fault."

"Thanks for that. But still…" On a shrug, Vanessa placed her burden on a table laden with traditional and gourmet fare. "Just look at this food. I feel like we're here for a medieval feast."

"The groaning board for sure." Laura smiled, glad to have her cheerful friend back instead of the stern government officer.

Munching on a miniature quiche, Vanessa quipped, "Of course I diet only in leap years."

Laura laughed. "I thought this was going to be a simple cookout with chicken and potato salad."

"So Stan said, but I think Joyce is a frustrated banquet chef." Vanessa took her arm as they strolled around the tables and toward the barbecue grills.

Laura wondered if the officer was back, herding her, to ensure more safety in the middle of the crowd.

Clutches of adults lounged and chatted in folding chairs. Toddlers played hide-and-seek beneath the food tables, and older kids stuffed their faces with chips and nachos from the appetizer array.

By the chips bowl, the Tolman twins and Kay clustered around a boy Laura hadn't seen before. His surfer-blond hair suited the dazzling flowered shorts and water sandals he sported. At least this boy was closer to Kay's age. And without Malibu Barbie mascara and hairdo, Kay looked fresh and sweet, as she should. Burt was nowhere in sight and hopefully out of the picture. Perhaps Laura's too-much-too-soon chat with Kay's parents made a dent.

Bea Van Tassel waved long-handled tongs at them. "You two have to taste this chicken." She licked her lips. The barbecue sauce's shade, a tomato-y deep maroon, amazingly matched her lipstick and her peasant dress.

The two grills were metal barrels sliced in half lengthwise and fitted with legs. Several dozen chicken pieces brushed with spicy sauce simmered over glowing briquettes.

Rudy Damon joined them. An elegantly tied royal-blue cravat—who but Rudy wore a cravat?—bloomed from the opening of his silk shirt. "Okay, Miss V., I'm here to relieve you."

Bea untied her apron and handed it over. "About time," she sniffed. "I'm supposed to be helping with the desserts."

"Smells delicious," Laura said. "Is that sauce… Bea's creation, Rudy?" The Van Tassel sisters were sweet to help out with the party, but she crossed her fingers that Bea hadn't also contributed to the cuisine.

"Never." The director fanned himself with a spatula. "Stan's secret family recipe. He wouldn't even let his wife watch him mix it. Do you want a breast or a leg?"

Laura could barely contain a laugh. Bea's only contribution was turning the chicken. "I'll have some chicken soon. Right now I want to watch the race."

After they strolled off, Vanessa chuckled. "For a minute I was afraid she'd poison the entire crowd."

"So she feeds you too." Enjoying a laugh together felt good as they made their way toward the starting line.

Vanessa gestured toward the racers. "For such a big, tough guy, Cole has a way with kids. My little nephews, my brother's two Hell's Angels, consider him their hero. He should have some kids of his own."

Laura's misty gaze followed her unwitting friend's gesture. She spotted Butch, paired with a dark-haired Asian man who looked exactly like him. Beside them Zach was finishing tying his ankle to Cole's. A grin on his face, Cole placed a steadying hand on the boy's shoulder.

Cole—gentle, protective, affectionate and affable

with children. Vanessa was right. He should have his own.

Seeing him with that boy and with the other men and their sons crowded an ache in her chest. When she saw him like that, how could she protect herself? How could she conceal her secret?

The startling thought hit her that Zach was only two years older than their son would've been. David would have been nine. Tears clouded her vision and clogged her throat. Her stomach heaved. She couldn't have eaten barbecued chicken without gagging. Like a panicked bird on a window, her heart threatened to beat its way out of her chest, and she had to turn away.

"What is it? Something between you and Cole is eating you alive. And it's not fear of the danger stalking you." Vanessa patted her arm.

"Ancient history, old business." Laura reached for a glass of wine from a tray. She downed two gulps as though it were water.

Vanessa snorted. "Unfinished business, if you ask me. The forest service should dial the fire danger to the red zone. When the two of you are near each other, the flames leap so high everyone within a mile gets singed."

A thousand emotions battered Laura in a barrage of invisible arrows. Each tiny missile drew blood. She needed a few minutes alone. "Excuse me. I'm going inside to see if Joyce needs help with the desserts."

She hobbled up the inn stairs and inside before the tears flowed. She ducked into the small TV room off the lobby and sank onto a loveseat. Her throat ached as tears slid down her cheeks. She willed the weeping to stop. She couldn't change the past any more than she could stem the tide. She couldn't change herself, to give Cole the family he wanted and needed. So it was idiotic to cry like this. She mopped at her eyes with the single flimsy tissue she found in her pocket.

"My dear, whatever is the matter?" Bea Van Tassel's gentle tone of concern only made the tears flow faster. The plump woman sat beside her.

"Here, Laura," Doris handed her a packet of tissues from her voluminous tote bag. "Sometimes a woman needs a good cry. You just get it all out." Folding her lanky body, she parked herself on a footstool.

"There, there." Bea patted her shoulder. "Man trouble?"

Sympathy only exacerbated her emotional dam burst. She hadn't considered the stress of pushing through every day with fear dogging her from all directions. Fear of Markos's hit man, of what new so-called accident he might try. But mostly fear of the emotional turmoil of living with Cole. She ached with love for him. Being with him was both torture and joy.

"Man trouble of my own making." She could barely choke out the words. She blew her nose into a tissue. "Drat, I'm making such a fool of myself."

"Nonsense, my dear, turn that flow into a gusher if you need to," Doris said.

"How can we help?" Bea said.

Their sweetness and understanding brought more tears. It had been so long since she'd had motherly comforting. She sobbed and sniffled, drawing her tears from a bottomless lake.

The two ladies let her cry, simply sitting beside her lending support. At last, she straightened and wiped the last of the moisture from her puffy eyes.

"I'm afraid there's nothing anyone can do." Her

sobs quieted to an occasional shivery whimper. Though she couldn't involve these gentle souls in her problems, they might be able to help in one way. "But let me ask your advice. This is totally theoretical, you understand."

"Of course, dear." Bea leaned in, her button eyes eager and alert.

"Ask away." Doris scooted her stool closer and nudged her tote bag out of the way. Her layered skirts spread around her like petals.

"Suppose you had a secret. An important, tragic secret you'd kept for years. A secret that would break your heart to reveal, but one that a person you loved deserved to know. What would you do?"

The elderly sisters looked at each other for a long moment.

Bea cleared her throat. "We've been in the theater all our lives. On stage and off, everyone has secrets."

"In *Arsenic and Old Lace*, the ladies' secret is murder. This secret is nothing so drastic, I expect," Doris said with the eager air of one hoping for more elucidation.

Laura drew back, horrified. "No, nothing dangerous or illegal, I promise you." Only agonizing to her, and probably shocking to Cole.

Outside, cheers erupted. The race was either starting or ending. She didn't have long. Cole would come looking for her.

"I never suspected it was, dearie," Doris said. "But let me say that I believe truth is usually better than deception. Look at all the problems in the world that could be avoided if people were truthful with one another."

Laura stood and helped the others to their feet.

"Thank you for your kind shoulders. You're generous friends."

Bea smoothed her sausage curls. "Doris is right. Most of the time, truth is preferable. On the other hand, too much frankness can hurt. If knowing a secret would cause the hearer pain, silence might be the wiser course."

"Then again," added Doris, "sometimes our emotions blind us. What we perceive as our show-stopper scene is only a walk-on in life's drama."

The Van Tassels departed, leaving Laura feeling guiltier and more confused than ever. No closer to knowing what to do.

****

The tracker in Laura's phone led Cole to the TV room. In her white pants and green shirt, she looked tailored and perfect, yet small and fragile. The attempts on her life and, he had to admit, his presence were taking their toll. What happened long ago had hurt her deeply. Losing the baby in an accident crushed her spirit. She'd believed that he didn't want her.

Not want her?

He'd never stopped. He knew that now.

"Laura, the twins are asking for you. They want you to sit and eat with them." Her slumped shoulders and red-rimmed eyes wrenched at his heart. "Are you okay?"

"I'm fine, just fine." She stuffed wadded tissues in her pockets.

"Sorry, sweetheart, but your Technicolor eyes don't agree." In two strides he reached her and wrapped her in his arms. "Whatever upset you had to be bad for you to go off alone. What happened?"

She stepped away from him, shaking her head. Pain and sorrow pinched her mouth. She searched his face, as if looking for the answer there. "It's everything— Janus, Markos, last night's attack. Us. All of a sudden I felt crushed, like being covered by a landslide." She managed a wobbly smile. "I'm all right. I'll go out now and see the kids."

As she walked away, he swore silently, his arms aching for her. But maybe she needed to keep busy. He looked through the screen door to assure himself she wasn't alone.

Sunglasses concealing her eyes, she sat at a table with the twins and Kay and their parents. Vanessa loitered nearby. Byrne on the other side of the crowd. Snow at a table with some of the other guests. Laura was safe for now. Physically.

Time and time again she'd berated him for dwelling on his dysfunctional and delinquent background. She ordered him to get over himself. And crowed when he acknowledged using his DARK credentials to open doors for Marisol.

He waited for his old man's voice to snipe at him from the depths of his soul.

Silence. No sneering voice.

Laura was right. He'd overcome the past and moved on. He didn't need to prove himself over and over. Success in his work and for the Colombian kids was a source of pride, but not hurdles with constantly raised bars.

If he applied the logic Laura so valued, no barrier existed between them. No more walls of stubbornness and self-doubt. Only the ones she erected out of pain and fear of the future. But he could knock those down.

For her.

For them.

He'd waited this long for her. He could hang on until she was safe from murderous importers and dodgy hit men.

His next order of business was to find out why Alexei Markos was nowhere to be found.

Chapter Twenty-Four

"THANKS, MAN," COLE said to Kent Isaacs. "I don't know if that information means anything. At this point I'll take whatever the hell I can get." They stood beneath a tamarack tree at the edge of the inn's wide lawn.

The DARK officer shrugged. "Fisher said to tell you one of the techs could fix the bum computer. I'll take it to him now if you like. I'm free."

"Great. The damn thing's not much good to me dead. Can't you fix it? You ATF guys are up on all the electronics." It was clear that Isaacs was trying to make up for the night before, for misunderstanding where he was supposed to be. If the guy wanted to run errands, okay by Cole.

"I can rig remotes to trigger bombs or deactivate 'em or block the signal. That's it."

Cole laughed. "Damn thing's on the front seat of the truck. You might as well drive that, for your trouble." He handed over the keys.

"Always wanted to tool around in that behemoth." Grinning, the other man waved a small salute and jogged away.

While Laura helped carry the leftover food inside, Cole gave a hand to Burt Elwell and Simon Byrne, who were folding the picnic tables and stashing them in the back of the resort pickup.

A while later, Laura came out carrying a paper plate covered with plastic wrap. When she spotted him, she straightened her shoulders and lifted her chin. Trying to conceal her exhaustion. Aches and pains from a tumble downstairs wore down even a woman with a steel spine. He'd pick her up and tuck her in bed, but she'd screech louder than a siren if he tried.

She cocked her head and smiled in a teasing way. "Bea wrapped up some lemon tarts. For a bedtime snack, she said."

"Think the chipmunks outside your cabin would like them?"

Laura descended the steps with care. "Not Bea's creation but Joyce's. Her cooking is blue-ribbon quality, not like Bea's black-ribbon cuisine, so you're safe."

Mouth watering, he peered at the crispy crusts filled with pale-yellow custard. He reached for the plate. "I'll eat one now. I didn't get any dessert."

She whisked it to her side, just out of reach, a sexy smile on her lips. "Not yet, mister. First, I want to know what has you looking like you swallowed a porcupine. Your jaw's as relaxed as a boulder. What did Isaacs have to report? Is it Markos?"

He took her free hand. "Not here."

They headed toward the lake, where no one would overhear. The aroma of barbecue blended with pine scents on the cool night air. Small brown bats scooped up insects on the wing.

"How's the knee?" he asked, swatting at the mosquito dive-bombing his ear.

"Not too bad. I'll be glad to put it up for a while."

She wasn't a whiner. That meant it felt like a heavyweight boxer had used it for a punching bag.

He moved her hand to the crook of his arm, to lend support—and better cover. "Nothing on Markos. That's a bust."

"Then what?" Her stubborn chin told him she was trying to sound casual.

"You heard me ask Stan about the gas heater. I want you to understand that there may be nothing wrong with it. Somebody may be deliberately loosening the valve and dousing the pilot light. Even with our surveillance."

Comprehension widened her eyes. "Do you still suspect Burt?" Her shoulders shook with a small shiver, as if a chill raced down her spine at the thought of that boy mixed up in this deadly game. She didn't want to believe it of him. God knew why.

He uttered a grunt of doubt. "I'd bet no. I want to eliminate him once and for all. When he comes to fix the heater, I'll talk to him."

Laura squeezed his arm, enjoying the feel of hard muscle beneath the skin. "Are you basing your skepticism on facts or on your spy instincts?"

"A little of both."

"Is it the note?"

"Think you're pretty smart." He grinned his admiration. "He's not clever enough for the so-called accidents. Janus wouldn't hire somebody so clumsy. Besides, the words on last night's note are spelled right."

She scuffed her sneaker toe in the sand. "My instincts about people are usually good. Burt may be lazy and not the sharpest pencil in the box. Rudy Damon may have dreams of returning to Broadway. Stan and Dr. Rhodes may be in debt. But none of them would take money from this hit man to murder me. They're no killers."

He brought her hand to his lips, kissing the palm. "I hate to point it out, but a year ago would you have guessed that Alexei Markos was a terrorist shill… and a murderer?"

Her heartbeat kicked up, and she could do nothing but shake her head. The chill she felt wasn't from the cool breeze wafting across the lake. "Do you believe it's one of them? Or do you think the hit man is here?"

"He's here." Cole's jaw was taut, his mouth grim. "But that doesn't mean he hasn't bribed or blackmailed an accomplice to help him."

She bit her lip in concentration, fighting the fear with cool logic. "And he seems to know where I am, what I do and what time I come home," she said as they meandered aimlessly. "Now that I think about it, the attacker last night seemed to know the theater in the dark as well as I did."

"He's sure as hell keeping a close watch on you. He seems to get around my officers to set up his damn accidents." Knuckles rasping against his whiskers, he wagged his head. "I should see a clue or two in that, but so far nada."

She trusted him to figure it out eventually, but hated seeing his frustration. "Your background checks have come up empty. That doesn't make sense. Someone should stick out."

"That's the hell of it, babe. I figure the hit man has to be somebody we both know. Somebody we see every day."

His gaze swept the area. The thickening clouds were deepening the shadows in the shrubbery. Every movement of the breeze shifted the shadows and rustled leaves.

"Let's head to the cabin. Too many dark places out here." He curved an arm around her waist.

They walked in silence until the cabin came into view through the trees.

She pointed. "I see Burt headed there. He doesn't look happy about doing repairs this time of night."

The cabin was dark except for the outside light. Its glow illuminated the silhouette of the young handyman, a tool kit in hand. He slouched along the gravel path.

"About time. Come on."

"Oh, no. Let him fix it." She placed a restraining hand on his chest. "You said yourself gassing someone that way was an unreliable and clumsy way to commit murder."

"Exactly. But it would look like an accident. Another in a damn string of accidents." He lifted her hand and kissed the palm. He flicked a glance toward the inn. Stan and Byrne were still loading tables. "I'm going in to keep an eye on him. And to see if the safety valve is defective or purposely disabled. You stay with Byrne until I give the all clear."

He sent Byrne a hand signal, and the officer replied with a different signal.

She didn't want to believe that someone she knew as a friend could be trying to kill her. Still, she had to trust Cole to know his business. "Don't be too hard on Burt if he's just doing his job."

"Please go back to the inn. I need to know you're safe." His eyes bored into her, seemed to reach out and touch hers with their heat. If she lived to be ninety, she'd remember the sizzle his gaze never failed to inspire. Now, with the added fillip of danger.

She sighed, and not entirely with resignation.

"Okay, okay. I'm going." She cut across the dew-damp lawn, but looked back at Cole as he continued along the path. He was only a dark silhouette against the fading sky as he approached the cabin.

A rumble like a waking dragon shook the ground.

The cabin windows burst outward in a torrent of glass splinters. The walls exploded apart with a thunderous roar and a burst of smoke and flame. A volcanic ball of fire shot through the roof.

The shock wave from the blast knocked Laura down. Roof shingles and broken glass fell on her head. A board crashed to the ground beside her. Broiling heat seared her skin and ignited trees. The old tamarack went up like a Roman candle.

Cole! Where are you?

Coughing and choking at the acrid stench of smoke and God knew what else, she scrambled toward where she'd seen him last. She pulled her shirt up to cover her nose and mouth. The heat was stifling. She could barely breathe. Black smoke curtained the path. She could see nothing.

"Cole!"

Only the roar of the fire and the serpentine flow of smoke responded.

Chapter Twenty-Five

COLE STUMBLED OUT of the choking smoke cloud and searched for Laura. Byrne was helping her to the safety of the inn. Coughing and wiping his eyes, Cole slogged in that direction. Every bone in his body ached like he'd been cranked on a medieval rack.

Sirens screamed in the distance, then blared louder as they approached.

Orange-red tongues of fire licked into the night sky from what was left of the small wooden structure. The tree beside it was a charred trunk, but most of the others nearby had only a few burnt limbs, like lightning damage. The recent rain must have soaked everything well enough to protect them.

One adjacent cabin had holes in the roof from the initial blast, but the wind blew the blaze the other direction. The fire was leaping across the open space to a cabin on the other side. He hoped the fire trucks would arrive in time to save them. Most employees were local and lived in town so both cabins were unoccupied.

Thank God he hadn't gone inside with Burt Elwell, the poor bastard. The valve must've been wide-open again, so the cabin filled with gas. The unhandy handyman probably clicked on lights, triggering enough of a spark to ignite the gas. A damn bomb.

The entire cabin was a bomb, rigged to explode.

Except Laura was supposed to be the one to die

inside. And probably him.

No doubt that the gas leak was deliberate. Too many contrived accidents for this to be a coincidence.

When murder was involved, he didn't believe in coincidences.

In spite of the heat rolling over him from the blaze, horror frosted him at what had nearly happened to Laura, and what could still happen if he wasn't more alert and careful than he'd ever been in his life. Fear for her coiled in his gut like a rattler ready to strike. A wave of dizziness hit and he had to grip the tennis court's chain link fence for support.

What would the bastard try next?

Cole shouldn't have listened to her plea not to go to a safe house. He should've hog-tied her and thrown her in the truck and taken off that first night before the head of DARK even thought of setting a trap.

They could still leave. Right now.

Hell, no cabin and no clothes, no reason to stay even tonight. He had the means to get them the hell out of here—his laptop and truck, safe in Alderport, thanks to Isaacs. His Harley hunkered safely in the theater lobby.

But he was close, so close, to trapping Janus and nailing Markos that he hated to give up. If it was the last thing he ever did, he would get the sons of bitches. Puzzling how to do that and protect Laura made him sweat and clutch at the writhing serpents in his belly.

Red fire trucks rushed onto the lawn. Men and women in black-and-yellow jackets and black boots raced to the lake with hoses. Soon plumes of water streamed over the blazing cabin and the small fires started around it.

"Cole! Oh, thank God you're all right." Laura

hurried to him and threw her arms around his waist. "I… I couldn't find you. The smoke…"

"I'm okay. The blast threw me backward, knocked me flat on my ass. Once I got my breath back, I got the hell out of the way."

She clutched at him. "That poor boy. Burt went in the cabin and…" She dissolved in tears that streaked down her soot-smudged cheeks. Ash smudged her blouse and pants. If she was smeared with it, hell, he must look like a coal miner.

He pulled her as close as he could without stripping off their clothes and holding her skin to skin. That was what instinct spurred him to do, to examine every inch of her skin to satisfy himself she wasn't injured. Instead, he kissed her, tasting her sweetness and filling himself with the fragrance of her hair, tinged with smoke.

The firefighters yelled at them to get back. Arms around each other, he and Laura walked to the inn.

Knowing she was safe uncoiled the snakes in his gut. An inch or two. He'd done the right thing to keep her safe. He'd sent her out of harm's way before the cabin blew. Maybe his instincts weren't all bad.

If he'd listened to what she called his spy instincts from the start, she would've been long gone. Out of harm's way.

Never mind Alexei Markos. It was time to get the hell out of Dodge. They'd head to whatever safe house his contact could manage. And they'd go tonight. No matter what Laura said. No matter what the general said.

A semicircle of people from the cabins had gathered to watch the fire and the firefighters. Grant Snow tipped his cane at him. Young Zach stood with a bathrobe-clad woman who must be his mother. He clicked away with his camera, retrieved from the police. The Van Tassel sisters huddled together and pointed at the flaming cabin.

At the inn, guests and employees hung out of windows and jammed the wide porch. DARK Officers Byrne and Ward stood at either end, watching the crowd.

Stan Hart slumped on the steps, his head between his knees. His wife Joyce, beside him, kept a consoling hand on his shoulder.

"Talk to him, Laura," Joyce pleaded. "He blames himself for Burt going in there."

Sliding her arm from around Cole, Laura went to sit on the step below Stan. "I'm so sorry about Burt," she said, her words slow and gentle. "We all are. But it's not your fault. It was an accident. That gas heater was faulty. It could have blown like that at any time."

The resort owner raised red-rimmed eyes to her. "He was just a kid, Laura. An inexperienced kid. Jake showed him a few things about the propane heaters, but not enough. I should've called the gas company to send out someone."

Cole couldn't let Stan believe the accident myth. Not since he was in on DARK's trap. Laura must know the truth, but was trying to save her employer from the reality of murder.

Placing one foot on the step beside her, he propped an elbow on his knee. He bent close so no one else could hear. "The gas explosion was no accident. Somebody tampered with the safety valve."

Stan was so still that for a moment, Cole didn't think the man heard him. Then he turned his head. "Not an accident? Do you mean it was part of the plot against Laura?"

"I wasn't certain until tonight," Cole hastened to

say. "The killer either meant to asphyxiate us or blow us up. I believe the thing was rigged so the safety valve was disabled. When the pilot light was extinguished, gas kept pouring out with nothing to shut it off. Burt must've ignited a spark in a cabin filled with gas. I'm damned sorry he got caught in this mess." He meant it. The kid had been harmless and sure as hell didn't deserve to die because he flicked on a light.

Stan rubbed his forehead and stood up. "Laura, I love you like a daughter, and I hope you're safe from now on."

He turned back to Cole. "I appreciate what you folks were trying to do to catch this killer, and I was glad to do my part. Insurance will cover the property damage, but this mess—" he waved his arms "—has endangered my people. My guests and my employees."

"Oh, Stan, I'm so sorry," Laura murmured.

He didn't look at her. "Enough is enough." His long face drooped with sadness, but his voice rang with determination. "You'll all have to leave."

Chapter Twenty-Six

LATER AFTER THE police and fire department finished and drove away, Cole lay beside Laura watching her sleep. Her back to him, she rested in exhausted slumber.

Not him. His brain and heart kept winding around and around and tying him in knots. Hell of a thing. He had no choice but to stick around and keep the trap baited. His contact officer had nixed their shutting down the trap and heading to a safe house. The same FBI informant who'd spotted Markos in Boston with Janus saw him renting a car and buying a Maine map. Since the bastard seemed to be headed for Hart's Inn Resort and Laura, they couldn't leave.

The cheese had lured the rat to the trap. Now the cats must be very, very wary. One cat especially.

Cole had managed to convince Stan to let them stay through the next day or two. DARK offered funding to make up what rebuilding insurance didn't cover. Wagging his head, Stan capitulated. Laura hadn't objected. Hell, no. More time meant she could finish the week with her students and the damn *Diner* troupe.

Cole pried one concession out of her. She wasn't to tell anybody they were leaving soon. As much as she might want to, no goodbyes. No sense alerting the enemy.

Following the fire trucks, Kent Isaacs returned in the

Cole's truck with the repaired laptop. The fire destroyed the satellite receiver, but he could get another in less than a day. So they had transportation and communication.

The Harts and some of the vacationing families offered clothing and toiletries to replace some of what was lost. Cole and Laura moved into the cabin he'd originally rented. After a shared shower, they fell into bed. He hoped to hell staying one or two more days wasn't asking for disaster, but—

Laura whimpered, rolled her head back and forth on the pillow as if in denial of whatever terrible vision passed before her closed eyes.

The nightmare again. No wonder after what she'd been through the past two days. He eased closer and put his hand on her shaking shoulder.

Her breath huffed out, then in with a ragged sob. "No! No! My baby…"

"Laura, sweetheart, wake up."

She sat up straight, eyes wide and breath chuffing in and out in shallow drags. The faint moonlight from the window winked on tears beading her lashes. "Thanks. Sorry I woke you."

He wagged his head at her automatic concern for him, not for herself. "You didn't." Their first discussion of her nightmare clicked in his memory. "Your dream. It's about the accident ten years ago, not the slalom ride in the hatchback."

She flopped back on her pillow, her pale hair haloing her face. Straightening her donated, oversized T-shirt, she sighed. "When you asked me about it that night, I thought at first you already knew. But of course you couldn't have."

"You want to tell me about it?"

226

"I can't really. The scenes are disjointed, a kaleidoscope of images and feelings. For a while after Kovar's attack, I saw knife blades and I seemed to be in a box. But that's gone."

"You triumphed in that case. You took control. Maybe that's why."

"I didn't think of that. Mostly the dream's about the accident. You were right. Some of it, like Angela's scream and the shriek of the tires, really happened. Others are creations of my pain. This time I saw Burt's face too."

Beautiful, sweet, generous Laura. Her torments and imperfections made her no less perfect as far as he was concerned. For years he'd had no idea the suffering she'd gone through. All while he nurtured hatred of her. "This will all be over soon. Will you go back to a counselor?"

She gave a wry laugh. "The problem's supposed to be post-traumatic stress. But the traumatic stresses keep piling up. Yes, I suppose I'll need help."

The bed jiggled as she propped up one elbow and leaned on her hand. "You said I didn't wake you. Can't sleep?"

Her voice, husky from sleep and tears, alerted at least one part of his anatomy. The part that didn't comprehend or care about the danger around them. "Just trying to figure things out."

"Based on facts? Or are you using your spy instincts?"

Gliding his fingers through her hair, he savored the moment of closeness. They'd found each other again, really found each other, without the prejudices and impulses of their youth. When she threw her arms around him after the explosion, he saw the love in her eyes. So this moment wouldn't be their last. He would see to it.

"Both," he answered finally. "Fact. Somebody opened the gas valve and doused the pilot light inside the cabin, for the third or fourth time. That somebody has a key or some other way in."

"So we were supposed to walk in and trigger the explosion... as Burt did?"

He considered. "That's my hunch. The killer continued rigging the heater to lull us into thinking it was faulty. If he's onto my real reason for being here, which is a distinct possibility, he has to figure that at least one time when we enter the cabin, I'll fail to detect the smell when I do a sweep. If we'd entered as usual, what would you have done first?"

"Turn on the lights. Maybe made tea." She put her palm on his bare chest. "Oh."

"Yes, oh. Boom. Another damn freak accident." He worked his jaw to ease the tension twitching at the muscles.

She shook her head before relaxing in his arms. In a short while, her breathing evened out. She was asleep. He hoped this time was without dreams.

Somehow he'd missed a clue. Something that niggled at his brain, at what Laura had called his spy instinct. If he could nail it down, he'd know who Janus was, who was after her. But the answer hovered just out of reach, fuzzy and indistinct like the shadows playing on the ceiling.

****

In the morning when they made love, it seemed their passion knew no bounds. One minute, Cole was tender, the next driven and demanding, stirring Laura's senses until the two of them soared together, closer than ever.

But she felt his tension as though the danger had increased. Her own desire simmered at feverish pitch, as though each time were the last.

One of these times would be.

She would have to end their affair. Pain speared through her. She closed her eyes and counted her breaths. She was standing on the rim of a great precipice. Like a mechanical doll whose key had been wound too tightly, at any minute she might burst into a dozen parts and fly over the edge, to be further smashed on the rocks below. Postponement magnified the heartache. But delay gave her more time in his arms.

She showered and dressed in Joyce's loaned royal-blue shorts and a Hart's Inn Resort polo. The swelling on her knee was no longer obvious, and she was grateful for the coolness of shorts. The greasy smoke smell no longer clung to her hair and skin, but it hung in the muggy air of the warm morning.

Once more she was reduced to almost nothing. This time not even a purse. Or her doctored driver's license. Only someone else's clothes and the gold crown charm. Slipping the long chain over her head, she tucked the charm inside her shirt. After Cole was gone, she'd have only that to keep next to her heart.

What was left of her heart.

When she entered the rental cabin's spacious living room, Cole looked up from his phone.

Clad only in a hastily pulled-on pair of denim cutoffs, he stood brooding, phone in hand. She stared, memorizing him—strong legs, slim hips, the line of black hair above the shorts. Up the ridges of his belly and broad chest to his neck, the angular planes of his face. And to the wolf eyes she knew so well. The dark stubble of whiskers and new abrasions from the blast added to his aura of danger.

She ached with love for him. She ached with the pain of having to let him go.

He crossed to the stove. "Zach's mother brought over coffee and muffins. You want some?"

"Not yet." Noting his taut mouth, an expression she knew well portended no good, she asked, "What's wrong now?"

Coffee sloshed into a mug and splashed onto the counter. He swiped viciously at it with a sponge. "More trouble with the plan for Marisol."

"The sponsor problem again?" If only she could make a phone call or two.

"That's not settled yet, but no. The airline won't let such a young child travel without an adult. Sister Josefa can't leave. The orphanage staff is too short-handed."

The opportunity lay before her. The precipice loomed. She had to do it.

Broiling heat rose to her cheeks. Good thing she'd eaten nothing yet. Food wouldn't have stayed down. "You can go to Colombia and travel with Marisol. Vanessa can move in with me. Byrne, Snow, and Isaacs are here to pounce on Janus and Markos. I'll be fine." Her words sounded so brittle to her ears, they might crumble apart and crash to the floor with their falseness.

Cole stared at her as though she'd punched him in the stomach.

Silence hung thick in the air. The only sounds were the low hum of the water heater and her heart, pounding like tom-toms in her chest. Time spun out on a thread of tension.

"Did I hear you right? You're telling me to leave?

And you don't mean just for Marisol."

She nodded woodenly. Her heart seemed to stop dead.

"Just like that?"

"Just like that. We both knew it would end sooner or later." Angling up her chin, she tried to convey detachment, as though exiling the only man she'd ever loved meant no more to her than refusing a telemarketer.

His eyes smoldered, and his low voice rumbled like approaching thunder. "Maybe you knew. I had other plans."

"I told you at the beginning this wouldn't work."

He reached her in two strides, but she stood her ground. His gaze captured her. She feared he could see into her soul.

His anger seemed to dissipate, to morph into vulnerability, an emotion more painful to see. He swallowed, clasped her shoulders with hands that trembled as much as she. "If you really believe we have no chance because of past hurt and misunderstandings, you haven't been paying attention."

"Please, Cole." She didn't know what she was asking, but if he continued, she'd break down.

"We know each other better than we did years ago. Trust and respect are a good start, but I need more than this short time together."

She averted her eyes, but he cradled her face in his hands, forcing her to look at him. "You can't deny that you have feelings for me, not after our nights, not after this morning."

Her lips quivered. She could scarcely form a reply. "No."

Before she could protest, he tugged her closer and

held her. At first she yielded, craving his touch. But she stiffened her spine and wrenched away from him.

"No! I can't. It didn't work then. It won't work now. And you... There's too much... too much."

His brows arched. He ran one hand through his ebony waves. "So, the princess has had enough of her fling with the biker?" His mouth compressed blade-thin. "I'm a damn fool."

The pain inside her was ripping her apart piece by piece. She forced anger at his accusation to override it. "Don't give me that biker bum-princess excuse. We've been through all that."

"Yeah, we've been through it. So much that you convinced me the differences between our backgrounds no longer mattered. You want a laugh? I even went so far as to think those differences never mattered except in my mind. Even ten years ago. But don't forget the other differences between us—the male-female variety you've been appreciating."

Blood roared in her ears and her stomach roiled. "Yes, the sex was good. The best. We always had that. But it's not enough. Go to Marisol. She needs you."

"And you don't." His voice was as glacial as the iceberg in his eyes. "I've got a news flash for you, Laura. You can't send me away. Only the DARK director can do that. So you're stuck with your shameful past—the biker, the hoodlum, the lowlife—until this damn trap catches a killer or two. Looks like I got over my past, but the princess didn't and slapped me back down where I belong. I won't forget again."

He stalked past her into the bedroom, every muscle and sinew bunched and leaped with tension.

Laura felt the painful throb of her heart with each

taut motion of his big body. Wadding his donated garments and his soot-stained sandal in front of him like a weapon, he slammed into the bathroom. A moment later, the shower was rushing full force.

Biting her fist to choke back a sob, she slid to the floor and dropped her head on her knees. Oh, God, what had she done? Her callous brush-off had hurt him more deeply than she'd anticipated. And in a way she didn't foresee.

But should have.

She couldn't allow him to believe the worst about himself. His inner doubt wasn't rational. Self-doubt is blind, a shroud of darkness over a glowing beacon. He had risked the light, but her clumsy rebuff snuffed out the flame.

Tears trailed down her cheeks. She clutched the chain at her neck. If only she could transform herself into the cold, unfeeling ore of Midas's daughter, she wouldn't feel this aching emptiness, this knot of pain constricting her breathing, crushing her bruised and tortured heart.

She had only one choice. She'd hoped for a reprieve, but time was her enemy. She owed him the rest of the truth, the secret she'd harbored in her soul.

And the truth would drive a wedge between them.

Not a wedge but a vast rift that would demolish any dreams he had of a future together.

Chapter Twenty-Seven

WHEN COLE OPENED the bathroom door, he clamped down his emotions and forced himself to think with the cool control that had saved him and his people from enemy fire. A different kind of danger, but as hazardous as a battle-field.

Laura sat at the kitchen table, shoulders slumped and bent over a mug of coffee. She looked drained, like trying to send him away was hurting her as much as him.

She was wrong. He hadn't lost his new belief in his worth. She'd urged him to get over himself, and with her by his side, he fought his way to that point. But her dismissal took him by surprise. Anger honed his tongue and he lashed out.

So if not because of their past or his bad-boy rep, why was she rejecting him? Last night he could've died with her in the explosion. Was she protecting him? She would risk endangering herself to save him, to send him out of harm's way. The need to protect her consumed him, the need to erase the smudges of worry beneath her eyes, to heal the cut marring that cheekbone. Deep within him, she'd kindled sparks where only cold and darkness had lurked.

Ever since she left him, he trusted no one. He never let anyone close to him, not his team, certainly not a woman. But life meant more than just surviving. She was the missing part of him. If there was a chance for them, he wouldn't give up without a fight.

No. Hell, no.

The stresses of being a murder target and the sorrows of the past were getting to her. That was the reason. After the tragedy ten years ago, depression and denial had set her course. He understood her burying herself in her work and charity tennis lessons. But that was an unfulfilled life.

She should have children—*their children*—to love instead of surrogates.

She was gentle and kind and so sharp she kept him on his toes like a damn ballerina. She was the sun coming out after a storm. He thought up stupid jokes just to see her smile.

And her tears made his soul weep. He wanted this trap sprung and the bad guys wrapped up like rodeo calves, so he could think without this massive vice binding his chest. So he could get on with making sure Laura never again had cause to shed anything but happy tears.

When he entered, she looked up with haunted eyes. She gripped her coffee mug with both hands, like a drowning victim clutching a life ring.

Before he could think of what to say, she held up a hand. "You were wrong, Cole. My reason for ending our affair has nothing to do with your past or our history."

"Then why? You can't tell me you don't care for me. I know better."

She nodded, her head moving mechanically as if blocking emotion. One hand flexed against her flat belly. "Because I do… care for you, I have to tell you the rest of the truth."

His heartbeat tripped on itself. What secret was she

still keeping? "The truth? Truth about… our son?"

"Not exactly." Her chin came up, but her eyes were dark and opaque as a moonless night, with no sparks to warm them. She set down the mug and pushed to her feet. "There's more about the accident that took our son. I couldn't bring myself to go into it before. Perhaps it's guilt for having let myself become pregnant in the first place. I don't know. I'm ashamed to admit that trying to spare myself only hurt you more."

He strode to her side. Started to reach out to her, but she backed away. "What then?"

"The crash damaged me as well." Her lower lip wobbled, and her voice caught on a suppressed sob. "Beyond repair. David was the only baby I can ever have."

Her words exploded in his face. They swirled in his brain in a language he couldn't fathom. His legs as weak as an invalid's, he sank into a chair.

Finally he made some sense of her new bomb. "You can't have children."

Shaking her head, she slid to the door. "The surgeon had to perform a hysterectomy. I'm barren. I can't give you babies. I can't give you the family we used to talk about, the family you've always longed for."

He sat quietly for a moment, then said, "I saw the scar. I figured it was from the accident." All the revelations of the past week poured over him in a flood of confusion and pain. He wanted to rub his eyes to clear the blur. "And you kept this from me until now."

There must be alternatives. But what? The impact of what she said evaporated his synapses and numbed his senses.

"I planned to tell you once this crazy trap ended, but

I couldn't go on allowing you to think you were that hoodlum you believed you had to be to survive. Toughness got you through hard times. You had nothing to be ashamed of then, and you have so much more to be proud of now."

She slipped her ash-smeared visor on her head, and jammed on her sunglasses. They concealed the melancholy in her eyes, but not the pain leaching all the color from her cheeks and lips. "I have to go. The sailing class."

He had to stop her. He strode closer to face her. "But—"

"No, there's no way around it. You may think now that we could make it, just the two of us, but one day you'd hate me for robbing you of your dream. That would kill me. And wound you far more. Ending it now is the only way."

"No. You love me. What we have together is too precious for us to walk away because you're afraid to take a chance. And it's not just sex. I want to be with you, to sit at the table and share morning coffee or a meal with you, to argue with you and make up afterward. In the past days, I thought I'd regained your trust, your smiles, your quiet moments and your passion. And I want them for the next fifty or so years. Marry me."

"Please don't ask me that. I can't marry you. I won't. It would never work. You deserve the family a whole woman can give you, not a hollow shell of one." She slumped against the door and hugged herself.

He lifted her chin so she had to look at him. "Sweetheart, you were the one who helped me to grow, to overcome my insecurities. You badgered me to change. You showed me that I had changed. Now it's your turn. Let me help you change things for you. For us."

A frown knit her brow. Tears clogged her voice. "What do you mean?"

"You're right that I've always wanted a family, a loving family with a bunch of children. But it's love, not blood that makes a family. We can't get our son back, but we can make a home for lost children who need parents. We can adopt kids."

"Adopt?" She pronounced the word carefully, precisely, like a strange word in Pashto. Shaking her head, she said, "It wouldn't work. One day you'd long for a child with your eyes or my mouth. You wouldn't mean to, but you'd resent me because I denied you that heritage. Eventually you'd detest me."

He clenched his fists so tight his nails bit into his palms. His heart pounded against his ribs like a desperate prisoner. But she was the one escaping. "You're wrong. If you run away because you're afraid to take a chance on me—on yourself, on us—you're not the woman of courage I thought you were."

Tears streamed down her face. "No. I'm not. I'm a coward. I love you, but I can't face seeing your love turn to resentment. To hatred."

A sob escaped her. She ran outside and down the path before he could stop her.

****

Enveloped in a pall of silence, Laura walked beside Cole into the theater that night. During the day, a front had moved in, bringing with it opaque fog and pewter drizzle heavy enough to sink her spirits to the bottom of Passabec Lake. The wind was the only thing picking up.

Stan didn't cancel the performance of *Diner* since so

many people had bought tickets ahead. Instead, before the curtain rose, they would have a moment of silence for Burt Elwell.

This was the longest day of her life. Laura was relieved to be in the theater, busy and surrounded by people. To avoid Cole between sailing and tennis classes, she'd manufactured mindless chores to do in the boat house and around the inn.

Avoiding him was impossible.

A taciturn and grim-faced Cole trailed along with her everywhere. He brooded in grim silence interrupted by an occasional phone call. Little communication passed between them other than the perfunctory kind.

The second weekend of performances opened to a packed house. After the flurry of costuming, makeup and props, the director and most of the stage crew milled around behind the orchestra seats and watched the performance. In the dark, Laura could barely distinguish who was there, but she thought DARK officers mingled with Bea and Rudy and the others.

The dark scowl on his battered face keeping everyone at a distance, Cole leaned against the tech booth alone.

Forbidding or not, she ached for him. Her hands itched to ease the tension in his broad shoulders. She longed to crush herself against his chest and absorb his essence and his strength.

She forced herself not to approach him, not to make an effort to soften the blow. She stayed where she was behind the right orchestra seats, the barrier of stage crew between them. Separation and distance were for the best. She'd known that from the start, but her heart had overruled her brain for a while.

Separation and distance. She repeated it to herself like a mantra, but repetition didn't ease the anguish stabbing her heart and scalding her throat.

When the third act was halfway through, Laura felt a sharp jab in her side.

"Come with me quietly or I'll turn this pistol on your boyfriend."

The whisper in her ear branded her brain. The coppery taste of terror froze her. "Who—"

"Shut up." The gun dug painfully in her ribs. A steel hand clamped her elbow and forced her to turn toward the door. "Move. Now. But nice and slow. Keep your hands where I can see them. Act normal."

She glanced at Cole, but he appeared absorbed in the play. He wasn't looking her way. How could she signal him? Her heart spasmed with fear and indecision.

"Don't. You warn him, and he's a dead man."

Her pulse tripping over itself, she managed to put one foot in front of the other as her captor herded her through the rear doors and into the lobby.

No one glanced her way. No one noticed their departure.

****

Cole fisted his hands in his pants pockets. Only his training kept him from jumping out of his skin. All day he'd spent trying to understand Laura.

Missions had gouged a few battle scars in him. Last night's explosion probably added one or two. The knife attack on her left gruesome tracks on her neck. But all of those together didn't match the internal scars. He was straining to understand how she thought, how she felt.

She was so terrified of his possible rejection of her that she had to cut him off first. Yes, her inability to bear children—his children—shocked him. He could make snap analyses and decisions in a tight spot with terrorists. Did his impulsive suggestion of adoption misfire? Or did it add to the past week's emotional minefield? Any misstep would blow up in his face.

So for the rest of the day, he'd guarded her from the distance she wanted and avoided the minefield altogether.

He allowed himself a glimpse of her. She was an exotic bird, an elegant bird in a borrowed yellow shirt that showed off her tan and jeans that were tighter than usual, just right in his judgment. Her bright facade might fool her friends, but not him. Renewed grief and pain faded the gold flecks from her eyes and smudged shadows beneath them. She might fool herself into believing their parting would be for the best.

Letting her go would be the worst possible thing he could do. That much he knew.

Happiness was beginning to trickle into the hollow places inside him. He was working at trust, at cracking the long-standing barriers built to protect his heart and soul. Only one person, only Laura had ever seen through those barriers.

With her, life had real meaning.

Because danger still stalked her, he couldn't take the necessary steps to heal their relationship — or lack of one. Making amends and making plans were impossible. Healing the pain, the breach, would take work. But healing had to happen. He would ensure it. She needed him. And the more he was with her, the more he needed her.

This distance between them hurt both, but gave him the space he needed to be more alert to danger. He glanced at her again. Safe enough with this harmless bunch. His teammates were stationed nearby, but if Cole couldn't spot them, neither would Janus. Or Markos, if he dared show his face.

If only they could have this business with Markos behind them.

If only Janus would make his damn move.

Cole wanted the trap sprung, so he and Laura could get on with building a life together. Sure, the thought of her belly never swelling with his child saddened him, but he could get past that loss.

As long as he had her.

Decision made, he turned his gaze to the stage.

Cliff Trigger, played by a fresh-faced new guy with script in hand, helped his new-found love Debbie and her father, the police lieutenant, close the trap on the killer. Using a deception carried off by the obnoxious dowager, played to the snooty hilt by Doris Van Tassel, Cliff tricked the murderer into incriminating herself.

No, *himself.*

Wait a damn minute. Cole had never read the script nor seen the final act, so he didn't know who committed the murders. He watched the climax in stunned silence, oblivious to the laughter and clapping around him.

As the denouement proceeded, Bea Van Tassel rushed over to him. She whispered, "Isn't that a marvelous ending? The audience is fooled every time. No one suspects Cookie is a man. Stan Hart is perfect in the role. And the wig! If only he had that much hair, poor man."

Cole nodded. In the unisex outfit of baggy pants, striped shirt and white apron, Stan sure as hell looked like a motherly, middle-aged woman. Cole had just figured they didn't have a woman to play the part. Duped him along with everybody else. And he'd watched a rehearsal or two.

Amazing. Cookie turned out to be the supposedly dead owner of a bankrupt ski resort, a man who for years plotted revenge against all the people who he imagined responsible for his ruin. He knew them, but they didn't know each other.

Devious. He watched Cookie, minus his wig and chef's hat, be handcuffed and led away.

A dual role. A successful hit man might have to play a dual role. One respectable for the public. One underground, clandestine.

Cole scraped a hand through his hair. More ways to examine the damn puzzle only gave him more headaches. No answers.

The performance would end in a few minutes. After the curtain calls, he and Laura were slated to help clean up. He turned toward where she was standing.

No Laura.

Shit! "Where is she?"

Bea clapped her hands together. "I have to see my sister when the play ends. Wasn't her fake death scene terrific?"

"Bea." He gritted the words through his teeth. "Where. Is. Laura?"

For his harsh tone, he received a schoolmarmish frown and a haughty sniff. "I saw her head to the lobby."

"Alone?"

"Someone was with her. I didn't see who. What—?"

The tracker on Cole's phone put Laura still in the building. He slammed through the double doors at the back of the theater.

Chapter Twenty-Eight

THE LOBBY WAS deserted. Where the hell did she go? The tracker still had her inside, but the damn app wasn't precise. He turned toward the door to the stairway, 9mm in his hand. He took the stairs to the lower floor two at a time.

With everybody onstage or behind the orchestra seats, the corridor of storerooms and dressing rooms stretched ahead lit only by dim emergency lights. Silence reigned except for echoes above of voices and creaking boards.

Was she down here? Who the hell had her?

He flattened against the wall. He adjusted the tiny microphone in his collar and tapped the button on his phone to call her.

No answer.

He tried again.

Nothing.

Why the hell wasn't she responding? Suspicion crawled up his spine.

Byrne and Snow were stationed outside. Isaacs ought to be in the theater, and Ward was backstage. He tapped the button to connect to them all. "Two and Three, come in." No response.

"Four, Five, you there?"

No response.

He shook the phone. It was working, but the

connection to his team—and to Laura—was dead. What the hell was it with these high-tech gadgets? His laptop freezing. Now this.

Wait and see. Maybe his alarm was for nothing and she'd gone up the other stairs. He'd find her happily congratulating the actors as they came offstage.

But the itching on his scalp said different.

Something about the play, about Cookie's dual role raked at his brain. A suspicion fuzzed and sharpened like a shadow puzzle. Staring at his phone, he almost had a grasp on how.

What if the signals were jammed? Or tinkered with? That was it.

Now for who. Slowly his mind made the connection.

Realization burned, an acidic poison in his veins.

Shoving away emotion, he inched along the corridor. At the first door, he crouched and stepped inside, sweeping the cramped space with his pistol. Prop storage. Old dummies, chairs, backdrops, the window seat from *Arsenic and Old Lace*.

Damn. There must be a dozen doors and little rooms like this one. The old box stalls from the structure's stable days. He turned and straightened, ready to perform the same sweep farther down the corridor as applause erupted from above.

The long black snout of a gun suppressor projected around the doorjamb.

Before Cole had time to react, the weapon spat.

The bullet hit him square in the chest. White-hot pain hammered his bones. Fire filled his lungs. The impact threw him backward onto the cement floor. Shards of pain exploded in his skull.

But he was right. He knew.

Janus. The two-faced god.

He knew the name, the face as the darkness dragged him down.

Too damned late.

****

Laura's captor shoved her down on the hard-packed dirt floor of the dark boat shed. With her hands tied and a gag in her mouth, she flopped to her side, helpless and numb. Her mouth and tongue were dry as sand, all moisture sucked out by filthy cloth.

A flashlight beam played over the walls. "Don't move or you'll be next." The voice was familiar.

The identity of her captor stunned her. Kent Isaacs.

No, Janus. Isaacs was Janus. He shot Cole.

Cole! Oh God, Cole!

The menacing hiss of the silencer echoed over and over in her head. It branded her brain and pierced her heart. A dark shroud filled every crack in her soul.

Isaacs had forced her to go down to the wardrobe rooms. Shocked and stunned at the identity of her enemy, she was trussed up and gagged before she could react.

Then they waited.

When Cole came down the steps, she struggled against her gag, straining to warn him. Powerless.

Her phone was in her pocket, but she couldn't reach it. The killer shoved her in among the soft folds of costumes, so she could kick nothing that would make noise. He kept her pinned to his side with one hand. With the other he held the gun, made more evil looking with the matte-black metal extension.

If she somehow escaped from this terrible mess, she'd never forget as long as she lived what happened next. Isaacs dragged her along the corridor to the next open door. They stopped just as Cole turned, his sidearm raised.

The killer didn't hesitate. He pulled the trigger.

Oh God, she could hear the muted sound of the gun firing. She saw the scene in slow-motion. The bullet slamming into Cole. The impact launching him backward. Then falling, falling with a sickening thump to the cement floor.

Where he lay motionless.

Her throat closed. She couldn't breathe. If he died because of her, she didn't want to live. Her chest ached as though her heart had been ripped out. She squeezed shut her eyes, the image of Cole, so still, branded on her pupils.

Then Isaacs had doused the lights and closed the door. He'd dragged Laura out of the theater building while the actors above were still bowing and blowing kisses during their curtain calls.

Was Cole dead? Or was he alive and bleeding? Would someone find him before it was too late?

Her pulse jittered, and her breath puffed in shallow pants. No, she couldn't let the agony of it break her. Nor let it suffocate her.

If Cole was alive, she was no good to him unless she could take control.

He had to be alive. She had to believe it.

She clung to the burning hope in her chest and worked to control her breathing. Slowly, in, out, until she was centered.

The boat shed's familiar smells of musty dirt floor, varnish and bottom paint calmed her nerves. Piled up in the corner were the sails for her class. Anchors, life jackets and boat cushions hung on the walls. Old friends.

Now she would see what could be done.

Across the room, the rasp of a match caught her attention. Its flame was the only pinpoint of light. A moment later, the lantern always kept in the shed glowed with a steady light, casting shadows in the back corners.

The glare set in stark relief the features of the man standing over her.

Gone, the affable gardener in his green work khakis. Gone, the government officer. The hit man looked malevolent and cruel in his black trousers and sweatshirt.

But she understood at last how Janus had fooled them all. How he'd known where she'd be and when Cole would be away. How he avoided the surveillance. Half the time he did the surveillance. What she couldn't fathom was why a respected DARK agent, supposedly the cream of intelligence officers, could also be a professional assassin.

She had tumbled down the rabbit hole.

The killer—oh God, *Cole's killer*—approached her. She recoiled, scooting back until she hit a plastic crate. But he only bent down and removed the gag. The smell of his sweat stung her nose.

"Don't want to bruise that soft mouth." He chuckled, more of a cackle. "This has to look like an accident. Stay put, or I'll tie your feet too." He walked away, weaving though the piles of boat equipment, and collected items that he piled close to the lantern.

The boat shed door stood ajar. The wind blew ragged curtains of fog and misty rain against the only window and through the narrow opening. The old sliding door creaked and groaned.

Working her cheeks and tongue, she forced saliva to moisten her parched mouth. A windmill of questions whirled in her head. "You can't hope to make my... death look like an accident. How can you explain the bullet in Cole?" Putting the events into words gave them too much reality. She trembled from the images in her aching skull and fought a wave of nausea.

She had to maintain her cool. She had to.

Thank goodness for Burt's laziness. Once the shed was cleaned up, he'd started leaving some garden tools inside. Within reach was a small folding saw, locked in the open position.

If she could saw through her bindings...

Isaacs barked a laugh that sent shivers down her spine. "It appears the lovers have had a spat. First you shot him with this gun. I'll hate to leave this little black-market beauty behind, but those are the breaks." He held up the small lethal instrument.

She had to keep him talking. If she could free her hands, she could reach the phone's panic button. Maybe it would reach one of the other officers.

No wonder the mysterious attacker Tuesday night had known the stage so well even in the dark. Isaacs had worked all over the theater side by side with the lighting techs.

"A lover's quarrel. No one will believe that."

On a shrug, he tucked the gun into his holster and began shredding a boat cushion with a pocketknife.

She backed away from him. And closer to the saw.

"Yeah, doll, they will." To hear this jackal's plot in matter-of-fact tones chilled her to the core. "Lots of people noticed that you weren't speaking to each other today. I made sure of it."

She rubbed her bound wrists across the blade. The jagged edge bit into her as it shredded at the rope. She controlled her breathing and ignored the sting, the feel of blood soaking into the braided material.

Such a small amount of blood. Nothing to her.

"Then in your panic," Isaacs continued, apparently proud of his plan, "you ran to the boat shed—which you opened up with your key."

He held up the padlock with her key inserted, then tossed it aside.

"Once inside, you bumped your head. When you fell, you knocked over this handy lantern. Too bad for such a classy chick to die in a fire. Hell of a shame. But my regrets will be overcome when I check my Swiss bank account."

She forced herself not to dwell on the future the killer mapped out for her.

She sawed at the rope.

A sneakered foot kicked away the garden saw. It landed with a clatter against the wall.

He slapped her. "I told you not to move!"

Fiery needles stun her face. "No!" She rolled to her side.

"I warned you, bitch."

Damn. She'd been so close. Tears burned, but she refused to let him see weakness.

He yanked at her hands and checked the rope. Unfortunately it was still whole. From somewhere he produced another length of the braided fiber. "Now you'll stay put."

While he bound her ankles together, she searched for flaws in his plan. "How will you explain my being tied up? Will you untie me after you knock me out?"

"I could untie you, but I don't think I will. Markos was right about you being clever." He twisted the cap off the lantern fuel can and grinned with satisfaction. "Those are custom-made paper ropes. They leave no marks, and the fire will reduce them to unidentifiable ashes."

He crossed the room and sprinkled the clear fluid over the cushions. The acrid petroleum smell stung her nostrils. Isaacs had once been an ATF agent, so he'd know better than most how to start a whiz-bang fire that looked accidental.

The lantern's flame flickered and danced. It animated his shadow against the wall.

She had little time. He was going to overturn the lantern and set the shed on fire. Her only chance was the phone. She prayed Isaacs didn't know she had it.

The serrated blade hadn't cut through, but her efforts had stretched the rope and loosened its grip. Her pulse skipped. Spreading the fuel around occupied her captor.

Keeping an eye on him, she lowered her hands to her right side. She twisted so she could inch her right hand into her pocket. Good. She touched the device. It might save both Cole and her. She prayed he still lived.

Shaking and sweaty and blood-smeared from the saw blade, her hands slipped on the smooth plastic. *Come on. Concentrate.* She turned the phone until she was sure of its orientation. The speed-dial button was at the bottom of the screen. There. At last.

She pressed, hoping she'd remembered correctly.

All she had to do now was talk. If Cole was conscious, he would hear her and know where she was. Or the others would. If he was de— No, she couldn't think about that. Maybe her voice would help the others find him. And her.

Please someone, listen to me!

"Why are you doing this, Isaacs? Are you really this

hit man, this Janus? Or is Markos blackmailing you into murder?"

The wind howled like a furious ghost. Rain sheeted through the rickety shed's opening. Thunder cracked the night and rattled the sliding door.

The stool where the lantern sat wobbled.

She chewed her lower lip. *Don't let it fall.*

Isaacs bent over her, grinning like a jack-o'-lantern. *That's it. Come closer. So someone can hear you.*

In the flickering shadows, his dark eyes were empty sockets. A frisson of revulsion skittered down her spine.

"Blackmail? Nothing so banal. Janus is my alter ego. The two-faced Roman god of doorways. For seven years, I've fooled them all. Occasionally government agents come under suspicion of espionage, but no one has ever suspected my little hobby."

"But why? You have respect, a decent salary, excitement in your work."

He stalked toward the shelving beside the lantern. "Excitement? Maybe that's how it looks from the outside. First in the ATF and now DARK, all I get handed is the boring background work, the surveillance. This gig is more of the same crap plus grunt work trimming hedges. So I make my own excitement. No one suspects. And I get well paid for it."

"You were spotted in Boston making the deal with Markos. Wasn't allowing your face to be seen dangerous?"

He tilted his head back and laughed, a hoarse rasp that grated on her nerves. "I'm smarter than the Feebs. That was my associate. He makes my… arrangements."

He hadn't caught on to her temporizing. Museum board meetings had taught her that inflated egos liked to expound on themselves. "You punctured my brake lines and fiddled with the gas heater? It was you who shoved the piano at me?"

"More than I should've needed to do. You've been a tough gig. Thanks to Stratton. Your macho lover kept turning off the gas valve. Ruining my plans. But a boat shed fire will be the final answer." Another hoarse laugh punctuated his grim joke.

"Won't the fire marshal know it was arson? What happened to your accident plans?"

He shook his head. "This old firetrap has too many fuel sources. They might guess arson, but they won't prove it. What difference it makes to Markos, I don't know." He lifted a paint can and set it back down. Next he hefted an anchor.

A paint can? An anchor? Her pulse shot to the roof. He was choosing something to knock her out with. Time was running out. "Switching the boats was a clumsy attempt. Not professional."

"Not professional is right. That lovesick idiot Burt bragged to me about his little boat-switching scheme. Thought he'd race to your rescue and be your hero. He didn't count on Stratton being Johnny-on-the-spot. So I backed up his story."

Poor Burt. Cole had been right about his feelings for her.

"But the ham-fisted plan worked for me. Made Stratton think Janus had paid the local yokel to do you."

The suspicion on Burt had been enough to confuse Cole temporarily.

The combustible fuel was soaking into flammables all around the shed. At any moment, the storm could rattle the shed and knock over the lantern without any help.

Her heart sank to her toes. No one heard her call. Or Isaacs's confessions. No one was coming.

Chapter Twenty-Nine

SHE HAD TO do something. Fast. Her captor's back was to her, apparently certain of her helplessness.

An old six-foot oar that didn't fit any of the newer, smaller boats lay on the floor where the now sunken skiff used to be. Laura scooted her legs around and rolled to her knees. Pulling the white-painted oar toward her, she judged its usefulness. Much longer than a tennis racquet, and heavier.

A weapon. Bracing herself with the oar, she pushed up. Up, up, inch by inch, until she stood wavering on her bound feet.

He didn't hear her over the roar of the storm.

With the oar as a crutch, she scuttled toward him. The dirt floor and the pounding rain covered her steps to within two feet of the man. Striking distance.

She lifted the oar high over her head.

Isaacs hummed while he worked. He picked up an old wooden lobster buoy. "Just the thing. It might even burn up in the fire."

She slammed the oar down on his head. Her overhand serve knocked the man to his knees. Still clutching her weapon, she hopped, hobbled toward the open door.

"No! You bitch. You won't escape again!"

An iron grip on Laura's ankles stopped her dead, sent her crashing to the floor. Pain splintered through her from her knees to her temples. Bruises on bruises, she thought inanely as she kicked at him.

"Let me go!" She struck out blindly with the oar. Heard the solid thud against bone and muscle.

He roared in pain, but didn't release her.

A shot rang out.

The hit man lay still. His hand fell away from her ankle. A flow of crimson soaked the dirt beside him.

Panting as though she'd swum the length of the lake, Laura scrambled away. Thank God. One of the DARK officers had heard her.

The man shoving the creaking door wider wasn't her savior.

The man who stepped inside was Alexei Markos.

****

Cole reached the boat shed as a gunshot split the night.

Laura! No!

He was too late. His blood ran cold. Then hot. "I'll cut out his beating heart!"

"Hold on, buddy." Simon Byrne, rain streaking his hair into his eyes, clamped Cole's arm. "That bump on the head is playing tricks with your vision. Look inside."

Cole squinted through the downpour that screened them from the view of those inside.

The prone figure was not Laura.

He swiped a hand across his eyes. Thank God.

Hands and feet bound, she was pushing to her knees. The man she confronted like a warrior held a pistol pointed at her. A .22.

Alexei Markos. Cole would recognize the smarmy Continental bastard whether he was drenched or dry. Perfectly styled ebony hair gleamed wet like shiny plastic in the lantern light. His dress pants and leather jacket were the real deal, designer expensive.

Cole flicked the safety off his 9mm.

"Be cool, Stratton," the other officer warned. "We need him alive."

Not knowing what Markos would do flayed strips off Cole's heart. His fear for Laura was huge, primitive, a fire burning him from the inside out. Blocking those thoughts, he reminded himself why they needed him alive. Husam Al-Din and the New Dawn Warriors, Markos's extremist playmates. Damn. "You'll get the bastard alive."

But maybe not in one piece. Not after what he'd done to Laura.

"What's the plan?" Ward, braid streaming over her shoulder in a wet ribbon, said in his ear.

Watching their backs, Snow waited at the corner of the building. He'd discarded his cane in favor of a pistol.

Cole rubbed his bruised sternum and thanked his instincts for making him don a Kevlar vest that evening. He might have a couple broken ribs and bump on the noggin, but he was alive. He'd swum to consciousness imagining he heard an angel calling him. The angel was Laura on her phone alerting him to her danger. Her words froze his veins, but propelled him to his feet. Moments later Byrne and Ward had found him as he staggered from the storage area.

"He'll be expecting his henchman. We'll use that." He waved them to positions beside the crooked old door.

He edged closer to the opening and peered inside.

"My dear, you have caused me an intolerable amount of trouble." The importer seized Laura's arm and yanked her to her feet.

Dirt smeared her shirt. Blood and dirt streaked her jeans and the white braided rope binding her wrists. And she had a new purpling bruise on her left cheek to match the cut on the other.

Another chunk he'd take out of Markos's hide.

Otherwise, she looked beautiful, just scared and furious. He allowed a second to feel relief. Then he concentrated on finding an opening, some vulnerability in his enemy.

"You'll be in a lot more trouble if you hurt me," she spat at the importer.

Yeah, sweetheart. Rile him. Distract him.

"I think not. Eliminating you once and for all will give me such satisfaction I won't mind having to leave this country for good. After a slight detour to my house. Too bad you can't accompany me." He pulled her close to him and caressed her bruised cheek with the pistol barrel. Used it to tuck stray strands of hair behind her ear.

Cole gripped his weapon tighter. If the bastard didn't have a gun at her head…

She averted her face. "What are you going to do?"

Markos dragged her closer to his employee's body and kicked the dead man's head. "The fool. He was supposed to be the best, but he failed at every turn. He would have permitted you to escape. However, his plan for this evening was sound. Time wasted on the confusion of one extra body will give me the time I require."

"You won't escape." Outrage burned in her eyes. She struggled, but the grip on her arm held firm. "Government officers are here. By now they've surrounded the shed."

Cole's jaw clenched. Damn. He ducked back an

inch.

Markos roared with laughter. "Ingenious of you, my dear. If your friends arrive, my man outside will alert me."

The maggot thought she was bluffing. Cole grinned.

Her eyes narrowed. "Are you certain of that?"

"You have not forgotten my colleague Kovar, have you, Laura?" When she blanched at the name, Markos nodded. "I see you recall his dexterity with a knife."

Pale but with fire in her eyes, she lifted her chin.

Markos turned away to examine the dead man's handiwork. "Ingeniously simple. A tip of the lantern and… poof!"

He was going to incinerate the place.

Cole backed up another inch. Uttering indistinct mumbles to mimic Markos's gorilla sidekick, he bumped the hanging door.

"Come in, Kovar," the importer said, a smile in his tone. "You're in time to watch me set off the pyrotechnics."

"Hurt," growled Cole, banging heavily against the door. He had to get the bastard to move away from the damn lantern. *Come on, come on.*

But Markos hadn't cozied up with terrorists without developing know-how on the subtleties of treachery. He clamped Laura against him with one arm. Together they stepped cautiously toward the door.

"See, I told you." She continued to strain against her captor. "The Feds are here. They've jumped your thug and wounded him. He can't help you. Give yourself up."

Markos didn't respond to her assertion, but tugged her around in front of him as a shield. He pressed his pistol to her temple. "Wounded or not, show yourself or

I won't wait for a fire to take care of her."

To Laura he said, "To Kovar, shooting you now will not matter, but to your friends…"

Cole sagged. He stepped into the door opening, his sidearm ready. His finger twitched at the trigger. "Federal officer, Markos. The lady was telling you the truth. You're surrounded. Put the gun down and let her go."

"Cole!" Relief lit her face like the sun coming out. "You're alive."

The importer took a step back, but quickly recovered his aplomb. "Ah, the lover. I should have known this piece of offal—" he spat on the hit man's body "—would also fail at eliminating you."

"Put the gun down and move away from her," Cole repeated. An ice cube's chance in hell Markos would surrender. He held his weapon steady.

The pulse beat frantically in Laura's throat. She was clearly terrified, but kept her gaze on him. He could see the trust in her eyes. He had to make this work.

If this madman shot her, killed her… But he wouldn't let himself think it. Couldn't.

He stared into her eyes, willing her to remember, willing her to understand his next move.

"Surrender? Hardly." A sneer on his snotty aristocratic mouth, Markos jabbed the gun barrel hard against her temple. "But I do have a change in plans. Laura and I are leaving together now. You will allow us to depart, or the lady will have a new hole above her lovely ear."

"You kill her, and you're a corpse."

The man's lips lifted into a cold curve as thin and deadly as a scimitar. "Then we both have much to lose."

Cole raised his pistol. "Laura," he said, his gaze on his target, "*Samla. Samla!*"

The wind howled, and the rain pounded at Cole's back.

Markos tilted his head. The hand with the gun wavered. "What trick is this?"

Laura's exhausted mind turned over Cole's cryptic word. Then she knew.

Samla. Get down. She went boneless in her captor's arms. Folding, she dropped to the floor. Distracted, he couldn't hold her. She tackled his knees.

Above her, gunfire exploded like thunder.

Cole dived at Markos. The two men crashed into the wall. As they fell to the floor, they bumped the stool.

Laura rolled away from flailing arms and legs. She stared helplessly as the fuel inside the sputtering lantern sloshed.

The stool rocked once…

Twice…

Over the edge crashed the lantern onto the shredded cushions and bunched sails.

A monstrous whoosh, and flames burst upward. Like a live creature fleeing the grappling men, the blaze leaped to the back of the shed. In seconds a raging wall encompassed everything. Her eyes and nose stung with the acrid fumes of the flaming synthetics.

Her eyes streamed, and she couldn't see Cole clearly. Was he all right? Had he been shot? The thunder outside was no match for the pounding of her heart. She rubbed her eyes to clear them.

The two men rolled and pummeled each other amid the burning cushions. Blood smeared them both.

One pistol lay beneath the fallen stool, out of reach.

But where was the other?

"Cole, oh God." What could she do? How could she help with her wrists and ankles tied? Scuttling across the floor, she searched for the other gun. Heat from the blaze seared her skin. Smoke sent her into a coughing spasm. "Help! Please help!"

Other figures wavered as ghosts, barely indistinguishable in the smoky haze.

Cole reared up. He landed a solid right on Markos's jaw.

The importer sagged to the ground. He lay still.

"Get her out of here," Cole shouted, his voice a harsh croak.

And then strong arms lifted her up and out into the night. Someone deposited her on the rain-soaked grass and ran back to the blazing shed.

The door was flung wider. People rushed in.

"Please," she gasped. "You have to save him."

Lifting her face to the dark sky in prayer, she didn't know if the welcome wetness was rain or her tears.

Chapter Thirty

BY THE TIME Cole finished with ambulances, the Alderport Fire Department and various law-enforcement agencies, it was morning. He'd be buried in reports for weeks.

But Laura was safe, thank God.

And Alexei Markos was in custody.

As soon as the fire started, Cole's fellow officers had called 911 and raced inside to pull everyone to safety. His shot found its target in Markos's shoulder, but the bastard's bullet grazed his arm. They grappled in the dirt and blood and flames until he knocked the crook out. Byrne and Snow dragged them outside.

Because the hit man was failing on his contract on Laura, Markos and his henchman Kovar had arrived that evening to spur him to action. Or to kill him.

During Snow's regular walk-through of the resort, he spotted their black sedan parked behind an unoccupied cottage. He alerted Ward at about the same time she and Byrne found Cole in the theater basement. Snow then followed Markos and his muscle to the boat shed. Luckily Kovar hung back far enough for the DARK officer to jump and hog-tie him.

Cole speculated that the importer had planned to eliminate both Kovar and Isaacs as unnecessary and dangerous witnesses before he flew out of the country. That little bit of information might induce Kovar to sing like a northern loon. Too bad the hit man wouldn't be able to talk.

Isaacs. A government turncoat. Cole had found no hint in his check of the DARK team. He tumbled to the man's identity as Janus too late. Too late he realized that the only person who had access to all their plans and to all the buildings could be only another DARK officer.

All of the miscommunication and absences were contrived by Isaacs. A former ATF agent who claimed no tech expertise but who knew how to mess with phone apps. After both Cole and Laura had disappeared from the theater, Byrne noticed the disabling on his phone and fixed it in time for Laura's warning to get through.

Coincidence, some might way. Cole called it good surveillance by the good guys on the DARK team. General Nolan would shit a brick when Cole informed him that one of his officers was the notorious Janus.

He kicked at a drift of ashes. The shed was a dead loss, only a pile of rubble by daybreak. Turning from what was left of the structure, he strode to his cabin.

Insisting insurance and a supplement from DARK would take care of the loss, Stan Hart was more charitable toward the new mess. He'd announced to the local press, present to review *Diner*, his undercover role in the "sting." He would spin what might have been negative press into positive publicity for Hart's Inn Resort.

Cole entered the cabin as Laura was emerging from the bedroom. After the medicos had pronounced her fit and at least one set of cops had taken her statement, Cole insisted she get some rest.

Showered and dressed in borrowed jeans and a resort polo, she made his heart soar. The twin contusions on her cheeks couldn't mar her beauty. The shirt collar lay flat, no longer flipped up to conceal the knife scars.

Badges of courage all.

"Going somewhere?" He hoped she didn't notice the hitch in his voice. He stood in the kitchen, unable to move a step closer to her without snatching her up in his arms. He doubted she was ready to accept his desperate relief and need.

"To my parents' in Maryland. They flew home last night. I have no ID for a plane ticket, so my father has sent a car." She walked hesitantly toward him, her gaze on his bandaged arm. Her lips forming a moue of sympathy, she reached out as if to check the wound, then drew back her hand. "Does it hurt much?"

It throbbed like a thousand killer bees had stung him, and he wanted her to cluck over him and pamper him. He shrugged. "It's not bad."

"You look red. Did the fire burn you?"

"A few places. My face, one arm. No worse than a sunburn. Rolling around in the dirt probably kept most of the flames away. Markos got it worse. Second-degree burns on his hand when he tried to grab his gun. Not nearly enough damage to make up for his sins."

External burns were nothing compared to the fiery need Cole had for her. How should he begin?

"Oh, I almost forgot." She darted to the bedroom and returned. She passed him a black mesh garment. "Here's the body armor you made me wear last night. Later when I thought about Janus shooting you, I remembered there was no blood. I should've realized you were wearing one too. At first I thought you were dead." Tears pooled in her eyes and she turned away.

He longed to hold her, but they had to settle things

before he let his desire for her cloud his mind. His gut twisted with the suspicion she might not forgive him for his carelessness, for putting her in jeopardy. "I thought the vest would protect you. You went off with Isaacs the hit man, and I didn't even notice. Damned lousy protection."

"It protected you, thank heavens." She offered him a small, sad smile. "And if I hadn't gone with Isaacs-Janus, who knows what he would've done next. He... he threatened to shoot you if I didn't go or if I warned you."

He breathed again. Just like her, not to blame him for making a hash of things. He didn't mention that Isaacs probably wouldn't have risked a shot in the crowded theater.

"You heard me on the phone, so you know what he admitted. Still, it's too bad you can't question him." Her chin came up. "But I'm not sorry he's dead."

"Sweetheart, you grilled him as thoroughly as a cop. I heard all his bragging. What you didn't know what that my phone recorded his every word."

She smiled, shaking her head. "You have it all!"

"And Markos's every damning word."

He couldn't help it. He needed to touch her, to know she was okay. He stepped closer and rubbed her upper arms. "You don't know how afraid I was last night that I'd lost you. When I heard that gunshot in the boat shed..." The memory clogged his throat, and he couldn't go on.

She pressed her hands flat on his chest, but the reason worried him. He didn't know if she was moving closer or pushing him away. "I—"

He shook his head to stop her words. "No, it's all over now. This nightmare brought us together, and it's given us a new beginning. Even when I thought you left me, you were embedded in my heart, part of me. I love you more than ever. I can't lose you now."

She averted her gaze and pulled away, walking to the kitchen. She glanced out the window, possibly looking for her ride, then went to the sink. She picked up a dish towel.

He let her fidget, but she would hear him out. She had to. "At first, I didn't believe we had a chance together. But the past doesn't have to govern our future. We're not the dumb kids we were ten years ago. What we have now is deeper, not a thin-layered infatuation to be easily pared away."

He could see she was fighting tears as she put away the plates from the dish drainer. Anything to keep busy. He knew the feeling.

She turned to face him, her eyes bleak. "Yes, I'm glad we could put the misunderstandings and judgments of the past to rest. But are friendship and intimacy enough?"

"Intimacy. That's an understatement. Between us there's magnetism I've never felt with anyone else, and more fire than in that blaze last night. I want you more than I believed it was possible to want a woman. When I saw you last night all bruised and wet, I wanted to hoist you over my shoulder and carry you off to my cave, bad guys or not."

"Cole, don't." She clasped her hands together. Her tortured gaze roamed his body, as if drinking in her last sight of him.

He had to convince her to cease lying to herself. "I saw the crown charm on your bureau. You kept it all these years and even brought it with you when you fled for your life. You're wearing it."

Her hand flew to the chain at her neck.

A black limousine pulled up outside. The uniformed driver stepped around it and opened the rear door.

She turned away from Cole. "My ride is here. But I need to tell you something first."

Desperation was burning a hole in him. Fear set it aflame. He scrubbed at his chin scar. "What is it?"

Laura twisted her hands together. She had to calm herself and get control before she began. "It's about the tennis lessons with my community center girls."

Unshaven and sexy, he was so strong, so confident and rugged in his black t-shirt and jeans. Except for the reddened skin on one side of his face and the white bandage on his upper arm, he looked invincible. His nearly dying had forced her to reexamine her heart and her fears. She had to make him understand what she'd figured out during the long night. She couldn't blame her white night on nightmares.

Only on squandered dreams.

Her heart pounded against her rib cage, fluttered like a wounded bird and sank. Regret was an ache in her chest so huge she could barely breathe. She prayed he'd give her this last chance.

"The ghetto kids," he said, his brow furrowed into a fierce glare. His hands clenched and unclenched. He looked ready to pounce.

A nervous laugh bubbled up. "I want to tell you the lesson they taught me. I finally learned it because of you. Do you remember Jamila and Desirée?"

"Is Desirée the one who wants to be Serena Williams?"

"That's Tanisha. Desirée has trouble at home, and

Jamila's gangster brother keeps bringing trouble home. For a while last year, both girls went to live with Jamila's grandmother, who already cares for two others. Only Jamila is the old lady's blood relative."

He edged forward, his blue gaze riveting her. "And what did you learn from that?"

She drew a deep breath. *Here goes nothing. Or everything.* "The grandmother tells the children she takes in that they're her family now, that love is thicker than blood. Jamila said she read it in an advice blog. Waiting for you to come in last night, I had a long time to think, and I remembered. That saying is like what you tried to tell me. Love, not blood makes a family."

Cole headed toward her.

"No, let me finish. I've made a terrible mistake, and it may be too late. I need to say this. So you understand."

Ignoring her protest, he cupped her shoulders in his cool hands. His gaze roamed over her features. The emotion in the depths sent fire racing across her nerve endings. "Say what you have to say, but I need to hold you while you say it."

His familiar scent filtered into her senses. She swallowed and had to look away from his mesmerizing gaze. "I should have seen it before. Bearing children hasn't made Desirée's mother a good parent. You were more parent to your dad than he was to you."

"Mine was definitely a dysfunctional family. But I understand your blindness. I can't feel what you suffered, are still suffering. You couldn't see through your pain." He kissed her temple.

She sighed at the warm support his lips conveyed. "And my pride. I should have given you more credit for your capacity to love and for changing from the youth of ten years ago. You love Marisol and the other orphans you help. I planned to adopt, as a single parent, but I never—"

"Shh, sweetheart. You were grief-stricken at losing a baby, then at learning you could never have another. And being in fear for your life skews all perspective." He skimmed a finger lightly as a feather across her cheek. "Let me help, Laura. Let me love you."

Tears welled in her burning eyes. She cupped a hand on his unshaven jaw. "Oh, Cole, I'm sorry I hurt you so badly. I love you so much."

He pressed her close so she basked in his heat and strength, felt his passion against her belly. His lips claimed hers, and the world ceased to exist. Salty tears seeping from beneath squeezed lids, she answered his tender assault with hungering lips and wrapped her arms around his neck.

"What hurt me was what hurt you. We can heal each other. Tell me you'll marry me." He lifted her up and carried her to the sofa. Cradling her in his lap, he stroked her hair and down her back. *"Zuh taso muhabbam."*

"That's not Spanish. More Pashto? What is it this time?"

"I love you."

"Zuh taso muhabbam." She clutched at his shirtfront, desperate to believe this wasn't a dream. In his eyes, she saw faith and honesty and trust. She cradled his face in her hands and kissed him with all the relief and happiness whirling through her. "And the baby? You forgive me for keeping that secret from you for so long?"

"There's nothing to forgive. You had no reason to trust me. God, I love you," he murmured against her mouth. He grasped her shoulders and held her away from

Susan Vaughan

him. A muscle in his jaw jumped. "But you still haven't said you'll marry me. I'm dying here."

"Cole, I love you. You're my other half. I love your self-made success, your protectiveness and your honor. You helped me overcome my guilt and pride. Yes, yes, yes, I'll marry you."

He beamed a jubilant smile. "Thank God." He kissed her again, gliding his hands over her breasts. "I need to feel you against me. How can I get you out of these jeans?"

A knock sounded at the door.

"What the hell?"

The limo driver. Her eyes widened in horror.

A giggle erupted as she pushed away from him. "Wait a minute." She whisked outside and dismissed the driver. Her father would understand. He had to. She wasn't leaving without Cole. Ever again.

When she returned, he was waiting for her on the couch. Desire rippled through her when he stripped away her jeans and wrenched off his shirt.

Once their clothing was banished, he knelt between her legs and smoothed back her hair as he joined them. He moaned with pleasure. "Ah, Laura, at last, nothing between us. No barriers. No secrets. Only love."

She would have told him again how much she needed him, how much she loved him, but his erotic caresses stole her power of speech. And then she was wrapped around him, and he was moving within her, and neither of them could speak except in the passionate welcome home their bodies and souls gave each other.

Epilogue

Two weeks later…

"MARISOL'S BEEN LOOKING for you all day, Ms. Rossiter," the floor nurse said cheerfully. "Every time I've been in to check on her, she asked for her *ángel dorado*."

Laura returned her smile and held up a book. "Thanks. I brought a Spanish language copy of *Goodnight, Moon*, but she'll have to put up with my faulty pronunciation."

She hurried down the Johns Hopkins Pediatrics hallway toward the child's room. Medicinal and lemon-scented disinfectant odors permeated the bright pastel corridor.

The four-year-old orphan had arrived in the United States ten days ago. Laura acted as sponsor, and Cole accompanied her from Colombia.

Marisol then underwent the corrective surgery on her foot five days later. The surgeon's words were guarded, but he admitted all signs pointed to success. The physical therapist had already begun exercises with the child to strengthen her muscles. Once the cast came off and therapy began in earnest, they'd have a clearer idea of long-term recovery. Judging from the girl's eagerness, Laura believed she'd walk normally.

"Oh, Ms. Rossiter," the nurse called. "Mr. Stratton

is already here, but I suppose it's all right if you go in. Try not to tire her too much."

Cole is here. She crossed her fingers he had good news about Marisol's future. And theirs.

She nodded, her pulse skipping in anticipation as she approached the room. The squeak of rubber-soled shoes on the tile floor and the clatter of trays faded into the background.

The patient label on the door read, "Marisol Ortiz." The door swung in so gently, the two people in the room didn't look up from their animated conversation.

Clad in the pink bunny pajamas Laura had brought yesterday, Marisol sat propped up with pillows on her hospital bed. One leg covered with bandages and a plastic cast from foot to knee lay on a U-shaped support.

Two heads nodded—one big and raven-haired, one small and blessed with a mop of raisin-brown curls—as they chattered in Spanish too rapid for her.

Her heart felt too big for her chest. Cole looked the same as he had that day in Maine when he'd suddenly appeared outside the tennis court. Closely cropped hair, eyes the color of Arctic seas, khaki cargos, military boots. The only changes were a tailored charcoal shirt instead of a t-shirt and a smile instead of a glower.

Seeing him with that darling child made her glow on the inside, as though she'd swallowed a sunbeam.

Hola, Marisol," she said. "Hi."

The little girl was small for her age, with too thin limbs that needed nourishment and exercise, but her lively spirit and bright smile lit the room. She laughed in welcome and wiggled her fingers to beckon Laura closer. "Laura, *mi ángel dorado!*"

From his position seated on the bed's edge, Cole

eased to his feet. His arms went around Laura, holding her tightly. He kissed her forehead.

She savored the strength of his arms around her, the solid proof that her happiness was real. Gratitude that they'd found love together again threatened to overwhelm her. Only because of the child, did she disengage herself. Reluctantly.

She turned to the waiting girl and gave her a big hug. *"¿Cómo te sientes?"* How are you feeling?

Taffy-brown cheeks flushed with excitement, Marisol replied in a flurry of childish Spanish that seemed to mean she was feeling chipper. She pointed to the picture book in Laura's hand. *"¿El libro, es para mi?"*

Was the book for her? That much Laura could handle. Of course it was for her. *"Sí, es para ti."*

A big smile on her pixie face, the child reached out with eager arms. Her big brown eyes sparkled.

Cole watched as Laura placed the classic children's book in small, eager hands. In her pale yellow linen dress that skimmed her hips, she was his *ángel dorado* too — his golden angel. Her recent injuries had healed, along with the pain in her soul, leaving behind only scars that no longer mattered.

Though she'd been through hell and back, her courage and generous heart had pulled him out of his black hole of bitterness. He couldn't take his eyes off her, especially with the child who would soon be hers. His. *Theirs.*

Laura ran a finger beneath the title. *"Buenas noches, luna.* I'll read it to you later." She lifted her shoulders and looked to him for help. "My Spanish is too rusty. I've forgotten how to say it."

"You did fine. We can read it together later." He translated for Marisol.

"Thank you," Marisol said in halting English. Then she turned the first page and fell into the colorful pictures.

He stepped away from the child's bed. He clasped Laura's hand. Her scent, apple and Laura, floated up to him, and he wrapped himself in its blanket.

"Good that you can sit with her awhile," he said. "I have to go soon. You wouldn't believe the red tape on this case."

"I've been tangled up in it myself." Her voice was tonic to his soul. "Has Markos told you what you needed? Have you gotten information about Husam Al-Din and New Dawn?"

He twisted his mouth in a wry grin. "His lawyers have him under wraps, but he's given us a little. He's more afraid of Husam than the courts. There was more for sale than Markos had you verify. And a great deal more profit. Millions. It seems our greedy importer skimmed a healthy chunk off the top, and the terrorists' money man figured it out. That's the real reason Markos was leaving the country."

Laura shook her head. "He stole from New Dawn? What does he do for excitement, play Russian roulette?"

"He sure as hell seems to be spinning the cylinder now. And we have to convince him we can protect him before the chambered bullet clicks around to blow him away."

"*Papá* Cole." Marisol launched into rapid-fire speech.

Laura sent him a questioning look.

When the child finally ran down like a wind-up toy,

he cleared his throat. It was time. His heart bounced like one of Laura's tennis balls. "She wants me to tell her *ángel dorado* the secret I shared with her today."

"A secret? The adoption?" Anticipation burned her eyes.

"You're leaking again." He dabbed at her cheek.

She blinked back the tears of joy. "Marisol won't return to Colombia? We can keep her?"

He lifted her hand to his lips. "We'll have a boatload of rigmarole to go through, but I got the word. How many bedrooms in that house of yours in D.C.?"

Her smile glowed. "Three. But I imagine we could find something bigger."

He grinned. "Marisol will only be our first."

"I can stay home with her while she has therapy. The museum replaced me with a series of interns. I'm working only part-time directing special projects."

"And I've put in for transfer from fieldwork to the analysis desk. I'll be D.C. based from now on."

"We have a wedding to plan. Then we'll be a real family."

"Es mi mamá ahora?" Marisol asked Cole. Her Cheshire-cat smile showed white teeth. She wriggled closer to them.

"Sí, niña, I am now your mama." Laura sat on the bed.

"Por favor, mami." A dimple winked in the child's cheek. *"Léeme el libro."*

Cole's heart leaped and kicked so hard he thought it might burst out of his chest and dance around the room. He'd damn well stay a while with his almost wife and daughter. DARK's reports could wait.

"Go ahead. We'll read her the story," he said. He

stood beside them, his arm around Laura and his hand resting on Marisol's small shoulder.

Stamps and signatures would make it official, but love already made them a family.

A real family.

This single moment beat anything he'd ever dared hope or dream. Happiness welled up until he could barely breathe past the football-sized lump in his throat. The dark memories of their past had miraculously led to a bright future.

Eyes misted over, he helped Laura read the simple text, as lyrical and beautiful in Spanish as in English.

A word about the author...

Occasional bouts of insomnia led to Susan Vaughan's writing career. When she couldn't sleep, she made up stories to fill the long, dark nights. Her stories throw the hero and heroine together under extraordinary circumstances and pit them against a clever villain. Besides curling up with a good mystery or romance, Susan enjoys walking her dog, boating, traveling, and volunteering. A former teacher, she is a West Virginia native, but she and her husband have lived in Maine for many years. Susan is the author of 16 novels and one children's book. Find her at www.susanvaughan.com, where you can sign up for her newsletter or contact her, or at https://www.facebook.com/susanvaughanbooks.

Thank you for purchasing
this publication of The Wild Rose Press, Inc.

For questions or more information
contact us at
info@thewildrosepress.com.

The Wild Rose Press, Inc.
www.thewildrosepress.com